Mosier's Raiders

Mosier's Raiders

✦

The Story of LST-325

1942–1946

David Bronson

iUniverse, Inc.

New York Lincoln Shanghai

Mosier's Raiders
The Story of LST-325

iUniverse, Inc.

For information address:
iUniverse, Inc.
2021 Pine Lake Road, Suite 100
Lincoln, NE 68512
www.iuniverse.com

ISBN: 0-595-31399-X

Printed in the United States of America

Contents

Foreword

There have been thousands of books written about the Second World War, covering nearly every conceivable aspect of that conflict. Authors more capable than I have written about the major events that form the backdrop of this story many times before, and it is not my intent to try to add anything new. The purpose of this book is simply to tell the story of one small piece of the broad mosaic of people, places and events from this particular period of our nation's history. This is the story of one ship, the *USS LST-325*, and of the men who served aboard her. This ship is no more remarkable than the others of her class; there were over a thousand just like her in both the Atlantic and Pacific fleets, each manned by crews very much like the men aboard the *LST-325*. Still, for the men who served on her and their families, the story of the *LST-325* is indeed special.

By and large, the sailors that made up the crew of the *LST-325* were young men, still boys actually, many having just recently completed high school. They came from all parts of the country and all different economic and social backgrounds. They came from some of our nations largest cities and from farms in the Heartland. At a time in their life when they might have been thinking of going on to college or starting careers and beginning their own family, the circumstance of war would change their lives forever. It took them away from their families and friends, their hopes and their dreams, and brought them together on a rather ugly and ungainly ship that would never have the glory of its more graceful sisters in the fleet. War would take these men to places they may not have even heard of before, let alone ever dreamed of seeing in person. Places like Algeria, Tunisia, Sicily, Italy, England…and a region of France's northern coast known as Normandy. The events that soon had the world in flames brought these men together as individuals and strangers but during the next two-and-half years the crucible of war would forge them into something more than just crewmembers…it would bring them together as brothers.

One of these men was my father, James G. Bronson. He was born on 1 August 1922, near the small town of Otsego, in the southwestern Lower Peninsula of Michigan. The second of four sons born to my grandparents, he was farm-born and raised, and it was here, helping his uncle and father run the family farm and working on its machinery that he learned the skills that he would later use to serve his country. He enlisted in Detroit ten days after his twentieth birthday, on 11 August 1942. It had only been two years since his older brother, Paul Jr., had died after being horribly burned in a welding accident. I can only imagine how my grandparents must have felt, having already lost one son and now another was going off to war. Another son, Elwin, would follow my father's footsteps and join the Navy in 1944. After Jim went through basic training and the Navy Diesel School in Richmond, Virginia he reported to the *LST-325* at the Philadelphia Navy Yard on 26 January 1943, where he was assigned to the ship's main engine room. During the next two-and-a-half years, the *LST-325* would be his home, and his shipmates would become his family.

After the war Jim came back to Michigan and like millions of other veterans, he settled down to make a living and raise a family. In 1947 he married my mother, Helen Hagenbuch of Three Rivers, Michigan, and together they raised their three daughters and two sons on the modest earnings of an automobile mechanic. As I was growing up my father would sometimes tell me about some of his experiences during the war. Mostly he spoke of the good times that he and his friends had together. He kept some old photographs in a small brown box in his den, taken by one of the ship's officers who after the war made copies available to all the ship's company. Most of the illustrations in this book are from that collection. He never told me much about some of the things I have since learned from other members of the crew, the close calls the ship had from German attacks, or seeing the terribly wounded casualties being brought onboard after the invasions. Moreover, he never spoke of the fear he must have surely felt when the ship was approaching an enemy beach, the sounds of explosions reverberating through the hull down to the engine room where he was stationed.

Years later my parents were able to attend a few of the annual ship's reunions that some of the crewmembers organized in the early 1980's. It was the highlight of his year, he eagerly anticipated the time to leave for the reunion, and he would talk excitedly about it for weeks afterwards. I know he couldn't attend as many as he would have liked to, for my mother had health concerns that made traveling difficult for her. She would tell him that he didn't have to stay with her and that he could go by himself, but Dad just wasn't the type of person to go and leave her behind. He died on 6 April 1994, from complications due to cancer, and he's buried in a small cemetery not far from where he was born, alongside several other members of his family…his father and mother, his older brother Paul and younger brother Philip, and his beloved wife Helen, who passed away in October 1998.

Shortly after he passed away, I thought about attending one of the crew's reunions. However, time passed by and the seemingly more pressing concerns of everyday life made me set those ideas aside. It wasn't until my wife and I went to see "Saving Private Ryan" that it again became a priority in my life. For the first time, I began to truly understand the enormity of the sacrifice these men had made, and the incredible debt we owe to the veterans who fought that war. There was a ghastly price to be paid for the destruction of Nazi and Japanese tyranny. Paid for in blood and in lives lost, and by the men and women that may have survived the war but whose lives were forever changed by the horror of what they experienced.

I was finally able, through the assistance the United States LST Association, a veteran's organization for men who crewed LSTs during WWII, Korea and Vietnam, and former crew members Clester Brown and John Roberts, to contact Emil Kolar, who was in charge of putting the 1999 reunion together in his hometown of Springfield, Illinois. That September my wife and I finally got to meet a few of the men who had been such an important part of my father's life. Only ten men were at the reunion but they, along with their wives, welcomed us like family. I could see in their eyes the love they had for my father, every time one of them looked at me. They were so pleased that someone remembered them and was interested in what they had been part of so many years ago. This surprised me at first, the gratitude *they* showed to *us* just for just the simple act of caring about what they had done for their country. The sad truth is many people today think that what this generation lived through and accomplished is just so much ancient history. They don't appreciate that the war and its outcome have had a deep and profound effect on everything that has happened since then, and will continue to do so for all time.

Shortly after we attended the reunion the idea for this book was born. It was then, and still is, my belief that the crew of the *LST-325* deserves to have their story remembered, as does every man or woman who put their country ahead of themselves and marched off to war. I felt the story of the *LST-325* should be documented so that the children and grandchildren of the men who served aboard her would have it to look back upon and understand just what it was that their forefather had been part of. The crew deserves no less than that. I sincerely hope that I am able to make this more than just a record of the places they were at and the events they took part in. I hope that despite my shortcomings as a writer I can convey to the reader the great camaraderie these men had, and still have, and the great affection they feel for one another. That is a bond that has never been broken, even after all these years and each having gone their separate way. I am so thankful to every one of them for what they did for us, and for having been my father's friend and brother during those great and terrible times. They are the true authors of this story, they created this history, and it has simply been my privilege, and my honor, to record it here.

I dedicate this book to the officers and men who served aboard the *USS LST-325*.

Acknowledgements

There are so many people that I would like to thank, but I hesitate to begin listing them because I know I'll forget someone. There are a few people though that I would like to especially thank, for their contribution has been what made this book possible.

To Bud Allgaier, Stan Barish, Bill Bliss, Chet Conway, Ted Duning, Ellsworth Easterly, Bill Hanley, Leo Horton, Emil Kolar, Howard Kramer, Dale MacKay, Don Martin, "Rem" Martin, Gerry Murphy, "John Bob" Roberts, Don Roy, "C. J". Mitchell, Dick Scacchetti and Harold Westerfield. Your contributions are the heart and soul of this book. They have allowed me to use the information they shared with me, mostly attained through written questionnaires and interviews. Throughout the text that follows you will see sections in italics that I have taken from their interviews.

And a special thanks to Stan Barish for his permission to use the photographs that appear in this book.

To Tom Sarbaugh, son of ship's officer John Sarbaugh, for all the groundwork he laid down researching the ship for years before I came into the picture, for sharing all his work with me and especially for the use of Bill Bodiford's personal diary from that time.

To Bette Thies, the younger sister of Clifford E. Mosier, Captain of LST-325. What a stroke of good fortune it was that put us into contact, your contributions have helped me so much in fleshing out your brother as a man, and not just as an officer. I only wish Bob was here to see the finished project.

To Captain George A. Hogg, RN, Honorary Curator of the Cornwall Maritime Museum in Falmouth, England, for his information on the men that *LST-325* carried from Falmouth on 5 June 1944, for the information on the convoy in which she sailed, and for the information on the German air raid on Falmouth on 30 May 1944.

To Salvatore R. Mercogliano, Professor at Methodist College in Fayetteville, NC, and at American Military University for his information on *LST-325's* service in the Maritime Sea Transport Service.

To all my friends and family that have given such tremendous support and encouragement. You are what kept this project moving forward and I could not have completed it without you.

To the people whose blood, sweat and tears went into bringing an LST home as a memorial to the sailors who served aboard the Large Slow Targets. Dad would have been so proud to know his LST now serves as a tribute to those brave men, especially those who gave the last full measure so that we may live in freedom.

But mostly I would like to thank my incredible wife, Donna. Her patience and understanding is always remarkable, it has been phenomenal since I started this project. She has never complained despite the many late nights I've put into this work, and all the added responsibilities she's taken on so that I could have the time to finish this book.

David Bronson, 2004

1

War

On October 27, 1942, the ship that eventually became the *USS LST-325* was launched at the Navy Yard in Philadelphia, under the sponsorship of Mrs. C. G. Wells. The stays holding the ship were released, and the 328-foot long and fifty-foot wide hull rumbled down the ways and into the Delaware River. One of the initial group of seven LSTs to be built at the Philadelphia Navy Yard, when launched the *LST-325* was little more than an empty hull. During the next four months workers busily installed, tested and put into operation all the equipment and gear necessary to transform the *LST-325* into a fighting ship of the United States Navy.

The *LST-325* was one of a new breed of ships, the "Landing Ship, Tank" or LST, designed to fulfill the need for a large, ocean-going vessel that could deliver a number of vehicles and men directly to an enemy-held beach, without the need of a developed harbor facility. In November 1941, just a week short of one year before the Philadelphia Navy Yard laid down the keel of the *LST-325*, John C. Neidermair of the Bureau of Ships submitted his initial design for the LST. Neidermair understood that his design had to be simple and economical, since large numbers of LSTs would have to be built in order to keep up with the demand in both fronts of the war. He would waste no materials or energy on making this ship beautiful; instead, he created a ship that would perform its mission beautifully.

With its boxy shape and high freeboard the LST was not as glamorous, nor as fast as her more famous sisters in the fleet. The top speed for a LST was, at best, just above 10 knots. Given the ships slow speed and its mission of beaching on enemy held territory, it didn't take long for some Navy wag to give new meaning to the acronym LST…"Large Slow Target." In fact, the Navy thought these ships would be just that. It was felt, by some, that there would be a high mortality rate among the LSTs during any amphibious operation and that if each LST made just one successful landing it would have more then paid for itself.

The most prominent feature of the LST design was the tank deck. Without any vehicles onboard, the tank deck was just a cavernous hold. The vehicles were loaded onto the ship through an opening at the bow, accessed through two large outer doors and an inner door that swung downward and acted as a ramp. The heavier vehicles such as tanks, bulldozers, heavy artillery, cranes, and the like were carried in the tank deck. Lighter vehicles, such as jeeps and trucks, could be carried topside on the ship's main deck, accessible via an elevator located in the forward part of the tank deck. Later LSTs were equipped with a ramp instead of an elevator, which helped to speed up loading and unloading. Located along both sides of the tank deck were storage compartments for the crewmembers and troop's gear, the boatswain's lockers and the carpenter, shipfitter and electrical shops. In the stern, aft of the tank deck, were storage compartments for the crew's food and supplies, and the ship's steering gear compartment.

Unlike a traditional ship, the hull of the LST was designed without a keel. Instead, the bottom was flat, with a one foot-in-fifty incline running from the stern towards the bow. This enabled the LST to land on a sloping beach and still remain relatively level. When the ship was fully loaded, the maximum draft was eight feet at the bow and fourteen feet at the stern. Empty, the ship would draw only two feet at the bow and eight at the stern. This combination of a flat-bottom and shallow draft ensured that the LST would have a tendency to roll even in the calmest of seas. During rough weather the ship could roll to an incline of 30° to each side, and in a strong gale it could even go as far as 45°. The LST was no duty for a sailor with a weak stomach.

To help compensate for the inherent nature of its design, the LST was equipped with a series of ballast tanks on the lowest level of the ship, the hold deck. While underway, these tanks were pumped full of seawater so that the ship settled lower in the water, thus lowering its center of gravity and helping to stabilize the ship. As they approached the beach, water would be pumped between these tanks to put the ship at the proper trim to get as close to the shore as possible. Then, once the tide went out, leaving the ship high and dry, the vehicles onboard could be unloaded directly to the beach. Located at the very bow of the ship on the hold deck were the beaching tanks, ballast tanks that performed another function when the ship was on the beach. These tanks were pumped full of water, so that as the ship became lighter while being unloaded, the bow would stay secure on the beach.

The LST's main and auxiliary engine rooms were also located on the hold deck level. Two large 900 horsepower General Motors V-12-567 diesel engines, the same engine used on diesel locomotives, dominated the main engine room.

Each drove an independent shaft and propeller and was equipped with a reduction gear for reducing the higher engine speed to the lower shaft speed. A pneumatic clutch system designed by the Falk Corporation allowed the propeller shafts to turn in either forward or reverse directions. Also located in the main engine room were the air compressors for the clutches, the lube oil purifier and pumps, engine coolant systems and the fire main pumps.

Just forward of the main engine compartment was the auxiliary engine room, housing three electric generators, each powered by its own 8-cylinder diesel engine. Rated to 440 volts at 1200 rpm, having just one generator on-line was enough to supply the routine electrical needs of the ship, but in times of increased demand, a second and even the third generator would also be brought on-line. Along with the generators, the electrical distribution panel, ballast pump, and the fresh water and fuel oil transfer pumps were also located in this compartment.

The enlisted men's berthing compartment was located on the next deck up, directly above the storage and steering gear compartments. Each sailor was assigned a bunk and a small storage locker for his personal belongings. The bunks were constructed of a metal pipe framework with a canvas bottom, on top of which was placed a thin mattress. They were mounted three high, leaving about two-and-a-half feet of space for each man. The inner edge of each bunk was hinged to stanchions evenly spaced throughout the crew's quarters. On the outer edge were two chains that linked the three bunks together and then hooked into the overhead. During the day, the bunks could be swiveled up and out of the way to make room for sweeping and cleaning the compartment. There was a head, or bathroom, located in the aft part of the crew's quarters. Two passageways ran forward from the crew's quarters, one along each side of the ship. In the starboard side passageway were the scullery and the ship's sickbay. Further forward in both passageways were the berthing areas for the soldiers while they were onboard. Near the bow were the ammunition magazines and the control room for the bow doors and ramp.

Situated aft on the main weather deck was the deckhouse. On the first level were the officer's staterooms, the wardroom and the galley. The staterooms were approximately eight-foot by ten-foot, the Captain's quarters only slightly larger. The wardroom was where the officers ate their meals and where they relaxed when off-duty. All of the crew's meals were prepared in the galley. At mealtime, the men would line up with their metal trays and go through the chow line in the galley, then descend a stairway (called a "ladder" in Navy terminology) to the crews quarters, which also served as the mess deck. Handling a full tray of food while going down a steep and narrow ladder could be a true test of dexterity during rough weather, and a bucket and mop were kept at the ready for the inevitable spills.

The wheelhouse, chart room, radio room and the degaussing control room were located on the second level of the deckhouse. All the equipment necessary for steering and keeping the LST on course were in the wheelhouse, including the ships wheel, the gyro and magnetic compasses, the engine order telegraph and the sound powered phones and voice tubes used for communicating to various parts of the ship. The 1MC, the ships public address system, was also located here. The degaussing control room housed the controls for the degaussing system, which consisted of a large cable that completely encircled the ship along the inside of the hull. An electrical current passed through the cable to neutralize the ship's magnetic field and offer some protection from magnetic underwater mines. For the degaussing system to work the ship's hull first had to be demagnetized, which was accomplished by running the ship under a network of crisscrossing cables through which an electric current was passed. Before beginning the process, however, the chronometer and all watches and clocks had to be removed from the ship, since the process would ruin their mainspring.

On either side of the deckhouse were two Welin-type boat davits that held the ship's LCVPs (Landing Craft, Vehicle, Personnel). Some LSTs had four or even six davits for carrying LCVPs. With a length just over thirty-six feet, the LCVP was the smallest of the Navy's amphibious landing craft. The LCVP could carry thirty men or one jeep. The davits could swing out over the side of the ship in order to lower the LCVPs into the water, and then swung back in to securely hold the boats while underway.

Aft of the deckhouse was located the stern anchor winch. The stern anchor was mainly used during beaching operations; as the ship approached the beach the stern anchor was let go and allowed to trail behind the ship. When the ship retracted, the winch would be engaged to assist in pulling the ship back off the beach.

On the main deck forward of the deckhouse were several tall, cylindrically shaped air vent housings. The vents drew out the exhaust fumes from the tank deck when the vehicles below were running their engines. These housings could be removed whenever the ship was carrying a smaller landing craft, such as a LCT (Landing Craft, Tank), on the main deck. The LCT was a 112-foot long landing craft designed to carry several vehicles to the beach at one time. While capable of making long trips over open seas, and having accommodations onboard for its crew of thirteen, the LCT was generally transported during long ocean voyages aboard an LST. It was hoisted onto the LST's main deck by crane, and held in position by brackets welded to the deck. After the ship reached the theatre of operation, another crane lifted the LCT off the deck. However, if no crane was available, the LCT could be unloaded by another method. Once the securing brackets had been removed, the LST would be put on a list by filling the ballast tanks along one side of the ship. Once the angle of list was steep enough, approximately 10°, the LCT would slide off into the water alongside the ship.

At the time she was commissioned, the *LST-325* was armed with a single 40mm gun and two 20mm anti-aircraft guns at the bow, and four 20mm guns mounted at each corner of the deckhouse on the navigation bridge level. At the very stern of the ship was a 3-inch naval gun which could be used against either air or surface targets. A circular wall around each gun position, called a "tub", offered some protection for the gun crew. Before the invasion of Normandy, the *LST-325* was fitted with additional 20mm and 40mm guns, and the 3-inch gun was removed.

As the workers from the navy yard completed their work aboard the *LST-325*, the first of the ship's officers and crew arrived in Philadelphia and reported onboard for duty. The ship's new commanding officer was Ira Ehrensall, a 22-year old Lieutenant who had served two years aboard battleships before he was given command of the *LST-325*. LtJG. Gordon Keene Jr. was the Executive Officer, or XO, and the ship's second-in-command. All the division officers reported directly to the Executive Officer. The First Lieutenant was Ensign Nathan Pritcher. As First Lieutenant, he was next in command behind the Captain and the XO and in charge of the ship's Deck Division. He was also responsible for the maintenance and integrity of the ship's hull and the ship's damage control and fire-fighting equipment. Ensign Guy Jackson was the Navigation and Communications officer; he was responsible for maintaining all the ship's nautical charts and records, the navigational systems and equipment, the radio, visual and sound signaling systems, the internal communication systems, and the safekeeping of all classified publications. Ensign William Bodiford was the Gunnery officer; he was responsible for all the weapons and ammunition aboard the ship and the training of the gun crews. Ensign Stanley Barish was the ship's Engineering Officer; his responsibilities included the main and auxiliary engine rooms, the steering gear, and all the electrical equipment on the ship. Ensign John Sarbaugh was the Stores Officer; he was responsible for all the ships stores and supplies, such as food, clothing and spare parts, and for the financial records of the officers and men.

As the first members of the crew arrived aboard ship from the Navy Amphibi-ous Training Centers and Advanced, or "A" schools, the job of organizing them into departments and divisions began. Every sailor had to be assigned to watch sections within his division for each of the various "conditions", or state of readi-ness. During routine operations while the ship was underway there were three watch sections, or shifts. Each watch section was on duty in their assigned area for four hours, followed by eight hours of off-duty time. The engineering gang stood watches in the main or auxiliary engine rooms, the deck division personnel stood watches as lookouts or on the ship's conn, and so on. There were other states of readiness too, for times when a heightened level of alertness was required. At "Condition III" there were three watch sections, and a third of the ship's guns were manned. During "Condition II", two watch sections stood four hours on, four hours off, and half of the guns were continuously manned. Each man was also assigned a "Condition 1" Battle Station, and a "Condition 1M" Beaching Station. When the "battle stations" or "beaching stations" alarm sounded, the men were required to remain at their station without relief until the condition was secured. Each division officer also had to assign his men to duty stations for collision, fire, abandon ship, and other emergencies. Finally, there was the Special Sea Detail that was set anytime that the ship was operating in shallow water, such as when entering or leaving port.

I was born on 8 May 1925 in Talmage, Nebraska. I graduated from Tal-mage High School in May 1942 and entered the regular Navy on 8 May 1942 in Omaha, Nebraska. I enlisted on my seventeenth birthday for four years. I was just a punk kid in a very small town in southeast Nebraska. I guess I was looking for excitement. I was intrigued by the uniform, knowing this was the one for me. While growing up I was taught to respect our flag and our country. I went through basic training at Great Lakes Naval Base in Chicago, Illinois. After one month at Great Lakes, I went to Norfolk, Virginia, for amphibious training. I then boarded the Joseph T. Dickman. I recall it took us thirty days to cross the Atlantic to be part of the invasion of North Africa at Casablanca. I then returned to the States. I served a short time on the Samuel Chase and the Susan B. Anthony. All three of these ships were troop transports and all were sunk later during the war. I boarded the LST-325 at the Philadelphia Navy Yard upon completion of building the ship, first part of 1943. I came aboard the 325 as a first class seaman; I was a deckhand. My General Quarters station was on a 20mm mount on the aft port side of the ship. Sometime later, I was promoted to Coxswain, which is still a division of the deck force. Chief Petty Officer Hughes was in charge of the deck division. He was a rough ol' boy, but he was one of the best sailors I ever encountered. He knew that ship from stern to bow.

—Harold "Icky" Allgaier, Radioman

I was born 31 March 1915 at Yonkers, New York. I attended the Philips Exeter Academy, Class of 1935, but did not graduate. I enlisted in the Navy on 13 March 1942 in Ft. Lauderdale, Florida. I didn't have basic training. I was assigned to Patrol Boat YP-331 before I had a uniform. After a month, I was made Officer in Charge. It was our duty to patrol a minefield near Key West. One night we stopped eight ships from entering the field. I transferred to the amphibious service in December 1942. I was assigned to the USS LST-325 in February 1943. I was a Coxswain Apprentice Seaman. My General Quarters station was as the pointer on the 3-inch stern gun, and then later on the 40mm gun in the same location. I was later assigned to Ship's Control and new rate Quartermaster 2/c. My duties were to check the logbook, check chronometer and relay messages to the Officer of the Deck.

—Bill Bliss, Quartermaster

I was born in Worcester, Massachusetts in May 1922. I graduated from North High in Worcester in 1940 and enlisted in October 1942. Since I was about twenty years old and the draft numbers were getting ready for me I considered my options. It actually came down to basic comfort. The Navy could supply a clean bed and not require a tight collar and tie for a uniform. That's why I chose to join the Navy. I wasn't drafted but I would have been shortly. I did not mind as my peers would all be doing similar duties and it would have been lonesome to be left at home. I went to basic training in Newport, Rhode Island and then went to Diesel School in Richmond, Virginia. I reported to LST-325 in February 1943. I was a Water Tender and after D-Day was in the auxiliary engine room. My GQ station was on the phones for the forward repair party, before D-Day I was put on a 20mm gun station on deck.

—Dale MacKay, Motor Machinist Mate

I was born in Philadelphia, Pennsylvania on 17 December 1919. I graduated from Taylor Allderdice High School in Pittsburgh and the University of Pittsburgh with a BS in Business Administration. I enlisted in Pittsburgh on 13 February 1942 in the V-7 Officer Training Program. I was in my last semester at Pitt and was able to finish before reporting to duty. I went to the USNR Midshipman's School, New York, located at Columbia University. Three weeks as an apprentice seaman, followed by ninety days as a midshipman. After graduation, I had a five-day leave, followed by ten weeks at Naval Training School (Diesel) at Ohio State University. After that, during a five-day leave, Shirley and I were secretly married. It was two years later until we were together again. Although I was commissioned as a Deck Officer and had ten weeks of diesel training that was strongly biased towards the engine setup of LCIs, after filing in to see the Lieutenant Commander in charge of assignments it turned out that there were positions to be filled for LSTs as well as LCIs and at duties in about all divisions. I requested and got the engineer's job with LST Crew #4079, which as it turned out was a wonderful assignment. On 27 January 1943, after an all night ride by train coach, LST Crew #4079 reported to Philadelphia Navy Yard and moved aboard LST-325 while workers were still painting, welding, etc.

—Stanley Barish, Engineering Officer

I was born in Canton, Illinois, and went to school there throughout my entire years at Canton. I graduated from Canton High School in 1938. I enlisted at Peoria, Illinois, and joined due to Japan bombing Pearl Harbor. I had to wait until 1942 in March due to my father being too sick for me to leave. I received my basic training at the Great Lakes Naval Training Station in Chicago. Basic training was not too bad, except for having to learn how to sleep in a damn hammock. Many times I was "flip-flop" around and on the deck, but I managed to get the hang of it after a few weeks. As to additional training, I was sent to Norfolk, Virginia to learn diesel engines on LCVPs. We did go out and participated in maneuvers with other LCVPs. We had a lot of fun but also a lot of work! I then was transferred to the USS Thomas Stone with the LCVP groups. This ship was a transport and we landed at Safi, North Africa (on the western coast of Africa) in 1942. We had a few harrowing moments there and several ship-

mates and I went into Safi, with a carbine and helmets, for a look-see! Little did we know that the town still had German snipers! But we got back OK, thank God! I was then transferred from that ship back to Philly where we picked up the LST-325 in 1942, and put it in commission! Everything on the ship was in turmoil at first, but we all got used to what went where, where we slept, etc. My assignment on the LST-325, at first, was as an Apprentice Seaman (deckhand). My GQ was on the 3-inch gun on the stern. We took turns loading and learning the ins and outs of working together as a unit.

—Harold Westerfield, Ship's Cook

I was born 21 June 1921 in Whiting, Indiana. My parents were Theresa and Frank Koncewicz. After the war, I had my name changed to Conway for reasons too long to mention. Graduated from Hammond High in 1939. I entered the service in 1941 in Hammond, Indiana. Just a little side note, I had a sister-in-law on the draft board but I still had to serve. I enlisted to stay out of the Army and knowing I would always have a clean place to eat and sleep in the Navy. I then went through four weeks of basic training at Great Lakes, Illinois and six weeks of Diesel School at Navy Pier in Chicago. I'm not sure of the exact date I reported to LST-325; best guess was in the late winter months 1942. Prior to that I had gunnery and beach landing training in Virginia. Once aboard the LST things changed, after a shake-down cruise the Captain revised all personnel. He went back to what the boys did in civilian life. Schooling didn't mean a damn. He assigned the crew to their new jobs. Me being one of the biggest onboard made me a Master of Arms. Nothing more than charge of cleaning the LST and security. I was in charge of a five-man crew. Got LST ready for inspections and made sure guys got out of their bunks in the morning and also tried to keep peace on ship. Mr. Sarbaugh was the supply officer a great guy and a great officer.

—Chet Conway, Motor Machinist Mate

I was born on 27 February 1914 in East St. Louis, Illinois. I graduated from Litchfield High School and enlisted in the Navy on 17 June 1942 in St. Louis, Missouri. I went to basic training at Great Lakes Naval Base and reported aboard LST-325 on 1 February 1943. My division officer was Mr.

Stanley Barish. He was a very nice and fair officer, treated all under him the same.

—Ellsworth Easterly, Chief Motor Machinist Mate

I was born in York, Pennsylvania on 29 November 1922. I graduated from William Penn High School in York and enlisted on 16 September 1942. I reported to LST-325 in February 1943. I was a Motor Machinist Mate and was in the main engine room. My GQ station was on a 20mm gun at gun tub #2. Stan Barish was my division officer, he was a good guy.

—Richard "Rem" Martin, Motor Machinist Mate

I was born in Newark, New Jersey 14 May 1922 at home, I cost Dad $50.00. I graduated from Central High School of Newark, 1940 after that I began a tool-making apprenticeship. On 3 March 1942 I took the oath, first at New York, NY (Church Street) and again at Newport, Rhode Island. Getting near draft age I prepared to be in the Navy. I took the chance to be around machinery, a clean sack and a hot meal. We were influenced by the Navy dress blue uniforms, bell bottom pants, Little Lord Fauntelroy collar and the thirteen buttons on your pants for a fly. Talk about patriotism, can you imagine our beer drinking liberties? I went to Newport, Rhode Island for four weeks of basic training, then Great Lakes Machinist School for twelve weeks. Then Cleveland Diesel School for six weeks. After Cleveland we were assigned to the Amphibious Forces, eventually we arrived at Solomon's, Maryland. Thence I was assigned to LST-325 in Philadelphia, then to European Theatre of Operations. I was Ship's Company until New Orleans when I reported back to Little Creek, Virginia for reassignment. My rate was Motor Machinist Mate. We had the responsibility to keep all machinery operable and keep out of sight of all work parties. Don't believe that, the engineers were a conscientious group. During General Quarters my station was in the engine room, either the generator room or the main engine room. During the real thing we were never the observer but we did listen. We did go topside at times to peek at the situation but after things quieted down.

—Bill Hanley, Motor Machinist Mate

I was born in St. Paul, Minnesota on 29 August 1920. I graduated from Faribault High School (Minnesota) in 1938. I enlisted in St. Paul in September 1942. I knew I would come up in the draft soon, probably a couple of months, and I thought I would rather go in the Navy, then to take my chances on where I would have ended up in the draft. There was no doubt in my mind about going into the service. I knew I would go in eventually and thought I would like the Navy the best. After basic training at Great Lakes Naval Training Station, I went to the Navy Gyrocompass School at the Brooklyn Navy Yards. I reported aboard LST-325, a brand new ship, at the Philadelphia Navy Yards, approximately January 1943. I was an Electricians Mate in the auxiliary engine room, the generator room. My other assignments were the on the repair party and, as a last resort, to pass ammo on the guns. My division officer was the Engineering Officer Stan Barish, a good officer.

—John Roberts, Electricians Mate

I was born in Westhope, North Dakota on 23 June 1922; the day a tornado came through and destroyed a farmhouse and barn two miles away. I graduated from a rural consolidated high school in 1939 at age sixteen. Rode horseback to school from age ten on. Over 1000 miles per year. I attended North Dakota State University for two terms until I ran out of money. I was sworn in to the Navy in Fargo on 29 September 1942. I enlisted not because the draft hadn't got to me yet, but because a classmate from our school, who was a year older, had the draft on his tail. I told him, "When you go, I go." I learned something when I was attending NDSU where their ROTC class was infantry. That taught me one lesson; my bed will be clean and dry at night and I knew about sinking ships but I'd take my chances. I went to Great Lakes Naval Training Center for six weeks and the U.S. Naval Diesel School in Columbia, Missouri for two months. Then one month at Advanced Naval Diesel School in Detroit, Michigan. I reported aboard LST-325 on 15 March 1943. I was a Motor Machinist Mate 2/c so the Auxiliary Engine Room was my "home". My GQ station was the "gun talker" for #5 and # 6 anti-air guns. On the trip from the Mediterranean I was the gun talker for the stern 3-inch anti-air gun plus two 20mm guns.

—Don Martin, Motor Machinist Mate

I was born in Minneapolis on 21 August 1921. Graduated from Deephaven High School in 1940. I joined the Navy on 13 August 1943 in Minneapolis. I went through basic training at Great Lakes and reported to LST-325 in February 1943. I was in communications as a Signalman. My GQ station was on the front 40mm gun turret.

—Don Roy, Signalman

I was born in a farmhouse three miles north of Ravenna, Nebraska on 28 July 1924. I graduated from Ravenna High in 1941. I signed up in the Navy in Hastings, Nebraska on 27 July 1942. Took a pre-exam in Omaha and swore in and a final exam at Great Lakes, Illinois. Then I went to a diesel school in Richmond for eight weeks and reported to LST-325 on 1 February 1943 in Philadelphia, Pennsylvania. I was a Motor Machinist Mate and my duties were in the auxiliary room where the generators were. My GQ station was on a 20mm gun starboard side in the rear of the ship.

—Emil Kolar, Motor Machinist Mate

I was born in Centralia, Illinois on 21 October 1921. I graduated from Centralia Township High School. I also attended two years of college in California and came home and enlisted after Pearl Harbor, as one brother was there in the Navy. I enlisted in February 1942 in St. Louis, Missouri. I went through basic training at Great Lakes Naval Training Station, Chicago and reported to LST-325 in November 1942. I was a Chief Motor Machinist Mate, head of all auxiliary engines, refrigeration, boiler and the care of the small boats. My GQ station was in the auxiliary engine room.

—C. J. Mitchell, Chief Motor Machinist Mate

At 0910 on 1 February 1943, Lieutenant Ehrensall began the ship's commissioning ceremony by reading his orders to the officers and crew assembled at attention on the main deck. Lieutenant Bailey, the Material Aide to the Chief of Staff of the Philadelphia Navy Yard, then read the document that placed the ship in full commission as the "United States Ship Landing Ship Tank 325." As he finished the order was given: "Hoist the colors!" The commission pennant and national ensign were smartly hoisted on the main mast at the same time the Union Jack was hoisted on the jack mast on the ship's bow. With that, the *LST-325* was now an officially commissioned vessel of the United States Navy. With the simple ceremony now complete, the officers posted the first gangway, security and engine room watch, and the shipyard workers came onboard to continue their unfinished work.

The ship's galley was still not fully in operation and as time for the noon meal approached, the mess personnel made arrangements to have the crew fed at the U.S. Naval Receiving Station. After the men returned from their meal, they were given their bunk and storage locker assignments.

Since I served aboard other ships prior to the 325 I can honestly say we had good accommodations. Our sleeping and bathroom facilities were on the second deck in the aft part of the ship. Our bunks were three-high stacked. Our "head", or bathroom, was tiled with marble over the steel deck. We all made sure it was kept clean. I could not gripe about our food.

—Harold "Icky" Allgaier, Radioman

We had chained bunks three high. The man on the bottom got all the end products from the guys above, if you know what I mean. No one wanted to be the low man on the totem pole. But all in all, things were great aboard ship; food was great, the service was great and above all a great, great bunch of guys. We had great desserts but you had to be careful, as guys were really good at stealing them off your plate.

—Chet Conway, Motor Machinist Mate.

We had very good accommodations considering that we were in the service. We had warm quarters, clean bunks…if we kept them that way. We had to put our stuff out to air periodically and it was our responsibility to keep our bed and our belongings clean.

—John Roberts, Electricians Mate

I had a bunk in the center of the main compartment aft. The chow was good most of the time. The ship itself was like a home away from home, though we were in constant danger when at sea in the English Channel from mines and torpedoes. On the cruiser (the USS Augusta) it was very formal and very military, but on the LST-325 it was informal, a more relaxed atmosphere and the men were friendly, like family. I liked living on the LST a lot better.

—Leo Horton, Gunners Mate

*It all depends on what you compared our accommodations with. If it was the foot soldier then we had it good. If it was "Home Sweet Home" it didn't compare. It depends a lot upon your Captain and we had a **good** one. It was a clean ship. Every so often, the Captain would hold inspections of the living quarters and workstations.*

—Bill Hanley, Motor Machinist Mate

Among the reason I had for joining the Navy was the knowledge that normally I would have a dry bed on which to sleep rather than a foxhole or whatever. Besides, though a landlubber, I had always been fascinated with ships. A cabin on the officer's quarters was designed for two persons and included bunk beds and storage drawers. The officer's head had a good shower and the wardroom with kitchenette was a place to unwind day or night when not on duty.

—Ted Duning, First Lieutenant

Next to the skipper's, my stateroom was the biggest and best. I had a desk with a shelf above on the bulkhead, where I kept the engine books. A phone connected me with the engine rooms. There was a cabinet for clothes, on top of which was Shirley's picture. The 2 bunks, one over the other, had real mattresses. Since my room was the biggest, when we carried armed forces personnel the one with the highest rank stayed in my cabin, but he still had to climb up into the bunk above mine.

—Stanley Barish, Engineering Officer

During the next few days, final preparations were made to the ship and civilian technicians came aboard to instruct the ship's leading petty officers on certain details of the electrical systems and diesel engines. A full load of fuel was taken onboard and the crew was given the order to make preparations for getting underway. At 0900, February 4, all lines were cast off and the *LST-325* moved away from the pier for the first time under her own power. The first stop was the yard's deperming station to have the ship's hull demagnetized and the degaussing system calibrated. The ship remained at the deperming station overnight, then returned to Pier 2 at the Navy Yard the following morning. That afternoon the first load of ammunition was received onboard from the Fort Mifflin Ammunition Depot.

After conducting a short trial run, the *LST-325*, now assigned to LST Flotilla 2, Group 6, Division 11 of the Atlantic and Mediterranean Amphibious Fleet, left Philadelphia for her shakedown cruise on the morning of February 13. Anchoring overnight near Solomon, Virginia, the next day the *LST-325* continued on Amphibious Training Base at Little Creek, Virginia.

On February 17 the *LST-325* had a change of command after Lt. Ehrensall received orders to replace the commanding officer of the *LST-391*. His replacement was forty-two year old Ensign Clifford E. Mosier. Mosier was originally from Juniata, Nebraska and had been in the Navy since 1920 as an enlisted man, before most of the men now under his command had even been born. After spending most of his career in the fleet as a Chief Boilerman, his most recent assignment before the war had been as a Navy recruiter. After Pearl Harbor brought the United States into the war, Mosier was given his commission as an officer in June 1942. On February 25, Ensign Mosier received his promotion to Lieutenant.

> *The Skipper was a serious person. I saw very few spontaneous laughs. In conversation he would force a smile every so often. Though his duty in the regular Navy was in the Engineering Division, he learned how to handle the ship very well. He ran a tight, fair ship. We were lucky to have him as Captain.*
>
> *—Stanley Barish, Engineering Officer*

> *He was a wonderful Captain; if you had any engine trouble of any kind he was always right there to help you. He was always partial to the engine room gang because he was in the engine room gang before he was made Captain. Good man always to everyone on the ship.*
>
> *—Ellsworth Easterly, Chief Motor Machinist Mate*

> *Captain Mosier (in the Navy it is customary to refer to the ships commanding officer as "Captain", irregardless of his actual rank) ran our ship with authority. He was restless and ambitious and expected a good deal from the officers and crew. He volunteered for missions and didn't like inactivity. He*

would walk the deck in the evening to keep fit. There were occasions when he would take our ship across the English Channel alone without waiting for a convoy to muster. He had the respect of everyone and was truly capable.

—Dale MacKay, Motor Machinist Mate

The *LST-325* remained at Little Creek for the next week, having final adjustments and calibrations made to the ship's radios and compass. During the evening on February 25 the ship was anchored off a beach not far from Little Creek. Overnight the wind grew to such intensity that, just before dawn, the force of the wind blowing against the hull caused the anchor to lose hold and the ship began to drift dangerously close to the shore. This was not an uncommon occurrence with the LST, due to its high freeboard. The Officer of the Deck immediately awoke Lieutenant Mosier, who ordered a general alarm and to drop the stern anchor. Before his orders could be carried out, however, the ship grounded onto the beach. He then had the main engines brought on-line but by the time they had warmed up, the ship had been left stranded by the receding tide. Ensigns Pritcher and Barish make a full inspection of the hull but reported no damage caused by the beaching. Later that morning, after the tide began to return, the Captain had a message radioed to the base at Little Creek, requesting a tug to assist in extricating the ship. Early that afternoon two LCTs and two tugs arrived from the base and helped pull the ship off the beach and out to a safer anchorage further offshore.

Later that day, the *LST-325*, along with *LST-355, LST-309, LST-394, LST-356, LST-337, LST-338* and *LST-307*, left Little Creek with orders to proceed to New York City for final preparations before heading to the Mediterranean and North Africa. The convoy of LSTs reached New York and anchored in the Hudson River on the evening of the 28th. The next morning, the *LST-325* and *LST-307* continued on to the Navy Yard in Brooklyn, and on March 2 workers from the yard came aboard to install the LCT loading brackets onto the main deck.

While the *LST-325* was on her shakedown cruise each department had maintained a list of items needing repairs and modifications to their equipment or spaces to better suit their needs. After they had installed the LCT skids, the shipyard maintenance men began working their way through the list, fixing, replacing or modifying as necessary. The work was finished by March 7 and the next morning a tug towed the *LST-325* to a new berth in the yard, directly astern of the massive battleship *USS Iowa*.

On March 10, the *LST-325* cast off from the Brooklyn Yard pier and, assisted by two tugboats, relocated to the Bush Terminals at Pier 3 in New York. Large wooden crates containing disassembled P-40 fighter aircraft were then loaded onto the tank deck. It took until the morning of the 12th to finish loading all the crates onboard, after which the *LST-325* shifted to a berth on Pier 45. On the 14th, a tug brought a floating crane alongside and hoisted the *LCT-202* onto the loading brackets on the main deck. Then, a LCM (Landing Craft, Mechanized) and a LCVP were loaded and secured inside of the LCT.

On March 18, the day before the convoy of LST's was scheduled to leave New York, thirteen Army Air Corp pilots and Quartermaster Corps officers from Fort Hamilton, New York reported aboard, followed by a company of the 794th Military Police Battalion from Fort Dix, New Jersey. The crew of the *LCT-202* had already reported aboard ship the day before.

At 0724 on the 19th, an overcast and drizzly Saturday morning, the lines were cast off and the *LST-325* slowly pulled away from the pier and made her way out of the busy harbor. Many of the men whose duties were topside paused to watch the Statue of Liberty as she slowly passed by in the hazy distance. Most must have wondered whether they would ever see this sight again, or return to the homes and families they were leaving behind.

At precisely 0900, the ships passed through the submarine nets guarding the entrance to New York harbor and formed into a column formation. Their first stop was Bermuda, where they would join up with a larger convoy before setting off across the Atlantic. After sailing through several days of fog and rain, the LSTs anchored in Bermuda's Great Sound on March 24, near the capital city of Hamilton. Here the crew of the *LST-325* would have a few days to bask under the warm tropical sun while waiting for the rest of the convoy to gather.

2

North Africa

On March 27, underneath the beautiful Bermuda sky, the *LST-325* hoisted anchor and made her way through the harbor now crowded with ships. As they waited for the rest of the convoy to form, the Captain held a General Quarters drill so the gun crews could get in some practice with their guns. One of the 20mm guns misfired and the ship's Gunnery Officer, Ensign Bodiford and Gunners Mate David George carefully removed the faulty round from the gun's breech and gingerly tossed it over the side of the ship.

By noon, the convoy was formed and ready to get underway. The first two days out of Bermuda the convoy sailed under ideal weather conditions, but during the afternoon of March 30 storm clouds began to gather in the west. Soon the ships were sailing through rainsqualls that reduced visibility to a minimum and after nightfall the convoy formation began to fall apart. As dawn approached the storm diminished, and soon the ships were able to return to their assigned positions in the convoy.

The *LST-325* was plagued with a series of mechanical problems during the crossing, the inevitable result of working all the bugs out of brand-new equipment. Throughout the morning of April 2, the auxiliary engines kept shutting down, causing the generators to kick off-line and the ship to lose power. After investigating the cause for the shutdowns, the engineers informed the Captain that it would take approximately an hour to complete the repairs. First, the ship moved out of formation and allowed the rest of the convoy to pass before securing the auxiliaries. By the time the repairs were complete, the convoy was nearly ten miles away and it took several hours for the ship to rejoin them.

Three days later, the air compressor for the port engine failed. With only the starboard engine they could not keep up with the rest of the convoy and again the ship had to move out of position and let the others pass by. It took over an hour to get both engines running and to rejoin the convoy.

On April 7, the port main engine had to be shut down again when the pneumatic clutch began to overheat. The engineers informed the Captain it would take several hours to finish the repairs; he then sent a radio message to the Convoy Commodore requesting a tow.

> *I remember when we left the States on our way to the Mediterranean, we were at sea about two weeks and our port clutch broke down. We could only go about four knots an hour, therefore the convoy we were with off and left us without any escort. The Skipper called me to his quarters and asked me if there was anything we could do. I told him that I had no idea what the problem was. But I had a little training on the clutch, so Captain Mosier told me that he would come down and help me repair it. The first thing we had to do was to stop the port screw from turning. We took a long crowbar and put it down into the shaft alley and jammed it into a coupling where it hit the catwalk, which stopped the rotation. We then went to the engine room and removed the cover off the clutch and found the air tube had broken, so we disconnected the reverse tire and plugged it off. This finally gave us power on both engines and we could return to our regular speed of twelve knots.*
>
> **—C. J. Mitchell, Chief Motor Machinist**

> *On our way to the Mediterranean we had a serious clutch breakdown before we reached the U-boat infested Gibraltar area. The Captain was in the bilge area working on the clutch along with the Chiefs and others. We had a tug alongside us to try and keep up with the convoy, but we felt really vulnerable.*
>
> **—Dale MacKay, Motor Machinist Mate**

The minesweeper *USS Steady* came to assist them and a towing cable was passed from the bow of the *LST-325* to their stern. By the following morning, Lieutenant Mosier informed the *Steady's* captain that the repairs to the port clutch would soon be completed, and that the *LST-325* would no longer need their assistance. At 0825, both ships stopped engines and the towline was cast off from the stern of the *Steady*. An hour later, the *LST-325* was underway on her own power and making revolutions for full speed to overtake the convoy.

On the 9th, problems continued to plague the *LST-325* when the fuel line to the auxiliary diesels became clogged. Throughout the day the ship was forced to stop several times while the engineers worked to clear the lines. It wasn't until after midnight that the problem was taken care of, and by then the convoy was completely out of sight over the horizon. The Captain ordered all engines "ahead full" and by daybreak the convoy was spotted bearing dead ahead, much to everyone's relief. No ship wanted to be alone without the protection of the convoy and the escort ships, especially now that they were nearing the hunting grounds of the German U-boat "wolf packs". The Germans had placed a picket line of submarines across the traffic lanes to Europe, when one of the pickets spotted a convoy they would radio its position to the others. The submarines would then swarm towards the convoy in order to attack it en masse, so that some of them might slip through the screen of escort ships and get to the vulnerable transports they protected.

It was close to midnight on the night of April 11 when the convoy reached the Strait of Gibraltar and passed into the Mediterranean Sea. Then, as the Officer of the Deck's (OD) relief reported to the bridge at midnight, the two officers discovered that the ships the *LST-325* had been following in the convoy were no longer in sight. The Captain was immediately called to the bridge where he ordered the helm to a course of 070° and by dawn, they had again rejoined the rest of the convoy. Further investigation revealed that during the 2000–2400 watch, the convoy had made three course changes, but the OD aboard the *LST-325* never received the orders for the last course change. When the convoy went to a heading of 077° at 2125, the *LST-325* continued on the last course of 083° and had sailed further and further away from the rest of the convoy. There were two reasons for why this had gone unnoticed for so long. First, all the ships in the convoy were sailing without topside lights as a precaution against enemy submarines, and second, LSTs at this time were not equipped with navigational radar.

On the morning of April 13, eighteen days after leaving Bermuda, the convoy reached the harbor entrance to the Algerian port of Oran. The ancient city of Oran had been one of the sites of a joint U.S.-British invasion in November of 1942, code-named Operation TORCH, that had defeated the Vichy French government in Algiers. After anchoring for several hours outside the harbor entrance until the harbor pilot became available, the *LST-325* entered the harbor and moored alongside the *LST-393*. That evening a crane lifted the LCT from the deck of the ship and lowered it into the water alongside the pier. By next morning the last of the cargo on the tank deck had been unloaded and the *LST-325* left its berth and anchored out in the harbor. At this time Lieutenant Mosier received orders assigning his ship to LST Flotilla 2, Group 5, Division 10 of Task Organization 81.1.2 commanded by Captain K. S. Reed, USN. The *LST-325* remained in Oran until April 26, when they, accompanied by the tanker *SS Polar Tank* and an escort ship, sailed for Arzew, three hours further east along the Algerian coast.

> When we were in Oran, Algeria, I went ashore alone and I was in a pub with two English sailors and a Canadian sailor. They got into a fight and I tried to stop it. At that point they all turned on me and I was lucky that some of my shipmates came in and rescued me.
>
> —*C. J. Mitchell, Chief Motor Machinist Mate*

> What I remember about Oran was the steep cliffs leading from the waterfront. Also the Red Cross building that held boxing matches and gave out bread and peanut butter for sandwiches.
>
> —*Dale MacKay, Motor Machinist Mate*

> I remember being in Oran when the USS Plunkett docked, the destroyer my brother was on. I do not remember the date, but we went on liberty together for about four hours. We had a wonderful time. A short while later a dive-bomber hit the Plunkett and he was killed.
>
> —*Howard Kramer, Coxswain*

> I'm sure it was awesome to all of us to see open view restrooms on the main streets of these North African cities.
>
> —*Harold "Icky" Allgaier*

> The first time on shore the odor of urine was terrible. We got used to it after a while.
>
> —*Don Martin, Motor Machinist Mate*

In Arzew, just after a tug had brought a floating crane alongside to remove the LCT loading skids from the ship's main deck, the sound of an air raid siren eerily wailed across the harbor and the crew experienced their first real General Quarters since entering the war zone. However, no aircraft appeared overhead and after a half-hour the "All Clear" was given.

During "General Quarters," each crewmember would proceed to their assigned battle station as quickly as possible, making sure to secure all hatches and covers along their way. Ships were divided into compartments, separated from one another with watertight hatches. The reason for this was in case the compartment's watertight integrity was breached by battle damage, the flooding could be contained to just the affected section of the ship. Some of the men were assigned to gun crews, manning the ship's anti-aircraft guns, while others had assignments with the Damage Control parties. The Damage Control parties had training in fire fighting and in methods of repairing battle damage. The Pharmacist Mates manned the sickbay and the battle-dressing station located near the bow of the ship and prepared for handling casualties. Both the main and the auxiliary engine rooms would be fully manned with the most experienced engineers, and the bridge and conning tower stations like-wise had the most senior and capable men in the division on station.

On May 1, the *LST-325* left Arzew and continued east along the North African coast to Mostagenem. On the 4th, the *LST-325* accompanied the *LST-383* to a training area called "Beach 11", located a few miles southwest of Mostagenem, where the two ships practiced beaching operations throughout the afternoon.

The "by-the-book" procedure for beaching an LST actually began several hours before approaching the beach, when the engines of the vehicles on the tank and main deck were tested. First, the exhaust fans were engaged a few minutes before firing up the vehicle motors. A close eye was kept on the carbon monoxide indictor located on the tank deck while the vehicles were running, an alarm would sound if the amount of this deadly gas reached a dangerous level. At this time, the traffic control light system was also tested. This control light worked exactly like a stoplight on any street corner back home; there was a red and a green light that would signal the troops when to begin driving their vehicles off the ship. After securing all the engines, the exhaust vents were allowed to run for a few minutes to clear out any lingering carbon monoxide and exhaust fumes.

As the LST drew closer to enemy territory the ship would go to "Condition 1—General Quarters." The Captain and the Gunnery Officer would man the ship's conning tower, or "conn". The Executive Officer went to his station in the wheelhouse and navigation bridge, and the Engineering Officer to his station in the main and auxiliary engine rooms. The First Lieutenant was in charge of the damage control parties; one party stationed forward and one in the aft section of the ship. Approximately three hours before the scheduled landing time, or H-Hour, the Captain gave the order to "Trim Ship for Beaching." With the use of the ballast pumps, water was shifted between the ballast tanks to put the ship at the proper trim, usually nine to ten feet aft and three to five feet forward. This enabled the ship to get in as high up on the beach as possible. Once the trim was properly set, the Engineering Officer then reported to the Captain. The Captain would then give the order to complete preparations for beaching. The third generator in the auxiliary room would be brought on-line to ensure that enough electrical power would be available to handle the additional load for the bow doors, ramp and winch motors. The un-dogging detail then "undogged" the outer bow doors, meaning they removed the large bolts that secured the doors and ramp in place and that helped to create a watertight seal. A report was then made to the conn that the doors and ramp were free and clear, which was then passed on to the officer in the bow and ramp control room. The ventilators were given a final check, a fire watch was set, the door and ramp motors tested and a final report made to the conn.

Thirty minutes before beaching the Captain gave the order to sound the beaching alarm. The ship would then go to "Condition 1 Mike—Beaching Stations." The First Lieutenant then made his way to the ramp and door control room on the tank deck. The ventilators would be engaged and the fire watch stood by with fire extinguishers while the troops started and warmed up the engines on their vehicles. The troops then removed the chains securing the vehicles to the tank and main decks. The elevator winch would be checked to make sure it was operating properly and ready to go. The stern anchor was readied for operation by removing the securing straps and making a check of the anchor winch.

Twenty minutes prior to beaching, the order would be given to prepare to open the doors and lower the ramp. One of the ship's Quartermaster's would be stationed at the bow of the ship with a sounding line that was marked at one-foot intervals. He would periodically make a check of the depth of the water to confirm the soundings recorded on the navigator's chart. When the ship was within a half-mile of the beach the sanitary system would be cut off, the corner ramp dogs would be removed and the First Lieutenant in ramp control would request permission from the bridge to test the ramp. The ramp motor would then be engaged and the ramp opened slightly. To save time after the ship had beached, the ramp was then un-clutched and put on the brake. Once the ship had beached, the brake would be released and the ramp could then be fully lowered in only twenty seconds. All stations for beaching would now report "manned and ready."

In the last few moments before hitting the beach, the Captain would give the command to open the bow doors. The First Lieutenant would then open the doors until they were parallel with the keel before reporting back to the bridge. The command would then be given to lower the ramp, which would then be lowered until it was about six feet or so above the waterline. When the ship was about two-and-a-half ship lengths from the beach, the Captain would then give the order to let go the stern anchor. The clutch on the stern anchor winch would be released until the anchor grounded, then the winch was allowed to run free and play the anchor cable out. As soon as the ship hit the beach, the order would be given to drop the ramp. The ramp was then lowered until it rested on the beach, the traffic light would flash to green and the first vehicles would begin moving off the ship as quickly as possible. It was very important to keep the ship at a right angle to the beach while unloading to keep from "broaching", or swinging parallel to the beach. Both engines would be kept running forward to keep the ship beached, while enough tension was kept on the stern anchor cable to keep the stern of the ship from swinging.

As the ship was unloaded, it would become lighter. Ballast would then be pumped to the forward tanks to keep the bow securely on the beach. When the last vehicle on the tank deck was unloaded the word would be sent to the conn, "tank deck clear", and the order would be given to begin unloading the main deck. The elevator pins would be removed from their sockets, releasing the elevator from its housing and the four corner elevator guides would be installed. The vehicles up on the main deck would one at a time be driven into position on the elevator and lowered onto the tank deck, where they would then be driven off the open bow ramp and onto the beach. When the last vehicle was off the ship, the ramp and bow doors would be shut, the forward ballast tanks emptied, and by putting the engines in reverse and engaging the stern anchor winch, the ship could pull itself from the beach.

On May 5, the *LST-325* and the *LST-383* returned to Beach 11 along with representatives from the 2nd U.S. Armored Division, onboard for an orientation tour of the ship and a beaching demonstration. The next day, the *LST-325* again left Mostagenem for exercises at Beach 11 with another group of soldiers from the 2nd Armored onboard. However, as the stern anchor was dropped during the approach to the beach it came undone from the cable and was lost. Since they would be unable to pull the ship back off the beach without the anchor the demonstration was cancelled. The ship returned to the spot where the anchor was lost and lowered the two LCVPs to look for it. They searched throughout most of the afternoon without success. Finally, the Captain ordered the boats back to the ship and the *LST-325* returned to Mostagenem. The Captain sent the ship's boats back to Beach 11 on the 10th, and after dragging grappling hooks in the area where the anchor was lost they managed to snag it and mark its location with a flag buoy. Two days later, the ship returned to Beach 11 and recovered the anchor.

On May 7, the American and British armies in Tunisia captured the ports of Bizerte and Tunis, marking the end of the campaign in Northern Africa. Before the Germans evacuated the two ports they destroyed most of the harbor facilities and deliberately scuttled ships in the harbor and channels in an attempt to render them useless to the Allies. It would take some time to get both ports back in operation, but both would be crucial embarkation centers and launching points for the upcoming invasions in Sicily and Italy.

Meanwhile, the *LST-325* spent the next few days in Mostagenem taking part in loading exercises with the U.S. Army. On May 15, the *LST-325*, *LST-386* and *LST-338* left Mostagenem to a training beach nine miles to the northeast. Onboard the *LST-325* was trucks and halftracks belonging to the 2nd Armored Division. The three LSTs anchored just offshore at 0135 Sunday morning. At dawn, the vehicles were offloaded over the bow ramp onto LCMs, which took them the rest of the way in to the beach. The LCM (Landing Craft, Mechanized) was a fifty-foot long landing craft designed to carry one tank or its equivalent in weight. It had a crew of four and carried two .50 caliber machineguns. After the LCMs were clear of the ships, the three now empty LSTs returned to Mostagenem. On the 19th, the Army began loading lumber and telephone poles for the Signal Corps onto the *LST-325's* tank deck. It would take until the evening of the 24th to finish loading all the poles and supplies onto the ship.

Red alerts were almost a daily occurrence in Mostagenem during this time, though typically the bombers were headed to other targets nearby. The evening of May 21 the air raid sirens went off again and the crew quickly secured from loading the telephone poles and manned their battle stations. Suddenly a barrage of anti-aircraft fire came up from the guns ashore and from the ships in the harbor even though there were no enemy aircraft in sight. The gunners aboard the *LST-325* also opened fire without receiving orders from the Captain to do so, much to his displeasure. The order was immediately given to cease-fire and eventually the gunfire across the harbor quieted down after the "all clear" signal was given. There was one casualty onboard the *LST-325* during this alert; Joe Snyder, a fireman in the engine room whose GQ station was as a loader on one of the 20mm guns, suffered a broken toe after a fully loaded magazine fell on his foot.

Each of the ship's six 20mm guns had a crew of three: a pointer, a trainer and a loader. The pointer was strapped into two shoulder supports that allowed him to aim and fire the gun. The trainer operated a crank on the side of the gun that raised or lowered the gun mount so the pointer's legs would be kept straight no matter where he might be aiming the gun at the time. The loader was responsible for loading the magazines into the breech of the gun. Each magazine contained sixty rounds of 20mm ammunition, which were designed to explode on impact. Every fourth round was a tracer so that the pointer could follow the line of fire from his gun and aim it accordingly.

There were four men assigned to the ship's 40mm gun: a pointer, a trainer and two loaders. The pointer and trainer sat on metal seats on each side of the gun. The pointer sat on the left side of the gun and operated a crank handle that controlled the rotation of the gun mount. The trainer sat on the right side and he controlled the up and down movement of the gun barrel with his crank handle. The first loader stood on a platform on the back of the gun and dropped the magazines into the breech. The second loader was responsible for keeping the loaded magazines coming to the first loader. The magazines were stowed in metal racks that ran completely around the inside of the gun tub. The 40mm ammunition was designed to either explode on contact or it could be set to go after a pre-determined amount of time. When the shell exploded it sent out hot, jagged chucks of metal casing, called shrapnel, in all directions that would damage any aircraft that happened to be within range of the bursting shell.

A single 3-inch naval gun designed for use against either surface or air targets was mounted at the very stern of the ship. This gun was manned by a crew of five; a pointer and trainer whose functions were the same as on the 40mm gun, two loaders and one hot shell man, whose responsibility was to clear away the empty casings as they were ejected from the breech. Each shell weighed twenty-seven pounds, so the men who were assigned as loaders needed to be quite strong to be able to slam these heavy rounds into the breech of the gun.

There were also men who were assigned as "talkers" for the gun crews. The talkers' General Quarters station was situated so that he would be able to communicate with several of the gun crews at one time. He was in contact with the bridge through a sound-powered phone and headset. His responsibilities were to report to the bridge when his stations were fully manned and ready after General Quarters was sounded and to relay information to the gun crews, such as when to open or cease fire and the location of incoming enemy aircraft.

The Army finally completed loading the telephone poles and Signal Corps equipment during the evening of May 24. The *LST-325* steamed from

Mostagenem the following morning to join a convoy headed to the port of Algiers, the capital city of Algeria and the principal Mediterranean port along northwestern Africa. The city's location and excellent harbor facilities made Algiers a very important base of operations.

I was on Shore Patrol once, I think it was in Mostagenem, when some were having disputes. I tried to take them back to the ship and keep them apart. That was a nightmare, push one ahead and try to hold the other one back. We got back OK without any real damage. When we got to the pier the ship was moving, only a shift for fuel or water or whatever. But as some of the guys came back and saw this they started to jump into the water, clothes and all! Even Paul Meehan with his pipe in his mouth! I guess the first ones thought they would be left, and then the others followed. No real problem, except the Executive Officer was up on the rail and yelled to me, as Shore Patrol, "Get those men out of the water!" Anyway, when the ship was tied up in the new location, everything was fine. Of course, there was a little "Vino" involved in this problem. That's one of the things I do remember well.

—John Roberts, Electricians Mate

While in transit the ships in the convoy would periodically and simultaneously steer in a pre-arranged zigzag pattern to prevent any enemy submarines from lining up a torpedo shot. Shortly after noon on the 25th, while the convoy was in the middle of carrying out one of these zigzag patterns, two of the convoy's escorts signaled that they had made contact with an enemy submarine and both immediately began dropping depth charges. The Convoy Commodore then radioed the convoy to make an emergency 45° turn to port to clear the area where the contact had been made. The depth charge attack continued until finally the British corvette *HMS Vetch* sank the German submarine *U-414*, which went down with the loss of all hands.

On May 26, the *LST-325* detached from the convoy and proceeded independently into the harbor at Algiers. On the 29th, workmen under the supervision of the British Army began unloading the Signal Corps equipment and poles from the tank deck.

When I got ashore I was rather like a sightseeing tourist, walking and taking photos. Every place we went was interesting. There were foreign cities, for-

eign countries and people. And the sight of them didn't let you forget that you were taking part in a war...bombed out buildings, ships sunk in the harbors, barbed wire, armed forces in uniforms from many different countries, etc.

—Stanley Barish, Engineering Officer

It took until June 4 to finish unloading all of the telephone poles and equipment off the ship. Afterwards, the *LST-325* remained moored at the dock to take on a load of U. S. Army half-tracks and miscellaneous engineering supplies. That night there was an air raid on Algiers, though no aircraft were spotted and no shots fired.

25 May 1943—Underway for Algiers. The best place since New York. One bombing here (June 4) but we didn't see anything or open fire. Sure I was a bit scared. Wouldn't you have been, there in the night, not able to see whether planes are right over you or not? Maybe a bomb is falling for you right now. You couldn't see it. Sure I was.

—Gunnery Officer Bill Bodiford's Diary

The last vehicles and equipment were aboard and secured for sea on the morning of June 8. That afternoon the *LST-325*, along with the *LST-385* and three merchant vessels and four escorts sailed from Algiers.

I remember the Red Cross in Algiers and other places, seeing the names of guys from my hometown. We all signed the book and it was a thrill to see one you knew.

—John Roberts, Electricians Mate

The *LST-325* anchored in the outer harbor of Arzew on June 9, having to wait until the 11th before they could enter the inner harbor and dock at the pier. On the 13th, the Army began unloading the vehicles and equipment onboard. During the next few days the crew took aboard provisions and supplies for the ship before getting underway on the 17th for Mostagenem, where they would begin preparing for the upcoming invasion of Sicily, code name Operation "HUSKY."

In Mostagenem on June 19, the US Army 1st Armored Corp began loading fresh water, PX stores, gasoline, ammunition and food rations onto the tank deck of the *LST-325*. Two days later they began loading their vehicles onto the ship's main deck. By 1700 a total of seventeen trucks, fourteen jeeps, one half-track and a motorcycle were loaded onto the ships main deck. The next morning they began loading the tank deck, bringing aboard nine half-tracks, six trailers, six light tanks, five jeeps, a truck and a motorcycle.

Throughout the day on the 23rd, ten more Army vehicles were loaded onto the tank deck, along with more supplies and ammunition. Since there wasn't enough troop berthing on the ship for all of the soldiers now onboard, temporary bunks were welded together on the tank deck. The next morning Army personnel began to embark on the ship. A total of thirty-one officers and 242 enlisted men of the 1st Armored Signal Corp and the 1st Armored Corp Reinforcements commanded by Lieutenant Colonel W. B. Latta came aboard and began stowing away their gear. Once everything was secured, the *LST-325* slipped her berth and steamed to Arzew.

The next afternoon a convoy of ships, including the *LST-325*, left Arzew for Tunis, which would be their launching point for Operation HUSKY. The convoy reached Tunis on the morning of June 28 and slowly the ships made their way into the bay and anchored off the city of La Goulette. During the next few days the crew of the *LST-325* had nothing to do except sit at anchor under the hot Mediterranean sun and wait for the word to go. The many months of preparation and countless hours of drilling and training were behind them now; ahead of them lay the island of Sicily and the un-tested crew's baptism of fire.

As a sentimental person I felt really homesick when the music by the big bands of that era were played. Glenn Miller, Artie Shaw, Harry James and Benny Goodman and the vocalist of that day were really a cause of homesickness. We missed our family and friends and eagerly waited for mail call. Shocking news of friends who lost their lives in the war were hard blows to take. We dreamed of what we would do when the war ended.

—Dick Scacchetti, Pharmacist Mate

Of course it got lonesome after awhile. You miss your home and the old things. But I had a girlfriend for a year or more before so I guess she was what I thought of most. But also family too. Dad and mother, two brothers and two sisters. Both brothers were in service, and my dad too.

—John Roberts, Electricians Mate

Being away from home was difficult at first. But in boot camp they kept you busy. Onboard ship there was always plenty to do. Overseas in a war zone you sometimes felt detached, as though home was a dream. I missed the good home cooking and the family. I was single while I was in the Navy.

—Richard "Rem" Martin, Motor Machinist Mate

At first it was hard, but if you kept yourself working that helped. Keeping yourself busy you get your mind on other things. I missed my parents the most but after about six months it got a little easier. It was my first time away from home.

—Gerry Murphy, Motor Machinist Mate

Even though you miss being home, being young and carefree with so many your same age made life a lot easier. Family responsibilities would change the outlook. Family is what one missed the most. The first leg of our voyage over the Atlantic brought out some signs of homesickness. One lad complained about a record sending out sentimental tunes.

—Dale MacKay, Motor Machinist Mate

It was awful hard to be so far from home, had never seen the ocean then ending up spending several years on it. I was one of the lucky ones to get to come home and get married and raise a family. I often think of the boys that we took in to the places that never came back…I remember the time I was taking muster one morning and I always let anyone sleep in if he had a rough night and I would count him present. This morning someone had hollered up for a mate that was ashore and I didn't know it. I turned my muster report in and later the Captain called me up to his office and said, "There's a mistake on your muster report. You have this guy marked as present and I saw him ashore last night. You know I could bust you down to Seaman for this?" I said, "Yes Sir, I know you could." After that I made them all be there for muster.

—Ellsworth Easterly, Chief Motor Machinist Mate

I was only twenty-two when I joined the 325, unattached, and to be quite honest, ready for adventure. After I married and had children of my own I finally realized what it must have been like for those on the 325 with wives and children back in the States. There was one officer whose name I no longer recall who joined the ship sometime after the invasion (Normandy). He had a wife and two children at home. When we were at sea he was a nervous wreck. He slept fully clothed in the wardroom rather than in his quarters. He was of little use to himself or the ship's company in that state and I'm sure his departure after a very short time was based on Captain Mosier's decision to that effect. One of the things I missed the most, chocolate milkshakes as well as real rather than powdered milk. I had grown up on thick milkshakes that back in 1943 cost all of ten cents. Other than that, since much of the time overseas was an adventure, albeit with unwelcome risks at times, I don't remember feeling that I was missing much.

—Ted Duning, First Lieutenant

We all realized that when we left New York it would not be a "piece of cake" so our minds had been programmed to do the best we can and finish it as quickly as possible. I personally took each challenge as a step closer towards home.

—Don Martin, Motor Machinist Mate

To be honest, things were going so fast and everything so exciting I can't say I was homesick. Naturally, I did miss my family but also thinking and knowing we were winning the battle gave all of us the "want to" to end the war.

—Harold "Icky" Allgaier, Radioman

Stars and Stripes at Sea

During the time they were onboard LST-325 the soldiers of the 1st Armored Signal Corp decided to print a newspaper, which they titled "Stars And Stripes At Sea." Each day for the next two weeks the paper was published for the benefit of the solders and sailors onboard the ship. The radio operators would take down the news headlines that were being broadcast via Morse code and the writers, editors and printers would get busy getting that days copy put into print. They also had articles explaining to their fellow soldiers this strange new world aboard a naval vessel as well as spotlighting certain departments or individual crewmembers. These articles offer a very interesting look into the day-to-day life aboard LST-325.

The Stars and Stripes at Sea

Vol. 1, No. 1
June 26, 1943

This is something to write home about because it's the first edition of the Stars and Stripes at Sea. Among other things, it's a reminder that Stars and Stripes will follow you wherever you go.

We started this paper with a big idea and a big hope. The idea was that everybody on this boat was hungry for news of the outside world. The hope was that there would be enough men willing to chip in and help. We got more than we asked for.

Our deepest thanks to:

Captain C. E. Mosier, skipper of this ship, and Lt. Col. W. B. Latta for their initial encouragement and constant cooperation; to Lt. Gordon Keene, ship's executive officer, who found us a place to work and gave us the stuff to work with; to Lt. Guy Jackson, ship's communication officer, who smoothed out our news source problem; to Chief Radioman Nicholas Cherok, who translated the dots and dashes into stories; and to all those Signal Corps boys who have volunteered to help him out and work in shifts so that we can give you complete coverage.

Seaman 2/c Lloyd Franklin Dewey, of Palmer, Mass., opened his mail the other day and said, "Whee!" The letter told Dewey that he was now a proud father. "I don't know whether it's a boy or a girl yet," said Dewey. "I'm waiting for the next letter from the Missus."

THINGS TO DO—As you've probably noticed, there's not much room for swimming or beach chairs on deck. As a matter of fact it would be a tough job to hold any kind of group entertainment onboard. Something might be worked out on the Public Address system; and if you've got any suggestions, put them down on paper and leave them at the Ship's Office, just opposite the kitchen.

Incidentally the Ship's Office is also the place where you can take out books to read. They've got several hundred titles listed and pasted outside the window. Pick out the one you want and drop around there in the afternoon from four to five and the storekeeper Russell will issue it out to you for 3 days. After that you've either got to re-new it or return it.

Vol. 1, No. 2
June 27, 1943

WHAT'S COOKIN' KID?—Talk to anybody in the ship's chowline and he'll tell you how much he likes the bread. "It's soft and light and fluffy—just like my girlfriend's dress," said one of the GI's with a faraway look in his eyes.

The most interesting thing about the bread, as far as we're concerned is that the two bakers who bake it are rookie cookies. Seaman 2/c Ronald Bibeau, of Nashau, N.H., was just broken in three weeks ago. As for Seaman 1/c William C. Yancy, of Portersville, Ala., he never saw the inside of an oven until six weeks ago.

Story behind the story is that Chief Commissary Steward E. M. Andrews of El Paso, Texas, really knows his dough. He had a bunch of bread recipes which he didn't particularly like so he juggled up some parts of each until he was satisfied—and the bread-eating crew was satisfied.

Andrews has been in the Navy for five years, spent four of them in the kitchens of a battleship, aircraft carrier, troopship and motor torpedo boat. "In the torpedo boat," said Andrews, "my kitchen was a four by five foot closet and if I was any fatter I'd still be there."

This is Andrew's seventh trip across—five of them have been across the Pacific. On his last ship he traveled 60,000 miles.

"Besides being the indirect father of 90 loaves of bread every day, I'm also the producer of a little baby which popped out of the oven on May 4, my wife writes me," said Andrews.

If you talk to a sailor about "storekeepers" the odds are ten to one that you are talking about two different things. To a soldier a storekeeper is a guy who stands behind a counter and sells things. But to the Navy boy's, a "storekeeper" is a chief clerk with 30 hands, like Howard Russell, SK 2/c, of Malden, Massachusetts.

Russell helps order the food, check it in, check it out, eat it, works with the supply officer, acts as ship librarian, ship secretary, worries about all the service records and takes care of the canteen.

This is his ninth month in the Navy and he's spent all of his time on LST's. Right now, Russell is only working with 15 hands instead of 30—he has an assistant.

Vol. 1, No. 3
June 28, 1943

Dear Editor:

Despairingly I beseech thee as a last means of delivering us, the ship's company, from a menace which is growing to such astounding proportions that we fear a complete relapse of our magnificent morale.

"Rebel" Hughes, our Chief Bos'n Mate, wakes us each morning with the same calls, which resemble a rhinoceros and a buzz-saw. "Hit the deck"—"out of 'em sacks"—"Make a move" and other such cat calls. Our gang has got together and we have decided that we want music, sweet songs, or a gentle tap to awaken us henceforth. Relying on the power of the press we anticipatingly await action upon this ghastly monstrosity.

Gratefully yours,

I.M. Pistof, Seaman 2/c

Vol. 1, No. 4
June 29, 1943

FROM THE BILGES—One of the most important jobs on the LST is the work of the "Black Gang"—the engineers of the Navy. These sailors, under the leadership of Engineer Officer Stanley Barish, form the largest division of naval personnel aboard this ship.

Usually laboring just above the bottom of the ship, they are charged with keeping the main engines running smoothly. In the generator room, they're constantly tightening and adjusting the engines which produce the ship's electricity.

Except for three members of the crew, all the men are without previous experience on diesels, coming directly from civilian life. "And a mighty fine job they're doing of it," says Engineer Officer Barish, who is proud of his men.

Besides oiling, cleaning and generally "manicuring" these powerful diesels, the boys are always applying grease to the shafts that turn the propellers.

Some of the men that breathe personality into these huge oil-driven monsters are Motor Machinist Mate 1/c E.L. Easterly, "Diesel Joe" Simondinger, who graduated from 15 years of auto engines to diesels, and Machinist Mate 1/c L.C. Turner, who is the only experienced navy man of the gang, having spent five years on all kinds of ships from sub-chasers to battleships.

The guys that probably get around the most on LST-325 are Electricians Mates 2/c Tom Crowley and his three "powerhouse" helpers. Everything electrical from light bulbs to the giant stern winch controller is their special job. "Oil King" W.R. Lee, another of the "Gang" got his nickname because he handles the transferring of thousands of gallons of oil and water all over the ship.

Grimy and greasy by day, the "Black Gang" sparkles on liberty nights, with Fireman 1/c H.B. Howard and "Jojo" Snyder in the van of the "Glamour Gang's" shore patrols.

ATTENTION JITTERBUGS—Our afternoon jive sessions got underway day before yesterday with Virge Anderson QM 2/c acting as musical selector. Anderson informed us that each department of the Ship's Company will take a turn at dishing out the jive recordings. Said Anderson, "We have a library of about 60 Victor, Columbia and Bluebird records, 4/5th of which are popular pieces." The sessions will start at the end of the crew's workday at 4:30 p.m. and will be terminated by the Lights Out signal at ten. Anderson tells us that only the inside speakers on the port and starboard sides and in the crew's quarters will carry the programs when the ship is underway.

NOTE TO SWIMMERS—Since there are no women within binocular-seeing distance of the ship, you can go swimming in your birthday suit every afternoon from two to 4:30 off the front of the ship. There's plenty of room for everybody.

Vol. 1, No. 5
June 30, 1943

PRIZE OF WAR—It was just a lonely, old rickety boat floating out in the middle of nowhere when somebody spotted it and sent the barge out to "capture it." The poor little eight-foot boat offered no resistance. In fact it seemed pretty happy about the whole thing. Especially when "Tex" Davis, RM 2/c, hitched it up to the barge and used it as a surfboard, racing as fast as the motor barge could go. Then the rope broke, and the boat slid to a slow stop. Tex rowed her over to the LST and hauled her in. Said Tex, "You never saw a happier little rowboat in your life. She stood up wonderfully." Tex hasn't named it but he's seriously thinking of calling her "Stinky Revivified."

SURFBOARD RIDER—Speaking of surf-riding, G.A. Bjargo, RM3/c, had a pair of home-made surfboards and yesterday he went bouncing all over the blue Mediterranean, until his boards broke. When his boards broke Bjargo's heart almost did too. "I like surfboard riding," he explained.

Vol. 1 No. 6
July 1, 1943

FROM PILOT TO PIPE-LEAKS—Mitch might have been soaring high above the rolling white caps of the blue Mediterranean today instead of spending most of his day beneath the surface, only the Navy medics pronounced him color blind.

For Motor Machinist Mate 1/c C.J. Mitchell, of Centralia, Ill., who has charge of the electric plant onboard, has 34 solo hours to his credit. He chalked up his flying time the hard way—soloing by day while pulling the "Swing Shift" at the Long Beach, Calif., plant of Douglas aircraft.

His dream of flying took him to California where he enrolled in the Civilian Pilot Training School. But that moved to Kingman, Ariz., when war broke out. Then came the medical exam, which wrote "finis" to his flying hopes.

So Mitch enlisted in the older branch of the Navy. His machinist background marked him for attendance at the Navy Diesel School, and after a sixteen-week course he was ready to join "the fleet."

Mitchell said, "My first assignment came as a charter member of this LST, when the ship was commissioned in February."

Leader of the crew that make up about half of the Engineers onboard, Mitch's men are known as the Auxiliaries. They're stationed all over the ship, but probably the most interesting spot is the generator room. There Raymond Hochwater Fireman 2/c, W.J. Hanley Fireman 1/c, Frank Jaworski Fireman 1/c, and W. Mack, Machinist Mate 2/c, are constantly stopping pipe leaks, cleaning valves and servicing the diesel engines, so we can have lights aboard ship. But the generator room is just one of Mitchell's responsibilities. He also has charge of the boiler room, where L. Bumgarner Fireman 1/c holds sway; and he has L.V. Mosby Fireman 2/c stationed in the refrigerator room to see that the refrigeration system functions smoothly so the perishable foods stored there do not spoil. The shaft house with C.O. Smith Fireman 1/c in charge is still another of his jobs. And he has to look in on the electrical maintenance room occasionally. Quite a job for this 21 year old guy, who only 14 months ago was a land-lubber from the Midwest.

Mitch has become quite attached to his diesels. He believes diesels will replace many gasoline-driven ones in the States after the war is over.

While speaking of diesels, we asked him how fast the diesel engines that run the ship could go. Mitch figured a moment before he replied, "Well, that depends on whether we're just operating or heading for the States."

TO MY OWN PRECIOUS WIFE

One year ago (Jan. 10—Sat. Nite 7:20), This night we wed,
In a very small town, where we both said,
That we would live together, 'til death do us part,
Living, helping, and loving, with all our hearts.
Never, Darling, shall I forget, that happy day,
Nor your beauty, your sweetness, and winning way.
Please God, may I have you, always to enjoy,
However, I'll share you, with our girl or boy.
Not once, in all my life, did I feel,
So happy, so gay—as when at last you did yield,
To become my partner, my own dear wife,
For from that night hence, began my life.
Nothing could be stronger, than my love for you,
I dream of your loveliness, your ivory hue,
Your sparkling eyes, your touch soft as foam,
Your kindness and laughter—our happy home.

Although our first anniversary, finds us far apart,
With this little verse, Dear, I'm sending my heart.
To prove that "I love you," 'tho I'm far away,
Also, Darling, to promise—I'll be back—Someday.

—Written especially for Mrs. C.B. Davis by C.B. Davis RM 3/c.

Vol. 1, No. 7
July 2, 1943

AT HOME ABROAD—War on the high seas is nothing new to this sailor. In 24 years of going to sea, Chief Bos'n Mate Francis Hughes has seen wars from the deck of ships all the way from the coast of China to the calm waters of the Mediterranean.

In fact, this is the second time that Hughes has shipped these waters. During World War I, as a member of the Merchant Marine, he was making Mediterranean ports of Gibraltar, Barcelona and Naples. "I saw so many sunken ships around Gibraltar then that the masts looked like buoys floating in the harbor," he said.

Back in China from 1925 to 1928, he watched Chiang-Kai Shek forming his Nationalist government, and was in Shanghai when he took control. "My ship docked in Canton when the 19th Route Army under General Lee swung over to the Communists, and they marched on that city and killed 5000 people," he related. Hughes and the Captain of his warship went ashore in order to make a report on the affair to Washington.

Hughes has been a member of the navy for nearly 12-½ years, and has seen service on battleships, gunboats, a supply ship and LST-325. He has had plenty experience in handling men (a Chief Bos'n Mate in the navy is equivalent to a topkick in the army), and when he retired from the sea in 1928, to settle down in San Francisco and get married, he became foreman of the Schenley Distilleries. "They're fine people to work for," commented Hughes. "They started a bank account for each employee in service and they put in one weeks salary every month."

Oddly enough Hughes has seen more of the rest of the world than he has of the States, for he has only traveled up and down the east and west coasts, while distant places like China, the Philippines, Honolulu, North Africa, Spain and Italy are familiar spots to this Navy topkick. Talking about the Far East, Hughes said, "Peking was the most interesting spot. You really saw the old China up there, you know." He thinks Barcelona is the world's best liberty port, since the senoritas of Spain include some of the most attractive women in the world.

When he joined the crew of our LST the last of February there were only two other men with previous naval experience among the enlisted men. "We had to whip a green crew into shape and I think we've done a pretty good job. We have a fine bunch of guys right now. Maybe they think I'm hard," said Hughes, grinning about the subject of the recent letter to the Editor, "But you've got to be tough when you're handling a lot of men." Then with a parting shot he said, "In the hammock navy of former days, the only music you'd hear if you failed to answer the first call was the swishing rhythm of the knife blade, and you'd be picking yourself and your hammock up off the deck."

Vol. 2, No. 2
July 4, 1943

SPECIAL MENU FOR FOURTH OF JULY
Chicken Barley Soup and Crackers
Southern Fried Chicken
Chicken Fried Beefsteak
Mashed Potatoes, Irish
Chicken Gravy
Green Peas
Buttered Lima Beans
Fruit Jello and Whipped Cream
Bread, Butter, Jam, Coffee, Lemonade
Cranberry Sauce

Submitted
E.M. Andrews
C.C. Std. USN

J.E. Sarbaugh
Supply Officer

NAVY PILL-ROLLER
"Doc" didn't want to talk about himself. "There's nothing interesting about me," he said. But we weren't there five minutes before we realized that E.R. Pittman, Pharmacist Mate 1/c, was a very important character on LST-325. Every passing sailor stuck his head in the door with some comment for "Doc". A soldier with

an infected foot sought his medical help; a captain with a blistered heel nodded gravely to his advice as "Doc" applied some medicine to the sore spot. Major Anderson of the Army Medical Corps, who was in the Sick Bay at the time, shook his head approvingly as Pittman prescribed for his patients.

When Pittman was only 17, he wanted to leave his Dad's farm outside of Smithville, N.C., and sail the seas. Four brothers had done that ahead of him (one of them is still in the Navy as a Machinist Mate 1/c). But his Dad thought he was too young, and "Doc" had to wait three more years before he could trade his plow for pills.

Because when Pittman joined the Navy 5-½ years ago, he went straight to the Navy's Pharmacist School at San Diego, California. After a four-month's course, he was ready for the Navy's Sick Bay life with enough medical knowledge to make a competent registered nurse.

"Doc" then saw 2-½ years service aboard a Destroyer Tender. This ship with a large crew serviced a squadron of Destroyers. Working directly under three doctors in ship surgery, Pittman really learned things.

Then came a couple years of shore duty, most of which was spent at the Naval Hospital in Portsmouth, Va. He was at Argentia, Newfoundland when the Destroyer Truxton and the Supply Ship Polox cracked up in a storm on the St. Lawrence. Flying to the scene of the wreck, Pittman told of his first sight of this disaster. "I'll never forget the sight of those broken ships—one was in three pieces and the other in two. Fifteen or twenty bodies covered the bank. We went to work reviving those that we could with artificial respiration, giving them dry clothes and warm drinks." It was a 48-hour stretch without relief.

In being appointed a member of the original crew of this LST the first of February, Pittman received his first assignment under what is termed "Independent Duty." His past record as a Pharmacist Mate having qualified him to be in charge of a ship's Sick bay.

So if you wake up some morning seeing mermaids, drop in and see the "Doc," he knows just what is wrong with you.

JUST A SAILING SAILOR—You'd never know there was a war on. There was Moe, in his little rowboat with a big sail on it, bouncing all over the blue. Moe likes to sail. He used to do a lot of that back in Bergen, Norway, where he was born. Moe's real name is Martin Malen, QM1/c. Moe was having a tough time yesterday with the wind blowing his little boat all over the place, first in one direction and then another. But when the boys started kidding him about it, Moe said, "That's OK, I'm not going any place anyway."

Vol. 2, No. 3
July 5, 1943

THANK YOU SO MUCH—Every Catholic aboard our ship was truly grateful to the officers who made the arrangements so that they could attend mass Sunday morning. Especially since this particular mass was a unique one to the men from the U.S.A.

Here before the eyes of the 20th Century Catholic Yank was a setting in which history was telescoped, and the universality of his Church became a concrete thing. Mass was celebrated by an English army chaplain and served by a French monk in a really beautiful French basilica. The architecture of the church was basically Moslem, but an atmosphere of the Crusades pervaded the inner structure for on the walls were small marble blocks bearing the Coat of Arms of many French Noble families of the past.

It was a thing to write home about (when censorship someday permits).

Vol. 2, No. 4
July 6, 1943

HANDS ON THE WHEEL—"Secure Special Sea Detail" comes the order from the Bridge. Andy relaxes in the wheelhouse just below and turns the steering over to the helmsman. Once more the steady hands and nerves of Virge (Andy) Anderson, QM 2/c, have safely guided the big ship through the narrow channel of some harbor to the open sea.

Although Andy has only 13 months of navy experience behind him, life on the water is nothing new to him. Andy comes from Brainerd, Minn., "The Land of Ten Thousand Lakes." There he spent his days sailing the Great Lakes, and in the evenings pounded away on his drums. Music and the sea were his hobbies. Later they were his life.

As a freshman in high school, he joined the school band, and for the next 11 years, he beat the "tom-tom" rhythm of the drum until he reached the tops in that profession—a Name Band. For one year he traveled over the United States as a drummer and vocalist for Hal MacIntyre, and then packed away his drums and headed back to Brainerd. Maybe his next job didn't carry the romantic glow of playing with a "Name Band" but Andy had found he couldn't keep another romance alive and travel from coast to coast. So he settled down in Brainerd and married the young lady.

Then came the war. So the guy who had toyed with sailboats took to the sea in earnest. He enrolled in the Navy's Quartermaster School at Great Lakes, Illinois.

After finishing a four-month course, he was ready for the big ships and life on the oceans. But it wasn't until this LST was commissioned in February that he got his first sea assignment.

As we've already told you, it's Andy's hands that dominate the mighty bulk of the ship as she eases in and out of the harbors, or cutting through the waves in the rough weather on the open sea. "But steering a ship is a round-the-clock job," Andy informed us, "and there are six other guys onboard who know their stuff about the work too." These fellows who stand their watches at the wheel are J.H. Hiley, S1/c; R.C. Lemieux, S1/c; H.G. Allgaier, S1/c; David George, GM3/c; and Cox H. White.

"Steering a ship is nothing like driving a car," Andy said when we tried to make the comparison. "When traveling the broad ocean storms, currents, tides and winds affect our course, and its nothing at all like driving your Ford Convertible across the smooth flat surface of a super-highway." It seems the helmsman, besides following the orders of the Officer of the Deck shouted to him through the voice tube from the Bridge, must keep one eye "peeled" at all times on the Repeater Gyro in front of him. He also looks out through the portholes at the sea as it rolls away before the bow of the ship.

"The most important instrument on any ship, and probably the most expensive one, is the Gyro System," Andy surmised. The Master Gyro is housed in a compartment below deck, and its readings are reflected on the Repeater Gyro in the wheelhouse. The Master Gyro system alone for a ship like this costs approximately $15,000.00 The Gyro is to a ship what a compass is to a person traveling across a trackless land.

The order from the Bridge that the Helmsman likes to hear is "Steady as she goes" for he knows then that the course he is holding meets with the complete approval of the Officer of the Deck.

But to Andy, as with all wandering sailors from the U.S.A., the most welcome command from the Bridge will be "Set Special Sea Detail" as ole' LST-325 rolls into sight of the Statue of Liberty, and his hands grasp the wheel to ease the ship along the piers behind which rise the tallest buildings in the world.

MOVING DAY—Bob and Pete have a new home—a bright new airy duplex. Bob and Pete are the two canaries onboard ship. They belong to E.M. Andrews, Chief Commissary Steward. Until yesterday our little seabirds spent their time in separate cages in the crews quarters or on the fantail. But the boys felt that the songsters would be happier if they could be together. So a brand new double cage was built to eliminate the possibility of Bob being left on the fantail and Pete down in the crew's quarters.

Now all Pete and Bob are looking for are a Patricia and a Betty to share their new homes

Vol. 2, No. 5
July 7, 1943

A LITTLE BIRD TOLD HIM—"Guess he read in the Stars and Stripes where we had a couple of empty cages since our canaries got their new ones," Said Tom Crowley, EM2/c. Tom was referring to the little ground-owl (he looks like a sparrow) that was picked up in the water yesterday afternoon by one of the crew. "Doc" Pittman, on looking the injured bird over, said that it had a "wounded rudder." "Apparently his condition isn't serious," Crowley said, "because he seemed quite friendly and not the least bit scared when he took over Pete the canary's former bunk."

3

Sicily

10 July 1943, was D-Day for Operation HUSKY, code name for the Allied invasion of Sicily. The invasion plan called for seven allied divisions to go ashore along a hundred-mile long beachhead along the southeastern coast of Sicily. Four divisions of the British Eighth Army would land south of Syracuse, while at the same time General Patton's Seventh Army would land three divisions in the Gulf of Gela, supported by airborne assaults behind the beachhead. After the beachhead was secure the Eighth Army would then push north along the eastern coast to the city of Messina and cut Sicily off from the toe of Italy. Meanwhile, the Seventh's main objectives would be to capture several vital airfields located through the heart of Sicily and to protect the Eighth Army's flank.

The American Western Naval Task Force would transport Patton's Seventh Army to Sicily. It would be divided into three Attack Forces: Task Force 86 (JOSS Force), commanded by Rear Admiral Richard Connolly, would transport the 3rd Infantry Division and two Ranger Battalions to Licata. Task Force 81 (DIME Force), commanded by Rear Admiral Hall, transported the 1st Infantry Division to Gela. Task Force 85 (CENT Force), commanded by Rear Admiral Kirk, would transport the 45th Infantry Division to Scoglitti. The floating reserve (KOOL Force), commanded by Captain K. S. Reed, would carry the reinforcements for the DIME Force. The *LST-325* was assigned to the KOOL Force.

One of the biggest worries for the Allies was the enemy armor divisions on Sicily. The Americans knew they would have to land their own tanks and anti-tank guns as quickly as possible before the enemy tanks counter-attacked and created havoc among the lightly armed assault troops. The tanks and anti-tank guns would be brought to Sicily aboard the fleet's LSTs and LCTs, but the beaches along the southern coast of Sicily would present the biggest obstacle to getting them to the troops ashore. Lying off the many of the beaches were sandbars that the smaller LCTs would be able to cross, but not the larger and heavier LSTs.

Between the sandbars and the beach were runnels, miniature lagoons deep enough to drown any tank or vehicle that attempted to drive through them.

Army engineers came up with a solution for this problem with the pontoon causeway. A number of standard 5' X 5' X 7' steel pontoon sections were joined together to form a causeway, or bridge, that could extend from the shoreline, span the runnels, and cross over the sandbars. The LSTs could then moor to the end of the causeway and the vehicles and equipment driven to the beach. LSTs would carry the causeways to Sicily by either having them slung alongside, or by towing them behind the ship. In addition, some LCTs were modified so they could dock on the open ramp of an LST and the vehicles could cross to a second LCT moored to the opposite end, bridging the sandbar.

Another new amphibious craft that would see action for the first time during Operation HUSKY was the DUKW, a 2-½ ton amphibious truck commonly known as the "Duck". The DUKW (an acronym based on D-model year 1942, U-amphibian, K-all wheel drive, W-dual rear axles) could be launched at sea and swim to shore using it's own propeller system, once it reached the beach it could be driven ashore just like a normal truck. Its primary use was to ferry ammunition, supplies, and equipment from the transport ships to the beach. The DUKW proved to be very successful in this and in every subsequent amphibious assault during the war.

> *Just before the invasion we were loaded with the Army and we had one of our auxiliary engines down, waiting for parts, and then the #2 diesel developed a bad knock and I had to shut it down. The bad thing about this was we had to have two engines to get off the beach. So we tore it down and the Army sent an Army engineer down to help us sand the shaft down and put in a new bearing, which worked fine.*
>
> **—C. J. Mitchell, *Chief Motor Machinist Mate***

At 0645 on July 8, the *LST-325* began making her way through the channel and out to the Gulf of Tunis. After the KOOL Force LST group had formed they steamed south along with LSTs from the DIME and CENT Forces. Later that evening, they turned eastward toward the Task Force marshaling point near the island of Malta. The purpose for this roundabout course was to hopefully confuse the enemy as to where the invasion fleet was heading, that instead of Sicily that Italy or even Greece might be their destination.

As the ships sailed east towards the Malta, a message from Admiral of the Fleet Sir Andrew B. Cunningham, the supreme naval commander in this operation, was broadcast to every ship:

> *"We are about to embark on the most momentous enterprise of the war—striking for the first time at the enemy in his own land. Success means the opening of the "Second Front" with all that it implies, and the first move toward the rapid and decisive defeat of our enemies. Our object is clear and our primary duty is to place this vast expedition ashore in the minimum time and subsequently to maintain our military and air forces as they drive relentlessly forward into enemy territory. In the light of this duty, great risks must be and are to be accepted. The safety of our own ships and all distracting considerations are to be relegated to second place, or disregarded as the accomplishments of our primary duty may require. On every commanding officer, officer and rating rests the individual and personal duty of ensuring that no flinching in determination or failure of effort on his own part will hamper this great enterprise. I rest confidant in this resolution, skill and endurance of you all to whom this momentous enterprise is entrusted."*

At mid-afternoon the lookouts aboard the *LST-325* spotted Malta along the southern horizon. Soon the LST force reached the marshalling point and came about to a northwesterly heading towards Sicily. The KOOL LST Group then separated from the convoy and proceeded independently under the command of Lt. Markham.

The weather had been clear for several days preceding the fleets sailing, but at dawn on the 9th the wind began to blow with ever-increasing strength out of the northwest. By nightfall the winds had reached gale-force intensity, and with the building seas the ships were having a difficult time maintaining their positions in the convoy.

> *When the ships were all loaded and "sealed" they all went out in some of the roughest seas you could imagine. The GI's were getting so sick you would wonder how they could go on an invasion. It was also rough all the way. When we got there I could see some of them were almost green in the face, I*

bet they wanted off! We were happy to unload and leave the area, back for another load.

—**John Roberts, Electricians Mate**

The LSTs had made their rendezvous with the KOOL Force section of LCIs on the 9th, as scheduled. By midnight, the smaller LCIs, unable to maintain their position in the high seas and gale-force winds, began to scatter from the rest of the flotilla. At that time the winds began to subside and the LCIs straggled back into formation throughout the early hours of the 10th. The LCI (Landing Craft, Infantry), designed to carry infantry, looked more like a traditional ship than the other types of landing craft because it did not have a ramp on the bow. Instead, two narrow ramps along either side of the bow were lowered after the craft had beached. They could carry up to 200 soldiers for more than forty-eight hours. Over 158 feet in length, an LCI had a crew of four officers and twenty-four men.

As we steamed through the night to a rendezvous off Malta the weather was very rough. I stayed topside to keep from getting seasick. There was talk of the invasion being cancelled. However, the weather improved and the invasion proceeded. We had aboard a group of General Patton's officers who had large, maybe six by eight foot, maps mounted and standing inside Army "Ducks", ready to go ashore when the time came. Meanwhile they were getting reports about the progress ashore and keeping track of it with pushpins on the large maps.

—**Stanley Barish, Engineering Officer**

At 0200 the KOOL Force ships began circling on station, fifteen miles south of Gela, while the DIME Force continued on toward the assault beaches. As the first waves of soldiers went ashore, the soldiers and sailors aboard the *LST-325* could see flashes from bombs and artillery along the horizon and the beams from enemy searchlights and tracer rounds arcing through the night sky towards the transport planes carrying the American paratroopers. While at most points along the Allied beachhead the resistance from the demoralized and war-weary Italian troops was relatively light, in the center of the American front around Gela there was bitter fighting as the soldiers and Rangers fought off determined German and Italian counter-attacks.

As soon as daylight came the troops on the beaches and the ships anchored offshore came under attack from German aircraft. At 0520, the *LST-325* went to general quarters when a large twin-engine bomber approached the reserve task force. Some of the bombs fell within a couple hundred yards of the *LST-325*, the explosions reverberating through her hull. No ships suffered any damage from this attack.

In Gela the Army was in desperate need of their tanks and anti-tank guns, most of which were still sitting aboard the LSTs, to fight off the enemy armored counter-attacks now bearing down on them. The army had hoped to use the large pier in Gela to help unload the ships, but as soon the first landing craft appeared the Italians defending the town blew it up. Only two pontoon causeways had been designated for the Gela invasion area, and one of those was with an LST that had gotten lost in the dark and was now miles away. The last remaining causeway was with the *LST-338*. Somehow, their crew managed to get the causeway deployed even as bombs and shells from German artillery fell around them. Other LSTs were offloading the weapons so desperately needed onto the smaller landing craft, but as the day went on the congestion and confusion on the beach continued to mount and few of the tanks and anti-tank guns were brought into action.

Late that afternoon the *LST-313* was attempting to rig another causeway when a German fighter plane came streaking in from out of the setting sun and released its bomb, striking her amidships. It tore through the main deck and exploded amidst the vehicles and ammunition below. Instantly the ship became a raging inferno. Sailors and soldiers on the beach rescued several men from the blazing LST by swimming out to the open bow of the ship and dragging them to shore. In a display of rare courage and brilliant seamanship the skipper of the *LST-311*, Lieutenant Robert Coleman, swung his ship around and placed its bow on the stern of the stricken LST. Eighty men trapped on the stern of the burning ship managed to escape death thanks to this courageous act. Almost miraculously, only 20 soldiers and one sailor were killed. For his actions, Lieutenant Coleman received the Navy Cross.

An LST had been hit by a bomb I think, anyway it was all burned out. Later, I went through it with a couple other guys and in the tank deck were several jeeps and trucks that were burned out.

—Emil Kolar, Motor Machinist Mate

At 0650 on the morning of July 11, the crew of the *LST-325* again manned their battle stations when a flight of fifteen Italian bombers attacked the ships anchored in the transport area. Again no ships were hit during the raid, but the explosion from a near miss did kill seven soldiers aboard the troop transport *USS Barnett*.

At 0900, the *LST-325* received orders to move in closer to the beach. As they prepared to get underway, the cruiser *USS Boise* crossed directly in front of the ship, firing her batteries of five and six inch guns inland. Until the Army could get more of their anti-tank weapons into the fight, they relied on fire support missions from the warships prowling offshore to counter the German tanks now approaching across the hills and plain north of Gela. Repeatedly the fire-control parties ashore would radio the location of the enemy tank formations out to the warships in the bay. Without the gunfire support from the Navy the soldiers ashore would have been at the mercy of the German armor and quite possibly been forced to withdraw from the beaches.

> *At Gela we witnessed the first naval battle with army tanks. On the first day we were at the verge of losing our beachhead when some Nazi tanks arrived. The Army sent messages to the USS Boise and "Bang!" That tank was scrap iron. More bit the dust too.*
>
> **—Don Martin, Motor Machinist Mate**

As the *LST-325* and the other transports moved closer in to the beach, they began to draw fire from German long-range artillery. As the guns began zeroing in on the flotilla, two rounds hitting within a hundred yards of the *LST-325*, the ships were ordered to pull back out of range.

Twice that afternoon the reserve fleet came under attack from German aircraft without suffering any losses, however their good fortune wouldn't last for long. Another flight of German Junkers Ju-88 bombers attacked the transports, scoring a direct hit on the Liberty ship *Robert Rowan*. The fires grew out of control and the crew was forced to abandon ship. Moments later, the flames reached the holds full of ammunition and a thunderous explosion echoed across the bay. A thick column of smoke billowed overhead from the shattered hulk of the *Rowan* as she burned for several hours before sinking.

> *An ammunition ship was bombed and burned for a while then all at once all hell broke loose! We had to pull anchor and move as debris was falling on us and we were probably a mile away. I have a news clipping from the*

United States saying a "heavy cloud" in the background; it was that explod-
ing ammunition ship.

—Don Martin, Motor Machinist Mate

After sunset, the *LST-325* and the other transports again were given orders to move closer to Gela. As the crew prepared the ship for unloading first thing the next morning, the transports were attacked by the largest German air raid of the day. The gunners aboard *LST-325* joined in as the fleet opened fire on the bombers. Just as the last aircraft of the raid were passing in the distance, the sound of more aircraft engines droned overhead in the night sky. What most of the ships below did not know was that these were American C-47 transport planes bringing in paratroopers of the 82nd Airborne Division. The pilots were bringing their planes in low over the bay to avoid the anti-aircraft fire now coming from further inland. The gunners on the ships below, exhausted after nearly two days of constant alerts and repeated enemy air attacks, opened up on the aircraft now over them in the dark sky overhead. In the next few minutes twenty-three transports were shot down and sixty pilots and crewmen and forty paratroopers were killed. The next day the Navy gunners were horrified to learn they had actually been shooting down their own aircraft.

The worst thing was one night all the Navy ships tied up together started
shooting at the aircraft going over. They were U.S. paratroopers in C-47's.
I don't think we hit any, but when we went on liberty the next few days we
got some awful looks from the GI's we met.

—John Roberts, Electricians Mate

We were on the beach the night they had that fiasco with the paratroopers
being shot down. I remember one of our planes trying to stop us from shoot-
ing, which we weren't, that as he flew by I could see his face very clearly. The
next day there were many bodies floating around in the water.

—Bill Bliss, Quartermaster

Shortly after the initial invasion I witnessed Hospital Corpsmen in a small
boat dragging something behind them, which I later found out was a dead
paratrooper shot down by the Navy. Another screw up of communication
that they call "friendly" fire.

—Bill Hanley, Motor Machinist Mate

The following morning, July 12, LCTs took the soldiers and vehicles aboard the *LST-325* to shore, after which Lieutenant Mosier received orders to accompany the *LST-307*, *LST-335*, *LST-4* and *LST-369* back to Tunis.

> *During the invasion we were anchored offshore waiting to unload. When we were in Standby GQ I would go topside. Each time I would see another ship burning. The last time was an LST on the beach. We still had to unload the Army. The next couple of hours I stayed in the engine room. When we were given the word to get underway I thought, "This is it." But then I was told we were heading back to Africa, we had unloaded to an LCT. That made me very happy. It goes to show you imagination was greater than realization.*
>
> **—Bill Hanley, Motor Machinist Mate**

The LSTs arrived back in La Goulette on July 13 and the *LST-325* was quickly reloaded with vehicles, supplies and U.S. soldiers. As the *LST-325* approached Gela on the 16th, the KOOL LST Attack Force Commander gave them orders to proceed to and unload at the beaches in the CENT Force beaches southeast of Gela. But after arriving there, the beach commander told Lieutenant Mosier to take his ship back to Gela. Returning to Gela, the *LST-325* anchored in the designated transport area for the night, then docked to a causeway on the western side of the assault area the next morning and unloaded. The ship then retracted from the beach and anchored a few hundred yards offshore for the night.

> *The Captain gave a few of us guys permission and the money to go ashore and get some fresh fruit, something we hadn't had for a long, long time. The end gate of this story is we ran out of room in the head and toilet paper.*
>
> **—Harold "Icky" Allgaier, Radioman**

Before dawn, the crew began unloading the supplies and ammunition remaining onboard onto landing craft docked to the open bow ramp. When the last boatload was away, the ship moved to the transport area to wait for the convoy returning to La Goulette to form. Just before the convoy sailed, the *LST-325* received orders to proceed to Scoglitti, a few miles west of Gela. After docking at the end of a causeway, 310 Italian prisoners-of-war were brought out to the ship and placed under armed guard on the tank deck.

I recall looking over a long line of Italian prisoners. One soldier told us he was an American who had come to visit his relatives and Mussolini had put him into the Italian army. The soldier also told us that he had fought in Madison Square Gardens.

—Dale MacKay, Motor Machinist Mate

We took many Italian prisoners back to North Africa. They were such a sad and beaten looking group of young men. I'm sure they were glad to be through with it.

—John Roberts, Electricians Mate

The convoy reached the outer harbor of La Goulette late in the afternoon of July 19. The rough weather, however, kept them from proceeding into the dock area until early the next morning. After the Italian prisoners were taken off the ship, vehicles, supplies and soldiers of the 814th Engineers, the 1059th Signal Battalion and the 1941st Quartermaster Company were loaded onboard. The *LST-325* sailed from La Goulette on the afternoon of the 21st, arriving back in the Bay of Gela the following day where the crew unloaded the loose cargo and supplies onto U.S. Army DUKW's for the trip to the beach. Next morning the vehicles and men were unloaded over the causeway on the Blue Beach sector; the *LST-325* then retracted and anchored in the transport area. That evening the ship went to battle stations when an air raid warning was issued. They saw bomb bursts and anti-aircraft fire several miles to the west, near Licata, but they came no closer than that.

23 July 1943—Got ashore last night. Just back of the first little hill, more like a high dune, running along the shore just a few hundred yards back, there is a very flat plain extending for a mile back from the shore. Here there are hundreds of our planes on this natural airfield. There were many wrecked vehicles and discarded helmets, guns, etc. The Captain, Pritcher and Jackson went ashore in our German jeep today and brought back many rifles and one small mortar.

—Gunnery Officer Bill Bodiford's diary

Returning to La Goulette on July 25, the *LST-325* loaded up with vehicles and men of the 205th Quartermaster Battalion, Company F of the 19th Engineers, and the First and Second Platoons of the 3407th Ordnance Company.

The wind was very strong and gusty that day, and as soon as the ship left the protection of the inner harbor, they ran into trouble. The ship passed too close to the Power and Light Pier and was blown by the near gale force winds into the pier. The Captain radioed Base Operations for assistance and soon a harbor tug came alongside and helped pull the ship back away from the pier. Ensign Pritcher and Ensign Barish made a thorough inspection of the bottom compartments for damage, but none was found.

> *26 July 1943—Arrived at Gela. Red alert tonight. Could see heavy AA fire and bombs some miles away. Heard one plane overhead. Saw none. They apparently hit ammunition dumps about nine miles off, starting fires.*
>
> **—Gunner Officer Bill Bodiford's diary**

The convoy reached Gela on the 27th, but at noon the following day the captain of the *LST-338*, the convoy flagship, signaled the *LST-325* to prepare to get underway and to follow them, giving no indication of where their destination might be. The two LSTs sailed to the JOSS Force transport area off Licata and unloaded. Military Police units then marched 730 Italian prisoners-of-war out to the ship, placing them under armed guard on the tank deck. However, the Army had not issued enough rations to feed the prisoners for the trip to La Goulette. Lieutenant Mosier contacted the Army port authorities and informed them of the shortage and shortly afterwards additional rations were brought to the ship.

> *27 July 1943—Went to Licata. Bought some melons costing about 20 cents, which in Tunis cast $1.00, which will cost that here soon. They just haven't got on to it yet.*
>
> **—Gunner Officer Bill Bodiford's diary**

The *LST-325* sailed with a convoy on the 29th. At 1956 the warships escorting the convoy signaled they had made contact with an enemy submarine and all ships went to battle stations. After nearly an hour of cat-and-mouse searching and hunting, the American sub chaser *USS PC-624* depth charged and sank the German submarine *U-375*. After midnight one of the escort ships off the port beam of the *LST-325* fired off a star-shell rocket, signaling another contact, and again general quarters was sounded. A second star shell followed and soon the distant concussion of exploding depth charges echoed through the hull of the ship, but this time the submarine managed to slip away.

29 July 1943—Underway for Tunis. Just before dark, at 7:55, as I was on the 8 to midnight watch, our escort started dropping depth charges. The order for GQ was given and we manned the guns for about forty minutes, then got tired and secured. We had another alert at 0230, but no subs sighted.

—Gunnery Officer Bill Bodiford's diary

After delivering the prisoners to La Goulette and reloading with the 15th Army Headquarters, the *LST-325* received orders from Lt. Markham, the convoy Senior Officer, to follow his ship, the *LST-307*, to Syracuse along with *LST-337* and the British destroyer *HMS Blankney*. Meanwhile, the rest of the convoy continued on to Gela. Lt. Markham reminded them that the ships needed to reach Syracuse before nightfall, since they could not enter the harbor except during daylight hours due to the risk of colliding with the wreckage of ships the Germans had scuttled in the harbor. Later that afternoon, the *LST-337* had a mechanical failure on one of their main engines and was forced to reduce speed. Soon it became apparent that the task force would not reach Syracuse in time, and Lt. Markham put the ships on a wide, circular course to delay their arrival in Syracuse until the next morning.

The four ships reached the entrance to Syracuse harbor just at daybreak on the 3rd. They were only there just long enough to unload, then immediately got underway for the return trip to Tunisia. After reaching La Goulette on the morning of the 5th, 202 men from the 55th Squadron, Royal Air Force and their vehicles were loaded onto the ship. The *LST-325* sailed for Licata the next morning. After unloading the RAF troops, the *LST-325* took aboard stores, equipment and vehicles of the 71st and 72nd U. S. Army Signal Companies to take back to Tunisia. They sailed from Licata at 1030 on 8th, reaching La Goulette the following day.

The *LST-325* remained in La Goulette until August 14, restocking the ship's stores and provisions. On the 14th they sailed with a convoy for Palermo, Sicily; onboard were sixty-five trucks, trailers and twenty-nine men of the 437th Aviation Signal Battalion, 160 officers and men of the Royal Air Force 255th Squadron, and 105 men of the 256th Army Medical Service. They reached Palermo on August 15 and unloaded, then were underway again the next day in a convoy of twenty-two LSTs, seven LCIs and five escorts for Bizerte.

While unloading we were given two hours on shore. The bombing damage was all over the port area. A crewmember, Mike Favazzia, had relatives in the area. He got permission to visit them. He came back and told the Captain that his family was starving. The Captain gave Mike permission to bring them food, which was nice.

—Bill Hanley, Motor Machinist Mate

Mike Favazzia had uncles that lived about forty miles inland and Captain Mosier let him take the jeep we had aboard and drive in to see them. He said everybody said they were his cousins.

—Emil Kolar, Motor Machinist Mate

The convoy reached Bizerte on August 17, the same day that the city of Messina fell to the Allied forces, marking the end of the Sicilian campaign. After mooring alongside the *LST-388*, welders from the base came aboard and attached a female coupling to the end of the *LST-325's* bow ramp, which would help to secure the ship when mooring to the end of a pontoon causeway.

Bizerte was where the Nazi's had sunk ships in the narrow channel into Lake Bizerte. Captain Mosier stationed men on all sides of the ship to report the location of the ships as we passed through the channel. If we had snagged one and cut our bottom it would have been "curtains" for us. The Base Officer had his pilots on other LSTs as they were in need of the base.

—Don Martin, Motor Machinist Mate

The night that the *LST-325* arrived in Bizerte there was an air raid; as the crew raced to their battle stations the smoke generators on the base began laying a blanket of thick, acrid smoke over the harbor. Ten minutes later a large formation of German Junkers Ju-88 bombers were spotted overhead and the guns on the base and the ships in the harbor opened fire. Captain Mosier gave the order for all the ship's guns to commence firing; immediately the word came back to the bridge that the 3-inch gun was malfunctioning. Moments later one of the 20mm guns was knocked out of action when a round fired before the breech of the gun was closed. One of the ship's stewards named Haynesworth was hit in his arm and leg by pieces of falling shrapnel, but fortunately his wounds were minor and he was able to return to his duties.

We were blessed with four good black guys on the 325. Vann, Haynesworth, Harvell and Brock. Their duty was serving the officers on the ship. They had

*their own quarters. I am telling this to point out that in 1943 there was seg-
regation between the black and white people.*

—Harold "Icky" Allgaier, Radioman

*Bizerte was so bombed out that there wasn't anyone living there at the time
we were there. Also we had the biggest air raid we had there. A plane flew
between our ship and the one next to us as the same level as the 20mm gun
tub; to be below all the anti-aircraft fire is my guess.*

—Emil Kolar, Motor Machinist Mate

The harbor facilities were hard hit during the raid, an oil storage facility ashore
had been set on fire and the glow from the flames lit the harbor for hours until
brought under control. Three ships were badly damaged and an LCI was sunk.

*17 Aug 1943—We have been up to Palermo and are now in Bizerte. It is
a toss up which of the two sites is wrecked worse, both are almost totally
destroyed. Why they call it "Total War", I guess...Tonight we had the worst
air raid yet. We saw no more planes—not as many even—as before, but
Haynesworth was hit in five places by shrapnel. All superficial wounds. My
#6 20mm blew up, ruining the magazine, and several ration cans on the
life rafts were hit. One had a hole about six or eight inches across. A man on
the ship tied up along our portside got a piece of shrapnel right on through
his head. We're still lucky. We go to Arzew tomorrow by ourselves with a sub
chaser.*

—Gunnery Officer Bill Bodiford's diary

The following afternoon sixty-six U. S. Navy officers and men who injured
during the previous night's raid were brought aboard the *LST-325*, accompanied
by an attending team of Navy doctors and corpsmen. As soon as the wounded
were secured, the ship got underway for Arzew accompanied by the *USS PC-625*.
They reached Arzew on the 20th, and immediately after docking the wounded
men were taken off the ship and transferred to the base hospital.

We carried seriously burned sailors from Bizerte to Oran in the crew's quarters so they could get continuous attention. We could see the cost of wartime actions.

—Dale MacKay, Motor Machinist Mate

22 Aug 1943—Reached Arzew without excitement. Hasn't been a raid here since I was here last. Very nice officer's club, movies, wine whiskey on order and…I hear…Coca-Cola!

30 Aug 1943—Went to Tenes. This is a resort town. Only place I saw with plenty of trees. A river runs between two mountains and waters the valley. These shore-based boys surely have the cream…nice clubs, meet people, plenty of everything, good food, movies, even whiskey. That's the life. Oh well.

—Gunnery Officer Bill Bodiford's diary

On August 30, the *LST-325* got underway, accompanied by the *USS PC-591*, the two ships reaching the channel entrance to Tenes at daybreak on the 31st. After mooring alongside the fueling dock, the main deck was then loaded with 50-gallon drums of lube oil while over 100,000 gallons of diesel oil were pumped into the ship's fuel tanks. The Navy was preparing to close the advance base at Tenes since the advance of the Allies across North Africa and Sicily had rendered this base unnecessary. The *LST-325*, now fully loaded, got underway in the early evening of 1 September along with the *LST-355*, *USS PC-625* and *USS PC-543*; arriving in Bizerte early in the evening of the 3rd.

1 Sept 1943—On our way to Bizerte. This little jaunt has been peaceful. I wish I had the words to describe the burning of the ship on July 10. It was loaded with ammunition and fuel and again and again would send a blast hundreds of feet in the air. When a magazine would go, it was like a fire in a firecracker factory. Tracers going in every direction. Even Hollywood can't afford a sight like this.

—Gunnery Officer Bill Bodiford's diary

4

Salerno

During the days after the *LST-325* arrived at Bizerte on September 3, there were several air raid warnings. Almost every time it turned out to be either a false alarm or the raiders were targeting another harbor nearby. However, during the evening of the 5th the sirens went off once more, and shortly afterward a large formation of enemy bombers appeared overhead. Instantly, anti-aircraft fire from the base and the ships filled the sky with tracers and bursting shells. Moments later a stray shell burst inside the ship's No. 4 20mm gun tub, sending red-hot chunks of steel into the legs and feet of the gun's three-man crew. The ship's Pharmacist Mate, "Doc" Pittman, administered first aid to the three men; Richard Martin was able to return to duty, but John MacPherson and Lloyd Mosby would require hospitalization.

With the bombers beyond the range of the smaller caliber guns, Captain Mosier ordered the 20mm gun crews below decks. Meanwhile the 3-inch and 40mm guns continued to hammer away at the bombers now caught in the glare of the base searchlights. The raid lasted for nearly an hour, and caused considerable damage to the port facilities.

The three men wounded during the air raid on 5 September 1943 were Lloyd Mosby, John MacPherson and myself. I am presently and have been for many years past the Adjutant and Finance Officer of the Military Order of the Purple Heart, York County Chapter #390, York Pennsylvania.

—Richard "Rem" Martin, Motor Machinist Mate

We didn't have aircraft superiority so we had many air raids. MacPherson, Mosby and Rem were injured at the #4 gun. The gun tub saved me as I was right beside but outside the tub. MacPherson lost a toe. Mosby had shrapnel in his ankle and Rem had shrapnel in his knee. I was their gun talker at the time. A 20mm was shot up at planes, which we couldn't reach, and what was shot up has to come down. Captain Mosier ordered everyone below after that.

—Don Martin, Motor Machinist Mate

9 September 1943 was D-Day for Operation AVALANCHE, the amphibious invasion of Italy. The plan was for the British X Corps to land at the northern end of the Gulf of Salerno, where they could capture the city of Salerno, the Montecorvino airfield and the important crossroads at Battipaglia. Meanwhile, the American VI Corps would land on the southern end of the gulf near Paestum, a town that was once the site of an ancient Greek colony. VI Corps would then protect the British flank and establish contact with General Montgomery's Eighth Army now making its way north from the "toe" of Italy. After all objectives had been taken, the allies would begin their push towards the vital port city of Naples, and then on to Rome. Lieutenant General Mark Clark, United States Army, was in overall command of the two corps.

As the invasion fleet approached Italy, the troops listened to General Eisenhower's announcement that the Italians had surrendered to the allies and many started to relax from their heightened state of preparedness. They assumed that since they were invading Italy and the Italians had just surrendered then they wouldn't be facing much resistance. However, what was being overlooked was that several crack German infantry and armored divisions would also be waiting for them after they got ashore. It didn't take long after the troops hit the beach for the Germans to shatter their hopes that this invasion would be a "soft" one. The landings that morning were among the most fiercely contested throughout the entire war and, just as they had during Operation HUSKY, naval gunfire was called upon to protect the allied forces from German armored counter-attacks.

On September 11, as the troops at Salerno and Paestum were slugging it out against a very determined German defense, tanks and vehicles of the British 40th Royal Tank Regiment were being loaded onto the *LST-325*. The next day, they finished discharging most of the fuel oil they had brought from Tenes into storage tanks on the base, and prepared to get underway. At precisely 1900 the ship hoisted anchor and joined the convoy now designated Task Group 85.9; their destination the British beachhead at Salerno.

The task group reached the Italian coast on the afternoon of the 14th, and made a slow circle to the northeast to begin their approach to the assault area. As the ships drew closer to the beach, the echoes of heavy artillery rumbled out from further inland. Just then, the lookouts spotted enemy aircraft diving from out of the sun directly towards the ships below. Fifteen fighter-bombers screamed overhead at mast-height, dropping bombs and strafing the ships with their machine guns. One low-flying fighter came in directly over the *LST-325* and released the two bombs slung under its wings. The first exploded a short distance off the port side of *LST-325's* bow. The second bomb, released a split-second after the first, narrowly missed a nearby Liberty-type cargo vessel. The fighter-planes were coming in so low that as the gunners on the ships tried to track them they were actually firing into the ships alongside. Once again, friendly fire proved to be more dangerous than that of the enemy when a 20mm shell fired from a near-by ship exploded among the group of men stationed on the bow of the *LST-325*. Ensign Nathan Pritcher (the ship's First Lieutenant), Ship Fitter 2/c Al Pollak, Coxswain White, and Water Tender 2/c Lee were all struck by shrapnel in the back and legs; four British soldiers were also injured in the blast. The medics immediately treated all eight men, but all were transferred later that day to a British Hospital Ship. Ensign Bill Bodiford assumed Pritcher's duties as First Lieutenant until his return.

> *During the invasion of Italy I was gun talker for #1, 2 and 3 guns. Our ship was straddled by bombs and strafed. Our GQ station was cancelled so I was in the engine room during this aerial attack. There were bullet marks on the deck where I had been standing moments before. A British soldier was sitting on the deck eating evening meal where I had been standing and a bullet took the spoon out of his mouth but wasn't hurt.*
>
> **—Don Martin, Motor Machinist Mate**

After the attacking aircraft had left, the *LST-325* anchored off the beach until the Captain received orders that evening to stand in to Green Beach, six miles southwest of Salerno. However, after the ship beached along the starboard side of the *LST-346* the British Beachmaster ordered them to relocate thirty-five yards further west from their present location. As the ship began to retract from the beach, enemy aircraft started bombing the front line positions north of the town, but left the beachhead alone. By the time the *LST-325* had beached again, the "All Clear" signal was given and the British tankers immediately unloaded. It was nearly midnight before the last tank was off and the ship retracted and anchored offshore in the transport area.

Our trek to Salerno maybe took a little of the bravery out of me. The one night German planes flew over, dropped magnesium flares and lit us up like a Christmas tree. We could not see them at all. I found out I could get scared.

—Harold "Icky" Allgaier, Radioman

The day before the *LST-325* arrived in the Gulf of Salerno, the Germans had launched a savage counter-attack in an effort to drive the Allies off the beachhead. Their armored forces struck along the left flank of the American VI Corps and drove them back while simultaneously attacking the British forces east of Salerno. Thanks in a large part to reinforcement airdrops of 82nd Airborne paratroopers the German drive stalled and the Allied lines held. As the heavy fighting continued on the night of September 14, the men aboard the *LST-325* could see the flashes and hear the reports of heavy gunfire coming from the mountains north of Salerno, just a couple miles inland.

The Salerno invasion was the worst as far as we were concerned. That is where we were strafed and had some casualties. We were scared. We had been carrying bag powder ammunition and aviation gasoline and why it wasn't set off when we were strafed I will never know. I got ashore once on the beach just to say I had been there.

—Bill Bliss, Quartermaster

Early the next morning the *LST-325*, in convoy with fourteen other LSTs, seven LCIs and four escorts, left the Gulf of Salerno for Palermo, Sicily. There, the ship was re-loaded with vehicles and troops from the U.S. Army's 3rd Division, getting underway for the return trip on the 17th. Late that night, as the convoy approached the beach area near Paestum, they received orders to to delay their approach as the beach area was currently under attack from enemy bombers. Heavy concentrations of anti-aircraft fire and exploding bombs lit the night sky and were clearly visible to the approaching ships. At 0300 the convoy were cleared to proceed to the transport anchorage. Later that morning, after sunrise, the *LST-325* docked on a pontoon causeway and unloaded. The convoy began the return trip to Palermo that evening.

Returning from Italy one night Bummie and I were sitting on a capstan or leaning on the railings. We had the Mediterranean, a full moon was shining and a nice warm breeze was blowing. Bummie said, "Wouldn't it be great to have our girlfriends with us tonight?" Little did we know that some stupid

British Naval Officer led us through sixty miles of our own minefield! Captain Mosier was mad!

—Don Martin, Motor Machinist Mate

18 Sept 1943—*Haven't written this up in a long time, have I? A lot has happened. We left Bizerte about 10 September with a load of Limeys and took them to the vicinity of Paestum or Salerno. It was still pretty hot there, though not like it had been a few days before. Just as we were leaving Bizerte the LST's came in that had hit Salerno. Three had 88mm holes in them (one had eleven hits) and one other had hit a mine. You know, two were torpedoed a month or so ago. We were talking to the Skipper of one of them the other day and he said the whole stern was blown out but that he filled up his bow tanks and took her into Palermo although it took him three weeks to make the trip. Just as we were steaming into the Gulf of Salerno something between one and twelve Me-109's dove on us and let go some bombs. One hit to port of our bow and one, well clear, to starboard. This one just missed the stern of a Liberty ship. The plane I saw was very low. It came across our bow from port to starboard. Only one of our 20mm opened up and the bow and stern guns. No hits on either side. One plane had had a little better luck however, because when we came in a Liberty ship was blazing ferociously. It burned completely and at great speed. Every once in awhile ammunition would go up with a terrific flash and tracers would go in every direction. I wasn't a bit afraid during the raid because I saw only one plane and it was past when I saw its bomb drop. This was the one that just missed the Liberty ship to our starboard. During the course of the action a stray 20mm hit the deck on our forecastle, injuring four British, four of the crew, and Pritcher. None were, as far as we know, too serious although one man's (a Britisher) radial nerve was clipped. Pritch got several small bits of shrapnel in the legs but he bled like a stuck pig. All were taken to a hospital ship. I forgot to mention that while we were in Bizerte, about September 6, there was a night raid. We saw a number of planes in the lights but got none. A stray 20mm shell hit in our #4 gun and injured the crew, two of whom were hospitalized with shrapnel in the legs. Yes, it does appear that 20's from other ships are more dangerous during a raid than the enemy bombs. Well, about the Fifteenth we went to Palermo. There were no more* *raids before we left Salerno but we could hear distant artillery and bombing back a short ways inland. We still just have a small strip of beach and the lines can be clearly seen from the ship. At Palermo we loaded an American combat team and the Seventeenth returned to Paestum where we are now. We have seen no enemy planes although we have a red alert every hour or so. The troops are now off and we are waiting to shove off. This is beautiful country and we can see some very interesting looking old ruins from the ship. We move out right after we unload and so don't get a chance to get ashore.*

—Gunnery Officer Bill Bodiford's Diary

After reaching Palermo on the 19th, the *LST-325* and six other LSTs received orders to proceed to Termini Imerese, located a few miles east of Palermo, to pick up vehicles of the 400th Anti-Aircraft Artillery Battalion. The LSTs returned to the Gulf of Salerno, beaching near Paestum on the 21st, and then anchoring off-shore. On the 23rd the captain of the *LST-308*, senior officer in the group, received orders to proceed to the northern end of the gulf, where two escort ships joined them. The convoy then sailed west, to where no one on the ship except the Captain knew. It wasn't until after the ships had passed through the Straits of Messina, the narrow stretch of water between Sicily and the toe of Italy, that Lieutenant Mosier informed the crew of their next destination.

25 Sept 1943—From Paestum on the night of the twenty-second, we moved along the gulf to Salerno. There is still plenty of artillery fire from the beach and a cruiser in the gulf was lobbing shells into the hills. So they can't be very far back. The mountains rose so precipitously from the water that I can't imagine much harder country to take. Tanks are no good at all. The country is so rugged that at least two LST's brought in loads of horses and mules. So now I've seen everything. We've carried everything from black, creosoted telephone poles to Italian prisoners (who are bad enough) but I hope we never get mules. We left Salerno on the night of the twenty-third and have been underway since, and are now going due south. To where, no one knows. I've never seen such a secret trip. Well, we'll know soon because they'll have to go one way or the other before long. I'll let you know…(later) I just heard from Malen that we're going to Tripoli, I wonder why?

—Gunnery Officer Bill Bodiford's Diary

The convoy had been given orders to proceed to Tripoli, Libya, where they would pick up their next load of passengers and vehicles. The ships anchored in the harbor of Tripoli on the afternoon of September 26. The next morning, the *LST-325* moored to the dock and took on 55 vehicles and 125 men of the Ceylonese Corp of the British Army. That afternoon the convoy prepared for the return trip to Italy.

> *26 Sept 1943—Reached Tripoli about noon. Liberty from 1300, but I lost. It's a beautiful looking place from the harbor, palm trees and mosque-like domes. I guess I'll get in tomorrow.*
>
> **—Gunnery Officer Bill Bodiford's Diary**

When the convoy returned to the Gulf of Salerno on September 30, the *LST-325's* starboard main engine malfunctioned and had to be shut down. They anchored offshore overnight and beached the following morning to unload the Ceylonese Corp vehicles. However, with just one engine functioning and having to fight against the strong wash kicked up by the rotating screws of the neighboring LSTs, the *LST-325* did not have enough power to retract from the beach. Finally, with some assistance from a tug, they were able to retract and anchor offshore. After he received orders for a return trip to Tripoli, Lieutenant Mosier informed his superiors that his ship could not comply with one engine out of commission and that repairs could not be completed except in port. The orders were then changed for the ship to proceed to Bizerte so that the necessary repairs could be made.

The *LST-325* sailed with the convoy bound for Tripoli until passing through the Straits of Messina, and then along with the *LST-308*, *LST-393* and *LST-314*, detached and turned west towards Tunisia. The ships steamed through rain, lightning and high winds throughout most of the two-day passage before anchoring in the Bay of Bizerte in the early evening of October 3. The next morning John MacPherson and Lloyd Mosby returned to the ship after being released from the Navy dispensary in Bizerte, where they had been recovering from the wounds they received during the air raid on September 6. The *LST-325* would remain in Bizerte for the next two-and-a-half weeks while repairs were made to the main engine.

> *A typical day in port was revelry, breakfast, muster, workstation, lunch, workstation, get ready for liberty or supper. Throw in a four hour watch now and then, a bucket of dirty clothes now and then, write a letter now*

and then and of course a good old Navy bull session. Liberty was granted every other day or every third day or not at all.

—Bill Hanley, Motor Machinist Mate

We all awaited liberty ashore but if we didn't get it we either stood watch, played "acey-duecy" or did one most hated job of doing our laundry. I don't know if you know what it was like to wash clothes in a bucket, a stick to plunge them and have only salt water to use.

—Harold "Icky" Allgaier, Radioman

A typical day in port was routine and boring. As one of the two Pharmacist Mates (Corpsmen) our responsibility was to open sickbay for treatment of minor ailments, scrapes and bruises. The two of us were excused from routine watches and kept out of the way of the routine duties of the rest of the crew. As Corpsmen, we were a separate part of the Navy and not subject to other than meetings of the crew. As a consequence, other than going ashore for routine medical duties, washing clothes, writing letters home and waiting for liberty (leave) it was boring. "Shooting the breeze" was a convenient way to pass the time.

—Dick Scacchetti, Pharmacist Mate

When we were in port we always kept busy in the Engineering gang to check over all the engines and everything that had to be ready to go anytime the Captain called to pull out. The Captain did not like to not be ready to go any time day or night, that was the number one priority to be ready anytime he called. You had no excuses.

—Ellsworth Easterly, Chief Motor Machinist Mate

9 Oct 1943—I did get in and rode the cycle all over. Not much there. From here we went to Salerno and just before we got there we lost our starboard engine. No raids. I rode all around on my cycle but so damn many convoys I couldn't get far. Got some onions and saw an old Roman road and an ancient Roman and Greek temple and other buildings. They are in no worse state of repair than most other buildings now. Just walls, no roof, windows or within…. We came back to Bizerte. Just heard that Pritch and Pollak got the Purple Heart. OK, let them have it. Captain said I was to be First Lieutenant. There's a hell of a lot more work to it than Gunnery. If Pritch wants it back I'll ask the Captain. I'd like to have it but not if Pritch wants it.

—**Gunnery Officer Bill Bodiford's Diary**

On October 20 a motor launch came alongside the *LST-325* and delivered a message that all vehicles now in possession of the ship would have to be turned over immediately to the Army base in Bizerte. The vehicle they were referring to was the ship's *kubelwagen*, a German version of the jeep, that had been earlier "liberated" by the crew of the *LST-325* from a U.S. Army captured vehicle dump. The crew then repainted the jeep Navy gray and painted a white five-pointed star on the side door panel. The Captain used this as his own personal jeep whenever he was ashore. Knowing full well that if he turned it over it would only end up being used by some Army officer, the Captain decided that if he couldn't use it, then by God, no damn Army officer should be able to either! He had a couple of his men take the jeep ashore, drain all the oil out of the engine and then ran it up and down the beach until the motor seized. Leaving it there, the Captain then sent the message that the jeep had been returned and where it could be collected.

The next day they received the *LST-325's* sailing orders to return to the base at Oran, Algeria, where they would prepare the ship for the trip to England. Many of the amphibious ships and landing craft that had taken part in the Sicilian and Italian campaigns were now being transferred to England for the invasion of France that, unknown except for a very select few, was being planned for mid-1944.

Later that afternoon Ensign Pritcher returned to the ship from the dispensary in Oran and reported for duty. He had been in the dispensary while undergoing treatment for the wounds he suffered during the German fighter attack at Salerno on September 13. The next day Chief Mitchell returned from the dispensary in Bizerte, where he had been since coming down with yellow fever in September.

20 October 1943—Bebe's 25. I'll bet she's no more lonesome than I am. I thought today about when we lived in Jax (Jacksonville). I didn't even come home to lunch. She must have been almost as lonesome then as she is now. We drove over to Tunis for the day Saturday, Sarbaugh, Jackson and I. We got very drunk on Anisette and I drove back. All I can say is that we made *it. How, I don't know. Latest on the Scuttlebutt <note: "scuttlebutt" is navy lingo for the rumor mill> front, we go to England, give the ship to the Limey's and go home for a new one. Not too creditable. Too much like wishful thinking. Scuttlebutt says we leave here on Sunday, stay fourteen days in Oran.*

—Gunnery Officer Bill Bodiford's Diary

The morning of the 23rd the *LST-325* left Bizerte as part of a convoy of eleven LSTs and five escort ships. Ten of the LSTs, including the *LST-325*, were towing LCTs behind them. In Oran, these LCTs would be loaded onto the main deck of the LSTs for transport to England.

I was glad to go. North Africa was too damn hot and liberty was not all the greatest and besides that we had lost our taste for wine.

—Chet Conway, Motor Machinist Mate

I was happy to go where they spoke English. My two years of high school French didn't get me far in French North Africa.

—Stanley Barish, Engineering Officer

The convoy reached Oran on October 26 and immediately the shipyard's welders began putting loading brackets for the LCT onto the ship's deck. Later, the Army loaded thirty-one rolled-up landing mats onto the tank deck. These mats were basically large metal grates that could be spread out over a beach during unloading to keep the truck and jeep tires from sinking down into the soft sand.

On November 2, a tugboat brought a floating crane alongside the ship, which then hoisted the *LCT-153* onto the loading skids on the main deck. Once securely chained down to the deck, an LCM was then loaded inside of the LCT. Shortly afterwards the crews of both landing craft reported onboard.

2 Nov 1943—We left Sunday, October 24 all right, we got here (Oran) on October 26. Two weeks from then is November 9. Our availability is November 8. How's that for Scuttlebutt coming through? No more about turning the ship over to the Limey's though. I'm pretty bored with it all and will be glad to get underway again.

—Gunnery Officer Bill Bodiford's Diary

The *LST-325* made the short trip to Mers el Kebir on the 4th, where they began loading provisions for the crew's mess. Overnight the weather turned rough as rainsqualls and heavy winds hammered the port. Early the next morning the *LST-157* frantically signaled that they were dragging anchor and were drifting on a collision course with the *LST-325*. Lieutenant Mosier immediately had the general alarm sounded and ordered all hands to stand by with fenders along the port side of the ship in an attempt to minimize damage from the pending collision. Meanwhile, the engineers raced to get the main engines on-line. Just at that moment the *LST-157* managed to get her own engines started and was able to maneuver clear of the *LST-325*.

Over the next few days the crew of the *LST-325* busily prepared for the long journey to England. The fresh water and fuel tanks were topped off and stores and supplies were brought onboard and stowed away. On November 9, six officers and ninety enlisted men of the 2nd Naval Beach Battalion embarked for transportation to England. The Beach Battalions were Navy units that were responsible for establishing ship-to-shore communication, marking lanes of traffic for incoming landing craft, and giving first aid and evacuating wounded from the beach during an amphibious invasion. The 2nd Beach Battalion would later be among the first waves of troops to go ashore at Utah Beach during the invasion of Normandy.

At last the *LST-325* was fully loaded and ready to go on November 12. The convoy of LSTs that the *LST-325* sailed with, designated Convoy SL-139, joined the merchant ship convoy MKS30 steaming west towards Gibraltar. Convoy MKS30 now numbered seventeen cargo ships and tankers, twelve LSTs and five escorts of the 40th Escort Group. They passed through the Straits of Gibraltar in the early evening of the 13th, where an additional fourteen merchant ships joined them. By midnight the convoy consisted of forty-seven merchantmen, eight escorts and all the LSTs of Flotilla Two, Group Five except the *LST-338*. For the first few days after passing through the Straits the convoy steamed due west. Things were relatively quiet and other than the obligatory General Quarters drills, the crew was kept busy chipping, painting and carrying out other routine chores.

15 November 1943—*Cruising as before. No excitement as yet. It's as cold as a well diggers ass. We're in a convoy of about sixty ships, in position 56. Very few escorts. The merchant ships just <u>won't</u> keep closed up. We've gone west since Gibraltar.*

—***Gunnery Officer Bill Bodiford's Diary***

When we left Oran we were loaded again with all the equipment we had carried over, LCT, LCM and several other LCVP's, etc. We went out through the Straits of Gibraltar, and we were headed WEST! We watched the compass for a couple of days...Great! Going back! We all knew better though, we turned north and of course we were going to England.

—John Roberts, Electricians Mate

Chief Boatswain Hughes had a pet dog he had picked up in Africa and which had scrounged off the ship garbage on the fantail. One day it slipped and fell into the ocean and was lost, as was usually the case.

—Bill Bliss, Quartermaster

However, after the convoy turned north on November 18, the peaceful period came to an end. Early that morning lookouts spotted two unidentified aircraft circling the convoy. The aircraft shadowed the convoy for the next hour, occasionally coming close enough that the escort ships could open fire before they could make a hasty retreat back out of range. But after all this cat and mouse, they finally were identified as friendly bombers.

Just before noon the escort ships scouting the waters ahead of the convoy reported making contact with an enemy submarine and began dropping depth charges. They stalked the submarine right through the heart of the convoy, but it escaped when the escorts lost contact.

A fresh wind sprung up during the night of November 18 and brought a few light passing rainsqualls with it. The crew exercised at General Quarters again that morning, as they would each morning while making the trip to England. That afternoon more unidentified aircraft were reported circling the convoy. The aircraft returned the wrong identification signals when challenged and immediately all ships went to battle stations. Several of the ships opened fire when the planes ventured within range of their anti-aircraft guns, but eventually they too were identified as friendlies and General Quarters was secured.

That evening, the escort ships radioed the convoy that an enemy submarine had been detected. Star-shell flares were shot off to illuminate the darkened surface of the sea, the escorts continuing the hunt on first one, then the other side of the convoy. Later a British medium bomber spotted and sank the German submarine *U-211* with depth charges.

Just before 0100 in the morning of the 20th, the escorts along the western side of the convoy began firing flares and dropping depth charges. This time the British frigate *HMS Nene* and two Canadian corvettes, *HMCS Snowberry* and *HCMS Calgary*, sank the *U-536*.

During the afternoon of November 21, lookouts spotted a large formation of German twin-engine bombers overhead. The bombers kept well beyond the range of the convoy's guns, which was puzzling to the men waiting on the ships below. Usually the Germans strategy was to attack as quickly as possible, before all the guns of the convoy could be manned and brought to bear on them. Then the officers on the bridge of the *LST-325* noticed what looked like a light glowing on the bottom of one of the aircraft. Suddenly this light detached from the aircraft and began to glide down towards the convoy. The object slowly made its way closer and closer towards the ships, until finally it was directly over one of the escort ships. Suddenly, it plunged straight down towards the destroyer and exploded just off its port side, sending a tremendous geyser of water into the air. Even though the bomb had missed, the stricken vessel began to take an immediate list to the port.

This was the *LST-325's* first experience with the German radio-controlled glider bombs. The bombers could stay at elevations that kept them out of the range of the ship's defensive fire while the bombardiers controlled the flight of the bomb with a joystick that transmitted radio signals to a receiver in the bomb. This operated a set of fins on the tail that directed its flight up or down, and left or right. The attack continued for the next two hours and it would be one of the most unnerving experiences of the entire war for the crew of the *LST-325*, since there was almost no defense against this weapon. One merchant ship was lost and several other ships were damaged in the attack, but the Germans suffered losses too this day. Two escorts of the 40th Escort group, the frigate *HMS.Foley* and the sloop *HMS.Crane* sank the submarine *U-538*.

My General Quarters station was in the main engine room. After having gone to GQ dozens of times I would sometimes stay topside for a few minutes to see what was going on. One such time was when, off the Bay of Biscay, we were attacked by bombers with radio-controlled bombs. I watched as a bomber released a bomb and guided it directly toward our stern. Apparently it was necessary for the bomber to be on the same course as the bomb. Our 3-inch gun on the fantail fired right on line with the plane and its bomb, but we were short. However, the pilot apparently wasn't yet ready to die for Hitler and swerved, almost hitting the destroyer escort on our port side.

—Stanley Barish, Engineering Officer

The *LST-325* didn't escape the attack on the 21st entirely unscathed. A sailor from the 2nd Beach Battalion was severely wounded when he was struck in the chest by a chunk of casing from an exploding shell while standing near the gun tubs on the bow of the ship. The medics immediately treated him with sulfanilamide, plasma, and an airtight dressing applied to his chest to cover the punctured lung. It was the best the medics onboard could do until the convoy reached England where he could be transferred to a hospital for more thorough treatment.

We left Oran on 12 November 1943 for England. On November 21 we were attacked by aircraft with glider bombs. It was overcast and one of the planes came out of the clouds right over us and banked upward when it saw the fleet. We saw the whole bottom of the plane and our gun jammed so we didn't fire on it. I was disappointed then, but I'm glad now.

—Emil Kolar, Motor Machinist Mate

During the morning of November 22, more bombers approached the convoy. Right after the aircraft were spotted, there was a tremendous explosion off the starboard side of the *LST-325* and immediately the Captain ordered General Quarters. There were no further attacks and thirty minutes later the German aircraft turned for home.

After the brief raid ended the Captain ordered a section of the crew moved into the troop compartments on each side of the ship. By doing so would help to minimize the loss of men if they should take a hit in the stern, where the crew's berthing was located. This was a common practice aboard LSTs when there was enough room available in the troop berthing areas.

Later that afternoon all of the LSTs separated from the rest of the convoy and turned eastward towards the English Channel. On November 24, as the convoy went through light rain and heavy following seas, the guide ship, the *LST-356*, reported that their gyrocompass had failed and ordered the *LST-325* to take over the lead position until repairs could be made. Just before sunset the flotilla of LSTs received a very welcome sight when a flight of friendly aircraft did a fly-by, assuring them that the convoy was now within range of allied air cover from England.

At dawn on the 25th, the coast of England came into view along the horizon. At 0930, the position of the LSTs in the convoy was changed so that all those proceeding on to Plymouth were in the starboard side column, and those going to Falmouth were in the port. Two hours later the Plymouth-bound LSTs detached from the remainder of the convoy with the *LST-325* leading the way.

As they entered Plymouth harbor, the crew of the *LST-325* did not miss the fact that they were, on Thanksgiving Day, entering the very harbor from which the Pilgrims had sailed for the New World in 1620. After anchoring, a British hospital boat came alongside and took the wounded Beach Battalion sailor ashore to the Royal Naval Hospital in Stonehouse.

> *25 November 1943—Thanksgiving! And after what we saw this trip, we have plenty to be thankful for that we've safely made harbor. We started finding subs in the vicinity about the Eighteenth. On the Nineteenth the escorts sank one. They radioed the Commodore whether to pick up survivors or not and he radioed back, "F—k 'em." The escorts had a sub contact practically the whole way here. Everyday more escorts would appear from somewhere. We started with six. On the Nineteenth I counted eight; on the Twentieth, twelve; and on the Twenty-first there were twenty of them. We had no torpedoing. On the Twenty-first however, about 1630 GQ rang. When I got up to my station on Conn, Dornier 217's were circling the convoy, out of AA range. That was peculiar because usually they came right on to the attack in order to get us before the guns are manned. They circled for ten or fifteen minutes, when Keene said, "They must be friendly planes. That one has a red tail light." Sure enough, under the plane was a big red light, like the glowing end of a giant cigar. About that time the light fell off and started gliding down towards the convoy. It was a "glider bomb", or "radio bomb", or "rocket bomb." By whatever name, it was sudden death. This one must have come two miles, losing altitude very slowly, and sometimes seeming to run along on a level, several thousand feet up. Then when it was about over one of the "can" escorts, down it came. It missed by about thirty yards but it rocked the can badly and it had a port list after the near miss. The bombs must be about 1000 pounders because the water went up hundreds of feet in the air. It was the biggest bomb I ever saw. The raid went on for about an hour and a half, and I don't mind admitting to anyone that I was scared. I never want to see one of those big things coming down for a ship I'm on. One poor straggler was bombed unmercifully and sunk. I saw three near misses, which must have caused severe damage. During the raid*

a passenger on our forecastle was hit in the lung by shrapnel. It went in one side and came out the other. I really hope our technicians can work out a way to jam the control of those bombs. They're rough.

—Gunnery Officer Bill Bodiford's Diary

5

England

On 26 November 1943, the *LST-325* (now attached to the 12th Fleet, LST Flotilla 2, Group 5, Division 10) moved to the dockyard in Plymouth, where the LCM and LCT were hoisted from the main deck. The crews then disembarked to their respective craft, and after fueling both craft, the *LST-325* backed away from the dock and moored in the harbor.

In Plymouth there were British young women in the armed forces, called WRENS, who handled our dock lines shore side. On liberty, I was impressed with how the British were carrying on under very adverse conditions, and with their fortitude.

—Stanley Barish, Engineering Officer

Much of Plymouth was bombed out but some sections remained intact and Mutley Plain was one area where you could dine well but simply. People were grateful for the American help in Plymouth.

—Dale MacKay, Motor Machinist Mate

Plymouth was a very beautiful city, at least what we saw of it. There was a great park, called the Hoe, I think. It overlooked the harbor and channel, and we could sit on a beautiful sunny afternoon and watch the Sunderland bombers, large seaplanes, land and take off on their missions. But the U.S. sailors had better not go through this park alone at night. Some came to very much trouble and worse. The British sailors were not too happy at all with all the U.S. sailors being around.

—John Roberts, Electricians Mate

On November 29, as the ship was preparing to get underway, Fireman R. Hochwater was helping to hoist one of the ship's LCVPs in the starboard boat davit. Suddenly, the cable to the forward shackle snapped and whipped about the deck, hitting Hochwater. The others in the working party rushed him to Sickbay, where Pharmacist Mate "Doc" Pittman treated the cut on his face and examined his leg, which had taken the brunt of the blow. Pittman recommended to the Captain that Hochwater's knee be x-rayed at the earliest opportunity to see if it was broken. There was no time to have this done in Plymouth, as the ship was due to get underway immediately to rendezvous with a convoy sailing to Falmouth. In fact, the ship had to sail before all the men on liberty could be rounded up by the Shore Patrol and ten men were still unaccounted for when the time came to get underway. Ensign Plumadore remained behind to take charge of these men when they returned to the base and see to it that they rejoined the ship in Falmouth.

> *Falmouth was another picturesque town that was pleasant liberty. Unfortunately, we were later turned away from the harbor because of taking some steel plates from the docks in order to repair our ship.*

> **—Dale MacKay, Motor Machinist Mate**

Shortly after midnight, the *LST-325* anchored in the Carrick Road estuary in the harbor of Falmouth. The port city of Falmouth was on a small peninsula between Falmouth Bay and Carrick Roads estuary. Two 16th century castles guarded the harbor entrance, Pendennis Castle to the west and St. Mawes to the east. The following day the ship moored to the West Dock in Falmouth's outer harbor, where Ensign Plumadore and the men left behind in Falmouth were waiting for them. That afternoon a working party from the base began unloading the gear on the tank deck, meanwhile Hochwater reported to St. Michel's hospital in Falmouth for x-rays.

> *Falmouth was where the boiler broke down. The watch did not check it and it ran out of water and burned out over half of the fire tubes. Here again, Captain Mosier came to our rescue. He knew all about boilers because he had served most of his Navy career on steam ships. He and I worked twenty-four hours repairing the boiler. We trained around Falmouth most of the*

time. We loaded the Army and unloaded them until we were blue in the face.

—C. J. Mitchell, Chief Motor Machinist Mate

During the morning of December 3, the *LST-325* was towed to the #3 dry dock in Falmouth to have the ships propellers replaced and to have the outer hull cleaned. The *LST-356* was brought into the dock at the same time and was positioned directly astern of the *LST-325*. As the water was being pumped from the dock, the yard workers began scraping and cleaning the bottom of the two LSTs. A group of yard repairmen came aboard to begin an overhaul of the main engines, assisted by the ship's engineers. Other members of the crew began cleaning and painting throughout the ship.

Just before dawn on the 4th, Gunners Mate 2/c David George was walking back to the ship with a shipmate. As they approached the ship, George missed the gangway and stepped over the edge, plummeting over forty feet to the bottom of the dock. The medical officer aboard the *LST-356* was immediately called to the scene, but by then there was little that could be done. George was rushed to St. Michael Hospital, where he was pronounced dead on arrival. The crew of the *LST-325* was stunned by the news of the sudden and tragic loss of their friend. George had been with them since the commissioning of the ship in Philadelphia. Later that day Signalman 2/c Bill Knierem was given the sad duty of accompanying George's body to London for internment at the Brookwood Military Cemetery. After the war, his body was relocated to the American Cemetery in Cambridge, England.

> *One of the worst things that happened to our crew was the loss of a buddy, Gunners Mate David Lloyd George, who walked into the dry dock and went to the bottom on a dark, rainy morning. We all had to go to the dock facilities for our morning chores bathroom-wise. There were no railings at all as I remember. Imagine what that would be today with all the lawsuits, OSHA and safety precautions, etc.*
>
> **—John Roberts, Electrician Mate**

The next day an official Board of Inquiry was held onboard the *LST-325*, under the direction of Lt. Keene, to investigate the fatal accident. The board determined that the major contributing factor to the accident was the absence of lifelines or safeguards of any kind along the edge of the dock. The night of December 4 had been moonless, and with no outside lighting of any kind allowed because of blackout regulations, George apparently thought he was stepping onto the gangway. Instead, with nothing in place to prevent just such an accident from happening, he fell to his death.

The *LST-325* remained in dry dock until December 9, when the ship was towed to the Falmouth outer harbor. The yard workers finished the engine overhauls on the 13th, then the ship got underway for sea-trials, making a four-day trip to Salcombe and back.

On 3 December 1943, Ensign Ted Duning reported for duty aboard *LST-325*...

I was born in Richmond, Indiana on June 17, 1921 and resided there through high school. I graduated from Morton Senior High in June 1939 and then attended Miami University, Oxford, Ohio receiving an AB degree in June 1943. I spent the last semester of college in Washington, D.C. as an intern in public service with the National Institute of Public Affairs. I took night classes at American University in Washington to complete requirements for the degree at Miami. On the afternoon of 7 December 1941 I was on a solo flight under the pilot training program at Miami University. Upon landing and parking the plane, I received the startling report about Pearl Harbor. There wasn't any question, of course, about my personally becoming involved in what would soon be a global war. The option that looked the best was the Navy V-7 program, one that would defer active duty status until my graduation. A week after Pearl Harbor several of us went to Cincinnati to join up. They built an obstacle course there at Miami University which many of us started to use daily to start building ourselves up to get in better shape. Naturally, we watched the progress of the war with keen interest knowing that at some point in the various engagement theatres we would be on hand for whatever was to be our lot in the war. I reported for active duty the first of July 1943 for my training at Midshipman School located at the downtown campus of Northwestern University in Chicago. Upon graduation early in November 1943, I received orders to report to New York City to await transportation to England where I would join my ship. After a three-day stay, I was taken aboard a tanker filled with aviation gasoline that got underway around midnight to join a convoy to England. We experienced a major storm on the way so severe that it caused one of the three fighter planes lashed to the deck for delivery to the ETO to be washed overboard. Having by that time mainly overcome my fear of the passage on that ship I recall going out on deck with a firm grasp on the handrail along-side the stateroom bulkhead to experience the thrill of a great storm at sea. On a very dark night late in November 1943 the train transporting us from the ship, which had docked at Liverpool, England, deposited us in the station at Falmouth. Lloyd Kurz and I were taken from there to the LST-325 being serviced in dry-dock. Everything was in blackout, of course, and the gangplank from the dry-dock edge to the 325's deck provided us our first training in blackout maneuvering. The next morning we learned of the tragic death that occurred that very night of one of the crew who missed the gangplank and fell to his death at the bottom of the dry-dock when returning to the ship from the head on shore.

—Ted Duning, First Lieutenant

During the months of December and January, most of the crew of the *LST-325* was granted leave on a rotating basis. For most of them London was the place to go and blow off steam, despite the fact that the city was still the target of frequent German bombing raids.

London was a busy place. I always think of the fish and chips, they served them on newspapers. They were really good. I was always hoping that they would not bomb while we were there, but they always did. We were very lucky they didn't hit us.

—Ellsworth Easterly, Chief Motor Machinist Mate

London was a wild liberty town! I carry some memories that I would have to sanitize before retelling! The U.S. Air Force owned the town, having permanent contacts, but the swabbies were given a few days to howl! I took a tour of Westminster Abbey, Hyde Park, 10 Downing Street, St. Paul's, Piccadilly, etc.

—Dick Scacchetti, Pharmacist Mate

It was interesting to see the people sleeping in the underground stations. While at the movies they announced an air raid, and no one got up.

—Bill Bliss, Quartermaster

In London, the strict blackout made it look like a dead city. But under the dark blanket the city was alive, people moving swiftly, theatres full, restaurants busy.

—Stanley Barish, Engineering Officer

I remember once I was doing liberty in London and I heard a buzz bomb go off but nobody did anything. One's nerves were used to such things.

—Don Martin, Motor Machinist Mate

I spent a five-day leave in London in December 1943. I stayed at the Piccadilly Hotel. It was blackout at night so you didn't see the city as you would have seen something like New York City at night. I also spent a leave there sometime in 1944 when the Germans were sending buzz bombs over and I heard two or three.

—Emil Kolar, Motor Machinist Mate

I hope all the crew had a chance to see London on leave. What a place and what an experience to be in the tremendous crowd milling about in the blackout in Piccadilly Circle each night. My first trip to London put me in the train station one very foggy night with no earthly idea where I would stay. I asked a cabbie to find me a place and he left me on a sidewalk pointing in the general direction of a doorway. I stumbled across the sidewalk, found a big drape (blackout you know) and eventually located the doorway behind the drape. Inside was a small lobby with a clerk ready to sign me in. He asked me, "Will it be one or two?" It was only then that I noticed a woman had quietly moved up and was standing just behind my right shoulder. I assured him one would be adequate and went forth to find my room down a long hallway on the second floor. I turned in right away, quite worn out, and was soon asleep. But, as one might guess from their experience in London at the time, within an hour there was a knocking at the door. Oh boy. I told whoever it was to get gone. That worked and I slept undisturbed until dawn. That was the last time a cabbie was asked to find me a hotel in London.

My older brother, a Master Sergeant with the 8th Air Force stationed up in the Midlands, met me the next day and we met again on the two more visits to London. During these times we did a lot of walking, a lot of talking, a lot of visiting historic places and monuments and even took a canal boat up a canal along the Thames to a place called Richmond. Remember, we were from Richmond, Indiana.

—Ted Duning, First Lieutenant

I came out of the Regent Hotel one day, it's right on Piccadilly Circus, and saw a GI standing in front I thought I recognized. I said, "Are you Clyde Grant from Faribault, Minnesota?" Yes, he was. We had a good visit, and it seemed a little like that the world was not that big.

—John Roberts, Electricians Mate

Liberty was few and far between but I do recall one trip to London. We got a little drunk and wandered down the street, singing and carrying on, and there was an air raid. It was so dark and we finally got to a doorway and had to go through several blackout curtains before we were able to see any lights. The bar was crowded with Limey's and Aussies along with the GI's and sailors. We drank and sang songs, and all the while the air raid was going on.

—Harold Westerfield, Ship's Cook

On December 21, the ship prepared to get underway for a vehicle loading exercises on a "Hard" in the Helford River. A "Hard" was a concrete ramp extending into the water, placed at the loading points for LSTs. After leaving their mooring, the base operations officer radioed the ship to postpone the exercise due to the high seas and gale force winds that were battering the area. The weather cleared overnight, and the next morning the ship completed the exercise with the 29th Infantry Division.

After several days of loading exercises with the Army, the *LST-325* was ready to take part in the first large-scale training exercise for the Normandy invasion, scheduled for early January 1944. On the last day of 1943, the *LST-325* moored to the Helford Hard and the troops assigned for the exercise embarked on the ship. Altogether eighty-two vehicles were loaded onto the ship, along with 21 officers and 285 soldiers of the 29th Infantry Division under the command of Lieutenant Kennedy.

The first exercise, code named DUCK I, was held in an area of Devon County surrounding a resort known as Slapton Sands, on the beaches of Start Bay. This site had been picked as a training area for two reasons. First, the terrain resembled that along the Normandy coast where the American 29th and 1st Divisions would go ashore on D-Day. The second reason was its remote location and sparse population that could be relocated with a relatively minimum amount of difficulty. During the months of November and December 1943, the British War Office evacuated more than 3000 civilians from the area surrounding Slapton Sands, all at government expense. This 30,000-acre region was then transformed into a military training encampment, with blockhouses and bunkers scattered among the hills and ravines facing the sea.

This series of exercises was designed to give the assault troops experience in the assignments they would be expected to carry out on the day of the invasion. The Army units involved had all undergone training on a regimental and divisional basis back in the States and at the Assault Training Center in Woolacombe, England. Here at Slapton Sands, they would bring the Army and Navy units together for the first time in joint assault exercises. The first large-scale exercise, DUCK I, was scheduled for early January 1944. The next two scheduled exercises, named DUCK II and DUCK III, would give them an opportunity to refine their plan based on the lessons learned in the previous operations. Small-scale exercises would follow, to give individual units an opportunity for further training in their own particular phase of the invasion. Finally, there would be two full-scale dress rehearsals, code named FABIUS and TIGER, in which every attempt would be made to duplicate the actual battle conditions the troops would face at Normandy.

> *The original 325 crew who had taken part in the Mediterranean action had "been there—done that", so training for Normandy was routine for those who had already had experience in troop and vehicle loading, transporting and then disembarking on the beach.*
>
> **—Ted Duning, First Lieutenant**

On New Years Day, 1944, the crew completed their last minute preparations for the upcoming exercise. Late in the evening of January 2 all of the ships taking part in the exercise left Falmouth for the Slapton Sands training area, anchoring in Start Bay before dawn. At 0950 Ensign English and two Army officers, temporarily assigned to the Navy Beachmaster, took one of the ship's LCVPs to the beach. Shortly after that, the Task Group Commander sent a radio message to the LST section of the convoy ordering all ships to proceed to the Line of Departure (LOD) at 1300.

In mid-afternoon the LSTs received orders to proceed to White Beach, at the southern end of the training area. The *LST-325* beached at precisely 1530, and as soon as the ramp was lowered the soldiers began driving their vehicles off the ship. The first three drove off without problem, but the fourth truck bogged down in the sand at the end of the ramp, despite the steel matting placed there specifically to keep this from happening. It took twenty minutes to get the truck unstuck, but once the ramp was finally clear the rest of the unloading continued without further delay.

The tide was now beginning to ebb and the time lost while clearing the truck from the end of the ramp had put the ship at risk of being stranded. As they tried to back the ship off the beach they discovered that the bow was stuck hard and fast. The *LCI-349* came alongside to offer assistance and a line was passed to them from the ship's stern. As the LCI pulled they attempted to swing the ship from side-to-side by running the ship's propellers in opposite directions, hoping to break the bow free. This failed, and there was nothing more they could do but wait for the tide to return.

Meanwhile, the *LST-372* beached alongside the *LST-325* on their starboard side. Finally, the tide returned and the ship was finally able to extract. As the *LST-325* backed away from the beach, they started to swing the ship around to the right. Unfortunately, they misjudged their distance from the neighboring ship, and the bow struck a glancing blow off the forward boat davit of the *LST-372*. The bow narrowly cleared the side of the *LST-372's* hull as it passed along the length of their ship, then struck another glancing blow on the portside bridge wing. Fortunately, both ships suffered only a few minor dents and some scarred paint in the mishap. Finally, the travails on the beach over, the *LST-325* returned to the Line of Departure and anchored.

The next morning, the *LST-325* returned to Plymouth in convoy with the other LSTs. The next two weeks were spent doing routine maintenance and taking on provisions and supplies in preparation for the next series of maneuvers scheduled to begin on January 19.

We went up a river and anchored near a very small village. This was prior to the Normandy invasion and the Captain had a very secretive meeting ashore. I, being the Coxswain, my machinist mate and bow hand took the

Captain ashore. He walked until out of our sight. We were ordered to stay with the small boat until his return. We tied up to the boat ramp. One of us spotted a pub not far away. We decided that we could go have a few and still be able to spot Captain Mosier quick enough to beat him back to the LCVP. He was gone quite awhile but we did spot him to beat him back to the dock. When we got there, there was the small boat hanging sideways! We had forgotten about the heavy tides there, and when it went out it left the boat hanging by the ropes we had tied to the dock! When the Captain got to the dock he was not too happy. We were totally blank as to what to do. The Captain asked if any of us had a knife. Well, we cut the lines, and the boat dropped...thank God...right side up in the water. The Captain didn't punish us, but we never tried this again!

—Harold "Icky" Allgaier, Radioman

During the time that the *LST-325* was in Portland, several Army officers were given orientation tours of the ship. On the evening of the 17th, Commander F. H. Newton Jr., the commander of LST Flotilla 12 Group 35, held an operations meeting onboard the *LST-325*. Present were the commanding officers of all the ships and landing craft that would be involved in the coming exercise. Commander Newton selected the *LST-325* as his flagship, and the next morning a LCT brought his personal jeep out to the ship's anchorage and the crew loaded it onto the tank deck. Additional radio equipment was also installed for the Commander and his staff. Soldiers of the 29th Infantry Division under Lt. Col. E. L. Meeks then embarked, along with a detachment of the 2nd Naval Beach Battalion under Lt. Walsh. Later that evening, the *LST-325* led a column of ships and landing craft from Plymouth Harbor, escorted by five English minelayers.

At dawn on the 19th, the flotilla of ships anchored in Start Bay. The weather this morning was less than ideal; at times the rain and mist reduced visibility to less than a mile. The Army and Beach Battalion personnel mustered on the main deck, then began lowering themselves down the cargo nets draped over the side of the ship and into the LCVPs bobbing alongside. By 0848 the last of the boats was loaded and away from the LST; they circled offshore as the warships launched a preliminary barrage of gunfire against the beachhead just as they would before the actual invasion at Normandy. When the barrage lifted the troop-laden landing craft made their run towards the beach. Meanwhile, the LSTs waited offshore until that afternoon when the Beach Battalion men, having completed their portion of the exercise, returned to the ship. Once they were back onboard and the

LCVPs returned to their davits, the ship weighed anchor and turned north for Dartmouth. After the *LST-325* had moored in the Dart River the soldiers from the 29th Division returned to the ship. That evening Commander Newton held a brief conference aboard the *LST-325* with the commanding officers of the ships and landing craft that had taken part in the day's exercise.

At midnight, the LSTs were again underway from Dartmouth to continue the exercise. The *LST-325* anchored in Start Bay at 0300 and immediately lowered both LCVPs into the water. Again, the 29th Division soldiers and Beach Battalion sailors scrambled over the side of the ship and into the boats and were soon on their way towards the beach. The Beach Battalion sailors returned to the ship shortly after 0900, and the *LST-325* hoisted anchor and returned to Dartmouth. That afternoon six officers and twenty-five soldiers of the 116th Infantry Battalion Headquarters came aboard and began preparing for the next phase of the exercise. Two U.S. Navy medical officers also reported to the ship; they were there to experiment with different methods of unloading casualties from smaller boats to an LST.

Back in Start Bay the next morning the Beach Battalion and the 29th Division infantrymen aboard the *LST-325* loaded into their landing craft at 1045 and headed to shore, following a brief artillery barrage from the guns of the 111th Field Artillery aboard the *LCT-80*. That afternoon two amphibious DUKWs, both carrying men from the 2nd Beach Battalion playing the part of simulated casualties, made their way out to the ship and were driven onto the tank deck as part of the Navy's casualty handling experiments. When the exercise was complete, the ships returned to Dartmouth.

Late that afternoon an air raid warning was signaled to all the ships now moored in the Dart River; enemy aircraft were reported to be within a few miles of the harbor and all hands were ordered to General Quarters. Soon they spotted three aircraft circling nearby, but they remained out of range of any of the anti-aircraft guns below. Apparently, their mission was strictly reconnaissance, and soon turned back across the Channel. Later in the evening two officers and two enlisted men from the British Royal Marines reported aboard the *LST-325* as observers for the maneuvers scheduled to begin the next day.

However, dawn on January 22 brought high winds and rain, and the forecasters were predicting that the storm would only get worse as the day went on. Finally, Commander Newton postponed the day's exercise. He also ordered all ships to have their guns manned at all times during daylight hours. The visit from the enemy aircraft the day before gave a good indication that the Germans were interested in the activity going on in that area and having all those ships gathered in one place could make for an irresistible target. After noon two of the 20mm guns and the 40mm gun on the *LST-325* were manned, as they would be from dawn to dusk each day the ship remained here.

The storm lasted until the 25th, and finally Commander Newton made the decision to cancel the balance of the exercise entirely. The vehicles and men of the 116th Infantry were disembarked from the *LST-325* onto LCTs and taken ashore. Most of the 2nd Beach Battalion and the four Royal Marine observers who arrived on the ship just before the storm hit had already disembarked the day before. The *LST-325* returned to Dartmouth on the 26th, where the next day Commander Newton and his staff disembarked along with the remainder of the 2nd Beach Battalion.

During the first two weeks of February, the crew busily prepared for the next series of training exercises, code name DUCK II, scheduled to begin on the 12th. One afternoon while in Plymouth the crew was treated to a very welcome break from the ship's routine when three American Red Cross volunteers brought freshly baked donuts and candy onboard. During the war American Red Cross volunteers made a significant contribution to the welfare of servicemen abroad, providing a wide array of services from supplying fresh donuts and other snacks, to running servicemen's clubs, helping servicemen contact home in family emergencies, providing care packages to American POW's, and assisting in the hospitals.

On February 8, Commander Newton held a conference onboard the *LST-325* with all of the LST commanding officers to go over the details of the upcoming exercise. On the 11th a flotilla consisting of the *LST-325, LST-336, LST-371, LST-388, LST-335,* four LCTs and several LCMs sailed from Plymouth. Lt. Mosier was Senior Officer of the group of amphibious ships, which were escorted by an American patrol craft and a British minelayer. Two of the LSTs, the LCTs and the LCMs continued on to Brixham for loading, while the *LST-325* and the remaining LSTs moored off Dartmouth to wait their turn. The following morning they continued on to Brixham and began taking on their assigned loads. The *LST-325* carried twenty-six trucks of the 29th Division, a platoon of "A" Company, 116th Infantry Regiment under 2nd Lt. Tidrick; "B" Company of the 81st Chemical Mortar Battalion under 1st Lt. John Riddle, "C" Company 121st Engineers under 1st Lt. Kahaniak and the Headquarters and Service Company of the 121st Engineers under Captain Roland McDonald.

On February 13, the ships and landing craft that were going to take part in DUCK II began to gather off Torquay. By the end of the day there were fourteen

LSTs and numerous LCIs anchored in the bay, along with several American and British escort ships.

The flotilla sailed from Tor Bay before dawn on the 14th for the short trip to Start Bay. The soldiers onboard the *LST-325* then climbed into the LCVPs moored to the open bow ramp. Once the soldiers were away, the *LCT-214* moored twice to the ship's ramp, taking most of the trucks to the beach. At noon, the LSTs received orders from the Task Group Commander to move closer in to shore off Red Beach. After anchoring there, the *LCT-554* docked to the ramp and the remaining trucks were off-loaded. With their part of the exercise now complete, the LSTs returned to Dartmouth.

The *LST-325* remained in Dartmouth until February 17, when the ship received orders to proceed to the U.S. Army Hard in Brixham to participate in loading exercises. During the next few days they practiced loading and unloading with the 190th and 186th Field Artillery, the 983rd Tank Destroyer Battalion, the 1923rd Quartermaster Truck Company, the 834th and 826th Aviation Engineers of the 9th Air Force, and the 83rd Mechanized Recon Company. Most of the exercise took place right there on the Hard, though they did practice unloading while underway, anchoring in Tor Bay and unloading the Aviation Engineer's vehicles onto LCTs.

On February 26, eight boys from the Brixham School for Boys came aboard for a tour of the ship and to have dinner with the crew.

> *I don't recall the port we were in at the time, it was somewhere in England. We entertained a bunch of kids aboard ship. They were war orphans from all over Europe. They ate white bread and thought it was cake. We had a ball. It was tough leaving them. They were given a royal treatment.*
>
> **—Chet Conway, Motor Machinist Mate**

With the loading exercises in Brixham complete, the *LST-325* returned to Plymouth on March 6 along with the *LST-388* and the *LST-392*. They would remain in Plymouth for the next three weeks, completing maintenance work on the main engines and having the No.1 LCVP repaired; it had been slightly damaged when it's battery caught on fire while the ship was in Brixham. On March 14, the ship moored to the Turnchapel Hard in Plymouth Harbor, for more loading practice with the U.S. Army's Transport Quartermaster School.

> *Plymouth was a good liberty town. Block after block had been leveled by bombs. They had movies, good dance halls and places where you could get*

food to eat. I was placed on report for being out of uniform when I was out on a work detail. The Skipper told me to forget it.

—Bill Bliss, Quartermaster

Plymouth was one of my favorite places. It is a historical place tied to American history too. I made it a point to go down to the Plymouth Steps, alleged to be the embarkation place for the Pilgrims. What appeared to be the entire center of the downtown section of Plymouth was gone, destroyed in a series of bombing raids by the German Luftwaffe. One of the local persons told me of spending night after night in the basement of their home during these raids never knowing whether the next bomb would be a direct hit on the only place they had for some measure of safety. It was here I met a Wren in the British Navy whose company I enjoyed when liberty was available to us in the area. We remained friends even after the war by corresponding from time to time. She married a U.S. Navy man, moved to the States and she and her husband had Waverly and me to dinner in a restaurant at the top of a skyscraper in New York City on the occasion of our being in New York for a meeting. Another interesting thing about Plymouth is that I learned years later that a close friend here in Lewisburg was in the Army and in charge of loading LST's with equipment and personnel at the same hard we had used to load the 325 there in Plymouth.

—Ted Duning, First Lieutenant

Ships officers, taken 29 July 1944
Seated (l-r): Lt. Clifford Mosier, Lt. Gordon Keene
Second row (l-r): LtJG Stan Barish, LtJG Guy Jackson, Ensign Lloyd Kurz,
LtJG Bill Bodiford
Third row (l-r): Ensign Ted Duning, LtJG Art English, LtJG John Sarbaugh

First day at sea, in convoy with LSTs after leaving New York for Bermuda,
19 March 1943

LST-325 main deck loaded with troops and vehicles for invasion of Sicily, Bay of Tunis, July 1943.

American soldier aboard *LST-325*, Bay of Gela, Sicily, July 1943.

LST-325 moored alongside *LST-387* in Bizerte, Tunisia after it had been torpedoed in route from Algiers, August 1943.

U.S. Army weapons carrier being lowered from the main deck on the ship's elevator. The ship's captain, Lt. Mosier, stands to the left on the corner of the elevator, 18 September 1943.

LST-325 moored to end of pontoon causeway near Paestum, Bay of
Salerno, 18 September 1943.

Jeeps and trailers driving over pontoon causeway to the beach at
Paestum, 18 September 1943.

Liberty party going ashore aboard an LCVP, Mers el Kebir, Algeria, November 1943.

Lt. Mosier using a sextant to get a fix on the ship's position, in the English Channel, November 1943.

In drydock, Falmouth, England. On 4 December 1943 Gunners Mate David George fell to his death here when he missed the gangway in the early morning darkness.

LST-325 on the beach at the Slapton Sands training area during the DUCK I exercise, 3 January 1944.

LST-325 in Falmouth Harbor, fully loaded for Normandy, 4 June 1944. Note the distinctive markings on the front of the soldier's helmets, identifying them as members of the 5th Engineer Special Brigade.

Standing in to Omaha Beach, 7 June 1944.

Omaha Beach, 7 June 1944. Note the artificial breakwater created by sinking merchant ships in a line. (*Courtesy Ted Duning*)

Offloading trucks through the bow opening onto *LCT(6)-550* during the afternoon of 7 June 1944.

Casualties from Normandy being taken ashore and loaded into waiting ambulances, Portland, England, June 1944.

Stern view of *LST-325* at Utah Beach, 12 June 1944.

796 German prisoners are unloaded at Portland, England, 28 June 1944.

LST-325 on the St. John's River at Green Cove Springs, Florida, fall of 1945, waiting for decommissioning. This is the only known picture of LST-325 with the Brodie Device, used for launching and retrieving L-4 observation planes from an LST. Note the Pacific theatre camouflage paint scheme. (*Courtesy Ted Duning*)

6

Preparation

On 22 March 1944, the *LST-325* left Plymouth for Londonderry, Ireland, where they would undergo extensive modifications to the ship's air-defense weapons. Before leaving Plymouth most of the 3-inch gun ammunition was transferred to the base Ordnance Department, except for a few rounds in case the ship ran into any trouble along the way. The *LST-325* and *LST-337* joined a convoy of nine merchant ships, two LSTs and six escort ships that was headed north. As the convoy neared the entrance of Bristol Channel near Lundy Isle on the 23rd, the two LSTs detached and continued north through the Irish Sea, finally reaching Londonderry on the overcast and drizzly morning of March 25.

> *I remember the time I was on the conn with Keene in a terrible fog on the way to Londonderry to get additional armament for the Invasion. We were off the southwest coast of England. It was before the 325 had radar and for a couple hours we couldn't even see the bow. Thanks to Bliss for keeping us on course. But if the crew had only known that afternoon how scared Keene and I were that we were about to land on a pile of rocks on the English coast they might have begun lowering the LCVPs from their davits!*
>
> **—Ted Duning, First Lieutenant**

After entering the River Foyle, the *LST-325* moored to the Lisahally Wharf in Londonderry, where the crew began unloading all the ammunition and pyrotechnics remaining onboard to the base Ordnance Department. Afterwards, yard workers came aboard and began removing the 3-inch gun from the stern gun tub. By mid-afternoon the crew had offloaded the last of the munitions, and shortly after the 3-inch gun was lifted out of the stern tub and the ship moved to a pier at the Naval Ordnance Base. The next morning workers from the Ordnance Base began to install the additional air-defense weapons to the ship. When they were finished, six 40mm, six 20mm and two additional ammunition magazines had been added to the ship's air defenses.

Before the ship left Londonderry on April 1, they took aboard crates of ordnance for the bases at Falmouth and Roseneath, Scotland. The ship left the Lisahally wharf after the cargo was stowed for sea, anchoring in Molville Bay for a few hours before getting underway later that afternoon for Roseneath.

By the following morning the *LST-325* had anchored in Gare Loch off the city of Roseneath. They moored to the Industrial Pier that afternoon and began unloading ordnance they had brought with them from Londonderry. The ship remained in Roseneath overnight, getting underway before dawn on the 3rd. Throughout the day, the ship encountered extremely dense fog. After midnight, with conditions gradually getting worse and visibility nearly zero, the Captain ordered the ship's running lights lit and reduced their speed. By dawn, they could not see more than a couple hundred yards ahead of the ship. The sun finally began to burn off the fog and soon the ship was able to resume full speed.

On April 4, the *LST-325* joined with Convoy WP502 for the last leg of the trip to Falmouth, which they reached shortly before noon on the 5th. There the crew began preparing and painting the new gun mounts and magazines topside and taking on stores and supplies. On the 10th, the ship moored to the West Wharf and offloaded the ammunition they had brought back with them from Londonderry.

Late in the evening of April 15, the *LST-325* received orders to proceed to Penarth, Wales to begin a scheduled overhaul of the ship's main engines. The the sailing orders weren't delivered until late in the day, after the off-duty section of the crew had already gone on liberty. They tried to recall as many of the men as possible before the ship had to sail, but there were still a dozen or so that hadn't been found and had to be left behind. Along with the *LST-332* and *LST-315*, the ship left Plymouth Harbor and joined Convoy PW507. Just before midnight, the ships reached Penarth, anchoring outside the harbor for the night, waiting until daybreak before proceeding into the harbor. Along with the engine overhaul, workers installed a smoke generator on the fantail of the ship. The smoke generator worked by burning a mixture of oil and water that created a dense smoke that would help to conceal the ship, hopefully, from aerial or surface attack. An additional smoke generator unit was stored away on the ship's tank deck, for later delivery to the *LST-376* now in Swansea, Wales.

> *While I was a Coxswain during a typical day at sea we took our turns standing watch or maybe chip the deck, reload ammo casings, splice rope or cable,*

etc. When I became a Radioman I had my regular four-hour duty in the radio shack sending and receiving messages.

—Harold "Icky" Allgaier, Radioman

While underway, one would stand a four-hour watch and have eight hours off. All were involved with this rhythm, which allowed for sleep and some daytime off. It made you feel that you were really in the Navy and there was a purpose for going to your destination. The engine rooms were fully manned and the deck forces were at the helm and look out posts.

—Dale MacKay, Motor Machinist Mate

At sea, we normally stood a watch by our station, usually four hours on and eight hours off. We all had special details such as getting underway, prepare for mooring, fire drill, setting the watch for underway and our battle station under fire. In your spare time you took care of your personal effects.

—Bill Hanley, Motor Machinist Mate

At sea, we washed clothing, tried to write home, I always had to keep check of all shifts on watch to see if everything was okay. If someone needed help, we would help out, kept really close check of the engines to see what had to be done in port that we could not do at sea.

—Ellsworth Easterly, Chief Motor Machinist Mate

Underway responsibilities weighed much more heavily on all of us than when we were in port. The English Channel was enemy territory, as we found out when called upon to rescue the troops from that torpedoed transport the last of December 1944. We each carried a responsibility for making sure the ship carried out its purpose, but more importantly, we had to constantly keep in mind that the lives of the crew as well as the troops being transported could be affected by the failure on the part of any one of us.

—Ted Duning, First Lieutenant

A day at sea was dependent on the weather. If it was good weather and the seas calm it was great. You could look all around you and see nothing but water. On the other hand, when the seas were rough it was hell. Most of our crew could handle rough weather but some, as well as Army personnel if they were aboard, would get sicker than a dog. Seasickness isn't something you take lightly. It can cause a lot of discomfort. Thank the Good Lord I wasn't one of them.

—Chet Conway, Motor Machinist Mate

We had no special duties at sea as the rest of the crew who had more active assignments. Surprisingly, I was usually sick back home when fishing with my family in the bays and on the Atlantic Ocean. When I was faced with sea duty I realized I might have a problem for a long time! I made my mind not to get seasick, and actually cured myself! Mind over matter!

—Dick Scacchetti, Pharmacist Mate

On April 18, the crewmembers left behind in Falmouth finally caught up with the ship and reported back onboard. The following day, LtJG. E. Jones, a U.S. Navy medical officer, and a team of twenty Pharmacist Mates and Hospital Apprentices reported for duty aboard the *LST-325*. Many of the LSTs were being assigned additional medical personnel for the upcoming invasion; they would play a crucial role during the early stages by bringing casualties back to England. Later, after airstrips were established in France, the wounded could then be airlifted back to England.

We carried about twenty Pharmacist Mates on the invasion and shortly after, to care for the wounded. They were a sharp impressive group of sailors.

—Dale MacKay, Motor Machinist Mate

On April 24, after making a run through the degaussing calibration range, the *LST-325* joined a convoy of LSTs bound for Milford Haven, Wales. They stayed there until the 26th, then continued on to Swansea, Wales. In Swansea, they loaded the smoke generator they had brought with them from Penarth into one of the ship's LCVPs and delivered it to the *LST-376*. After the LCVP was away the ship moved through the tidal lock and moored to the Hard at the Queen's Dock. There bulldozers, cranes and other equipment belonging to the 336th and 348th Engineer regiments of the U.S. Army were loaded onboard.

The *LST-325* left Swansea in convoy on April 27, reaching Falmouth the following morning. It was during the early morning hours of the 28th that a group of LSTs taking part in the Operation TIGER training exercise was attacked off the coast of Devon by nine German torpedo boats. Fast and maneuverable, the

German boats evaded Allied patrols that night and attacked the group of LSTs without warning. The *LST-507* was torpedoed and the crew abandoned ship. The *LST-531* was torpedoed and sank within minutes. The *LST-289* was able to open fire on the attackers but was also torpedoed, though they were able to get their crippled ship back to port. Casualties from the attack were high; a total of 198 sailors and 551 soldiers were killed or missing. The reports of this attack and the losses suffered were kept under wraps by the Allied high command, and even though members of the *LST-325*'s crew heard rumors about the attack the details of the losses that night were not made public for many years. While revisionists tried to paint the cover-up as a conspiracy by the military to hide an embarrassing incident, the truth is that the High Command was trying to keep the Germans from learning the extent of their losses, especially to the LSTs which were in short supply already and were absolutely crucial to the success of the invasion. In fact, the demand for more LSTs at one point drove the British Prime Minister Winston Churchill, exasperated by the time it was taking to gather the required number of LSTs for the invasion, to say, "The destinies of two great empires seem to be tied up in some damn things called LSTs!"

> *We heard rumors of the attack. But after reading the details it was hard to realize that the LSTs were left out at sea without convoy protection, air cover and without radio communication with each other. How many snafu situations existed in war is hard to realize. In case you don't know the meaning of snafu, "Situation Normal, All Fouled Up." We used different words but these will do.*
>
> **—Bill Hanley, Motor Machinist Mate**

Before dawn on April 29, the Germans attacked Falmouth by air. Shortly after going to battle stations, the mean could hear heavy anti-aircraft fire coming from north of Falmouth, near the small town of Foway. The large smoke generators on the base laid a smoke screen down over the harbor, above which they could hear more aircraft passing overhead. A short while later more anti-aircraft fire was heard coming from further off to the east and to the west of Falmouth.

About an hour after the raid ended, the *LST-325* left Portland accompanied by the *LST-281* and two escort ships. The *LST-325* was towing a "rhino ferry" behind them for delivery to Poole, England. A rhino ferry was a barge constructed with the same pontoon sections used to build causeways. Rhino's were six pontoons wide and thirty pontoons long (41 feet X 176 feet), powered by two large outboard engines. They were nicknamed "rhinos" because of their large size and lumbering speed and were used to transport vehicles from LSTs stationed offshore to the beach. Smaller versions of the rhino, three by seven pontoons in size, were known as rhino tugs, and were used to assist the ferries. After the ships reached Weymouth, two tugboats came alongside and took the rhino the rest of the way in to the harbor at Poole. The two LSTs anchored off Weymouth for the night before returning to Falmouth.

We practiced loading and unloading troops and equipment, vehicles, small tanks, gun tracks, etc. all winter. We were able to have liberty about every third day and saw a lot of the area in southwest England. Falmouth and Weymouth mostly…we had to make sure that the bow doors and the ramp and elevator would all work, if not we were in trouble. We were able to keep them going, thankfully with a lot of luck and the Lord's help.

—John Roberts, Electricians Mate

I liked Falmouth, that quaint English port, very much and enjoyed liberty many times there. When we were on a visit to England with another couple in 1986, I had listed Falmouth as one of our must-see places. Driving down from the crest of a hill as we came into town we could see the dry-dock as the waters edge below. It was where I had joined the 325 in 1943 and it was still in use. I remember returning from liberty in Falmouth one night, stepping across one liberty boat to get to ours just outboard when someone with me (perhaps with good reason) asked if I could make it all right. As I was answering, "Of course, I'm fine", I stepped between the boats and went down with one leg fully in the water.

—Ted Duning, First Lieutenant

My buddy and I went on liberty that day and as we're riding along in a cab we passed a couple girls standing on the corner. We went by them but I told the cab driver to turn around and we went back to them. They got into the cab and it was there I met the girl I later married in England. I had to go through a lot of red tape and talks with Captain Mosier as to whether I wanted this. We were married in England, had a son, and were later divorced in 1961.

—Harold Westerfield, Ship's Cook

May would be a busy month for the crew of the *LST-325* as they prepared for the upcoming invasion of France; though still unknown to any of the officers or crew the invasion was now tentatively scheduled for 5 June 1944. On the morning of May 5, the crew prepared for getting underway for training exercises scheduled that day in Gerran's Bay. Just as the ship began to make its way out of the harbor they received word that the exercise had been cancelled due to strong winds and high seas in the English Channel, so the ship came about and returned to its mooring. On the 7th the *LST-325* anchored in Falmouth Bay to train with rhino ferries docking to the open bow ramp. Other sections of the crew not involved in the docking exercise underwent training with small arms and in casualty handling procedures.

On 12 May 1944, Pharmacist Mate Dick Scacchetti reported aboard *LST-325*...

I was born on September 11, 1925 in Jersey City, New Jersey. I graduated from Emerson High, Union City, New Jersey and attended one school year at New York University—a stern school. My family doctor told me that because I had a punctured eardrum that I would be rejected for the draft and I was dejected. Frankly, as an active sports-minded young man to be out of the war effort was unacceptable. In all honesty I wished to do my part as a citizen. Most of the older men by mid '43 were in service. Those who were not had something "wrong" and appeared deficient. Together with a recent classmate we planned to go to South America to "do something" rather than be obvious rejects. My college freshman classes were composed of young women, which made me uncomfortable. More than courageous, I felt I had to do something to look back on in the future, providing I survived. So, I took the chance and volunteered for the Navy, and was happily surprised to be accepted! I enlisted on 10 September 1943, as I always wanted to be a Navy man. I could not imagine being trained to kill anyone. I went through basic training at Sampson Naval Training Station, New York and the Pharmacist Mate School in Bainbridge, Maryland. I departed New York City, Easter Sunday 1944, for Roseneath, Scotland. Transferred shortly to LST-325 on 12 May 1944, from Milfordham, Wales...I was the second of two ship's company Pharmacist Mates. I reported to Pharmacist Mate 1/c Charles Hutchens and was part of a surgical team to treat the wounded being transferred from Omaha Beach. The surgical team was trained as an operating team for the wounded until they could be returned to the English hospitals for more intense treatment and recovery. My assignment during General Quarters was to dog the hatches along the port side and go to my battle dressing station on the bow.

—Dick Scacchetti, Pharmacist Mate

On the morning of May 10, the *LST-325*, accompanied by the *LST-513* and *LST-521*, left the Fal River to take part in exercises off Foway. After the *LST-325* passed through the boom gates at the entrance of Falmouth Harbor they stopped long enough to take a rhino ferry in tow, then continued out into the English Channel. The three LSTs headed northeast along the English coastline until they reached a point off Par Sands. Here, the *LST-325* anchored and waited while a Navy tug came alongside to take the ferry the rest of the way to Foway. As soon as the tug and ferry were clear, the LSTs hoisted anchor and returned to Falmouth.

The following day, the *LST-325* moved back up the Fal River to King Harry's Reach and moored alongside the *LST-338*. During morning muster on the 12th, all of the Navy issue Mk6 gas masks onboard were replaced with the Army issue Mk3 version. Later that afternoon the ballast tanks along the starboard side of the ship were filled, putting the ship on a list to that side so that the crew could paint the hull on the port side all the way down to the waterline.

The Fal River gave the U.S. Navy a new first! Our LST-325 went up the Fal River and tied up to a tree! There was getting to be so many LSTs and other ships that they decided to hide some up by King Harry's Ferry. We called it King Harry Carrie.

—Don Martin, Motor Machinist Mate

During the next three days the waterline along both sides of the ship were painted and the #1 LCVP was taken to the Base Maintenance Shop in Falmouth for some minor engine repairs. On May 16, the *LST-325* moored to the Turnware Hard so that the 336th Engineers could practice loading their vehicles onto the ship. While the exercise was underway the ship's crew exercised at Condition 1 and Beaching Condition 1M drills, during which they practiced removing simulated casualties from the gun tubs. Since the Allies thought the Germans might resort to using poison gas against the invasion force, they instructed the crew in chemical warfare defense. Later all of the ship's company was instructed on the operation of the 20mm and 40mm guns.

I remember one incident that I believe was during a period we were tied up in one of the rivers leading into the English Channel and I was an officer of the deck on an afternoon watch. A Machinist Mate was down in an LCVP tied alongside trying to remedy a problem involving engaging the propeller shaft. With the engines sounding as though it was wide open he tried to engage the shaft gear and created a horrible grinding sound. The Captain came out on deck shouting down to the man as he continued to try and engage the gear with the same loud, ear-splitting results. The Skipper turned to me, .45 by my side, and ordered me to give him the gun so he could shoot that man. It was an order I decided not to obey under the circumstances.

—**Ted Duning, First Lieutenant**

While we were docked in Falmouth I had liberty that day and since I was a cook I cut four large, beautiful steaks and tucked them down the waistline of my dress blues. I had a date with my future bride and her family. I walked up to the O.D. and asked permission to leave the ship. About the time I saluted we had General Quarters. Of course, I had to take my station and for two hours I stood GQ with those steaks slowly defrosting! When I finally got to my girlfriend's house I looked like I was "belly-shot." What a sight! But they tasted good!

—**Harold Westerfield, Ship's Cook**

The ship remained moored to the Turnware Hard until the afternoon of May 17 when they returned to the Fal River. Later that day, the crew gathered on the tank deck to watch training films on aircraft identification and use of the 20mm and 40mm guns. The next day more films on fire fighting, first aid and damage control were shown to the crew. In anticipation of having to feed the German prisoners they expected to transport back to England, additional food stores for POW's were issued to the ship and stored away that afternoon.

On 12 May 1944, Fireman Gerry Murphy reported for duty aboard *LST-325*...

I was born on 18 February 1926 in Syracuse, New York. After graduating from Vocational High School, I enlisted in February 1944 in Syracuse. When I enlisted, I had to get my parents to sign for me. It was the best thing I ever did. A lot of my friends went into the Army and the stories I got were not for me. Digging holes was not my way of thinking. I'd rather sleep between white sheets and be able to shower every day. I had basic training at Samson Naval Station in Geneva, New York and joined LST-325 in May 1944 when the ship was sitting in the Falmouth River in England. I was a Fireman 1/c and my GQ station was in the main engine room.

—*Gerry Murphy, Fireman*

On May 19, the crew went through more drills, including a simulated gas attack so the men could familiarize themselves with the new Army gas masks. That evening, the Stores Officer transferred all the crew's service, health and pay records from the ship to the Group Disbursing Officer aboard the *LST-338* for safekeeping.

We had gas mask training and on D-Day and for three or four days after we had them with us and wore gas proof suits. We had to sleep in them too. Germany did not use poison gas though. To show you how "matter of fact" we handled the coming invasion, I told "Rem" (Richard Martin) if he doesn't make it I'll go to your Mom and if I don't make it you go see my Mom. OK, we agreed.

—*Don Martin, Motor Machinist Mate*

The *LST-325*, along with the *LST-511*, *LST-391*, *LST-393* and *LST-337* left Falmouth on May 20 for gunnery practice. When the ships were in position on the practice range a Royal Air Force "Hurricane" fighter plane towing a target sleeve made a series of fly-bys. It first made three passes along the ship's port side from bow to stern, then three more passes along the starboard side. During each fly-by, the gun crews of each LST had forty-five seconds to fire at the target sleeve. The fighter then made one pass across the bow of the ships, traveling from starboard to port. When the Hurricane made its approach, several gunners aboard the *LST-325* opened fire prematurely and immediately the Captain ordered them to cease-fire. After making one last pass from across the bow, the fighter reeled in the target sleeve and returned to its base.

The ship prepared to return to the range the next day, but just as they were about to leave the harbor, a message was received from Base Operations that the exercise had been cancelled and to return to their mooring. Instead, the crew exercised in handling casualties to the ship's main deck from LCVPs alongside and then lowering them down into the tank deck. Another Condition 1 drill was held, involving a simulated bomb hit on the forward and aft sections of the ship.

On 13 May 1944, Gunners Mate Leo Horton reported for duty aboard *LST-325*...

I was born in Pontiac, Michigan on 15 June 1923. I graduated from High-land Park High School, Highland Park, Michigan. I enlisted in Pontiac on 8 April 1941. I shipped out of Detroit with other recruits on the Grand Trunk railroad to Chicago. Took an "El" the rest of the way. We got to Great Lakes after 10:00 p.m. without getting any supper. After basic I was sent to the USS Augusta, a heavy cruiser. I reported to LST-325 in 1944, just before the invasion of Europe. I was a Gunners Mate 2/c and my station was the 40mm tub in the fantail...Eugene Hendricks, Gunners Mate 2/c, was my best friend and a dedicated Christian. We used to have prayer together for the ship and for our work. He had served on a battleship and was transferred to LST-325 at the same time I was for the invasion. We came across the Atlantic together on the Queen Mary, assigned to the same stateroom. Both Gunners Mate 3/c and both with a Bible in our hands. We were both given an advance in our ratings to GM 2/c as soon as we came aboard the LST-325.

—Leo Horton, Gunners Mate

On the 23rd, the *LST-325* left its mooring on the Fal for the Turnware Hard, where an Army truck and jeep were loaded onto the ship's tank deck so that mea-surements could be taken for the two vehicles. These measurements were used for figuring out the optimum arrangement for each individual ship's assigned load. While on the Hard, twenty-one day's worth of U.S. Army rations were brought aboard and stowed away, along with 800 Army issue blankets.

The ship returned to the Turnware Hard on the following day and four cater-pillar tractors, four cranes were loaded onto the tank deck, the first of the vehicles that the *LST-325* would take across to Normandy. The next day the ship moored to the Eastern Arm pier in the outer harbor and the Captain had the crew go through gas attack, abandon ship and fire drills. On the 26th a U.S. Army Air Corps medical surgical team, Captain James T. Glazier, Sgt. T. Turner and Pfc. Art Campbell, reported onboard the *LST-325* for assignment through the initial stage of the invasion.

On May 27 the ship entered the #3 dry dock in Falmouth for minor alterations to the bow doors and to replace the ship's supply of lube oil, test the smoke generators, painting the ship's bottom and for an inspection of the ship's propellers. The next day, the *LST-325* left the dry-dock and moored off Messack Point, where later in the day more medical supplies were brought onboard.

During the morning of May 29, most of the registered government publications onboard were removed from the ship and placed into storage ashore to prevent them from falling into enemy hands, in case anything happened to the ship. Later that day 2nd Lt. E. M. Thornton and five enlisted men from the 30th Chemical Decontamination Company, 5th Engineer Special Brigade Group, came aboard for an orientation tour of the ship. A platoon from this company and their vehicles would make up a large part of the *LST-325*'s first load for Normandy.

That night, German bombers again attacked the harbor of Falmouth. All the ships anchored in the harbor went to battle stations as the guns ashore opened fire on the raiders. The ship's gunners stood by and watched as the planes flew overhead but they were under strict orders to not open fire so that the Germans wouldn't be able to estimate the number of ships. During the raid, the Germans bombed the fuel depot near the town of Swanvale, setting it ablaze, and they also dropped parachute mines into the bay, which had to be cleared out by minesweepers the next day.

We left from Falmouth to invade Normandy. I remember the air raid just before the invasion and we had to hold our fire so not to give away our locations. That called for discipline as bombers flew low overhead.

—Dale MacKay, Motor Machinist Mate

May 30 was the last day that the crew would see liberty until well after D-Day. From now, until the invasion, all the sailors and soldiers were restricted to their ships or marshaling areas in an effort to keep any information from leaking out. The Germans knew the invasion was coming, the only trump card the Allies had to their advantage was "where and when." The Allies had gone to fantastic lengths to trick the Germans into believing the invasion was going to take place at the Pas de Calais, the shortest distance England and France. They would take no chance on letting the Germans find out at the last minute that the actual invasion would take place at Normandy.

At 0615 the morning of June 2, the *LST-325* moored to the Turnware Hard and the rest of their first load for Normandy was brought aboard. By 0915 a total of sixteen DUKWs, twelve jeeps, four bulldozers, fifteen 2-½-ton trucks, two weapon carriers, three trailers, four cranes, a compressor truck and a repair truck were loaded onboard. As the vehicles were being securely chained to the deck, 31 officers and 408 enlisted men of the 30th Chemical Decontamination Company, under the command of Captain Milton E. Moore, embarked aboard the ship. Once the vehicles were secured and the soldiers aboard, the ship retracted from the Hard and returned to it assigned anchorage in the harbor, now crowded with LSTs and other assault craft. A pontoon causeway section and the rhino tug that the *LST-325* had been assigned to tow across the channel was brought out by tugboat and attached to cables off the stern of the ship. Later that afternoon Lt. Keene held a training session for the benefit of the Army personnel onboard to explain the ship's general alarm signals.

> *As a cook I had to get supplies, cook meals ahead, keep the "joe" pot filled so the crew could have their cup of "joe." We did bake a lot of bread that we stored in the freezer and I had the cooks make a lot of roast beef so we could have them for meals when the invasion came.*
>
> **—Harold Westerfield, Ship's Cook**

The day before the ship's scheduled departure from Falmouth, many last minute details were taken care of, both materially for the ship and spiritually for the crew. Once again, General Quarters and fire drills were held, still more medical supplies were brought aboard, and the LCVP's fuel tanks were topped off. Late that afternoon a Protestant chaplain held a church service for the crew and soldiers on the ship and later an Army Catholic chaplain came aboard to take confession. At 2015 nineteen U.S. Navy "Seabees" of the 1006th Construction Regiment under Warrant Officer A. K. Butterfield reported aboard.

> *As we, along with other LSTs were loading and standing by in Falmouth Harbor awaiting the order to get underway we had another LST come alongside to tie up with us. I was out on the starboard side watching our men take up lines when, looking up at that ship's conn, who should I see commanding that ship but Jim Elleman. Jim and I were in the same Morton*

High School graduating class in 1939 and at that time he lived just a block from my home in Richmond, Indiana.

—Ted Duning, First Lieutenant

The weather had been quite pleasant during the first three days of June but by 0400 on the 4th, as the crew was making preparations for getting underway, the weather turned rainy, windy and cold. The crewmembers whose duties required them to be topside wore specially treated clothing, issued to them just days before, that would protect them from possible German gas attacks. At 0520, the order came to hoist anchor, and the ships began to slowly make their way out of the harbor entrance and into the English Channel. However, after most of the ships had left the harbor, the word came that General Eisenhower, the overall commander of the Normandy Invasion (codename Operation OVERLORD), had ordered a 24 hour postponement of the invasion in hopes the weather would clear. The ships then came about and returned to Falmouth to wait out the storm.

The weather remained miserable throughout the day, but by evening the storm began to break up, just as the forecasters had assured General Eisenhower that it would. At 2145, Eisenhower made the decision that the invasion was a "go" for June 6. He then issued this following proclamation, a copy of which was to be read to each of man who would be soon be on their way to an uncertain fate in France:

Soldiers, Sailors and Airmen of the Allied Expeditionary Force!

You are about to embark upon the Great Crusade, toward which we have striven these many months. The eyes of the world are upon you. The hopes and prayers of liberty-loving people everywhere march with you. In company with our brave Allies and brothers-in-arms on other Fronts, you will bring about the destruction of the German war machine, the elimination of Nazi tyranny over the oppressed people of Europe, and security for ourselves in a free world.

Your task will not be an easy one. Your enemy is well trained, well equipped and battle-hardened. He will fight savagely.

But this is the year 1944! Much has happened since the Nazi triumphs of 1940– 41. The United Nations have inflicted upon the Germans great defeats, in open battle, man-to-man. Our air offensive has seriously reduced their strength in the air and their capacity to wage war on the ground. Our Home Fronts have given us an overwhelming superiority in weapons and munitions of war, and placed at our disposal great reserves of trained fighting men. The tide has turned! The free men of the world are marching together to Victory!

I have full confidence in your courage, devotion to duty and skill in battle. We will accept nothing less than full victory!

Good Luck! And let us beseech the blessing of Almighty God upon this great and noble undertaking.

Dwight D. Eisenhower.

At midnight, 5 June 1944, the first LSTs once more began leaving their berthings. At 0410, Lieutenant Mosier gave the order to start main engines and prepare to get underway. At 0530 the anchor was hoisted and the ship again slowly made her way out of the harbor to the English Channel, trailing the causeway and rhino tug behind her. Once clear of the harbor the ship anchored to wait for the rest of the convoy to gather.

Finally, the months of tedious training and exercises and waiting were behind the officers and crew of the *LST-325*. Now, as the greatest invasion fleet the world had ever known was getting underway, the crew of the *LST-325* faced with grim determination the task lying before them. Most of the crew had been through the invasions of Sicily and Salerno; those that reported onboard after the ship had arrived in England had heard the stories from the veterans. They all fully understood what might be lying in store for them when they reached the French coast. The question going through many of their minds now was what their fate might be once they reached the "Far Shore" of the Channel.

> *We got underway from Falmouth for the Normandy invasion, moving out into the Channel. There was a gray, light fog, and a long, long line of ships steaming in line. Then we turned back to do it for good the next day. Thoughts were spinning through my head as to what awaits us, what would happen?*
>
> **—Stanley Barish, Engineering Officer**

7

Normandy

The *LST-325* sailed for Normandy as part of Convoy ECL-1 in Task Force 126, or Force "B", the floating reserve for the assault force going ashore at Omaha Beach. By 0800 on 5 June 1944, all the ships assigned to Convoy ECL-1 had assembled. The three-column formation of LST's looked like this:

533	331	266
5	325	388
61	306	389
212	7	27
307	392	28
335	393	262
355	59	538
338	391	326
197	516	369
336	381	337
356	523	16
	532	

The Senior Officer of Convoy ECL-1 was the skipper of the *LST-331*. Providing the protective escort for the LST's was the destroyers *USS Hambleton, HMS Volunteer, HMS Vimy, HMS Boadicia* and *HMS Bluebell.*

Once the *LST-325* was in her asigned position, the stern cable to the pontoon causeway and rhino tug was let out to a distance of 400 feet, and the barrage balloon that had been installed on the ship a few days earlier was raised to an elevation of 800 feet. A steel cable connected the balloon to a winch on the forecastle; its purpose was to keep enemy aircraft from making low level attacks on the ships, if they did they risked flying into the cable and damaging their aircraft.

Later that afternoon, nine LSTs from Salcombe joined the convoy, bringing the total number to forty-three.

The more-than-5000 ships that made up the invasion fleet sailed from several different ports in England, Wales and Ireland. The planners had worked out a strict timetable of departure times so that all the various elements of the different assault groups, the faster warships that would be supplying gunfire support during the assault and the slower amphibious ships and troop transports, would all arrive at the proper place at the proper time. All the ships converged at a point called "Point Z", located approximately thirteen miles southeast of the Isle of Wight. Around Point Z was a five-mile circular zone swept clean of enemy mines, code-named "Piccadilly Circus." From here the ships would go on to their designated assault zones through lanes that the minesweepers had cleared through the minefields off the Normandy beaches. After the Force "B" ships reached Piccadilly Circus, they maintained position while the Force "O" and Force "U" groups carrying the initial assault forces, headed for the Omaha and Utah beaches respectively.

> *It was a very slow trip to Normandy in the convoy with an Army rhino barge being towed behind. Everybody was grim. The Air Force covered the sky like ants. Various levels of aircraft overhead filled the sky above the invasion forces. They gave the appearance of insects crawling on high with deliberate precision. At apparently various levels were aircraft from English bases flying to and over Normandy, while others were apparently returning from bombing runs. The skies were literally alive with activity, which added to our confidence below.*
>
> **—Dick Scacchetti, Pharmacist Mate**

Shortly before dawn on June 6, the preliminary naval bombardment of the German fortifications on Omaha Beach began. Even though the *LST-325* was more than fifteen miles from the beachhead, they could still hear the distant rumbling of the fleet's big guns. Flashes of gunfire, tracers and explosions lit the southern horizon. As dawn came the men could see for the first time the enormity of the invasion fleet gathered about them. Hundreds of ships of all types and sizes were in every direction as far as the eye could see. Hundreds of bombers, fighters and troop transports flew overhead in steady streams to and from the coast, giving the men on the ships below a much needed boost to their confidence and morale.

> *To see the horizon full of ships surely meant that something big was in the offing. When we saw the American planes, we knew that the coast was being*

battered. Also to see battleships and cruisers nearby and lobbing shells over-head impressed us.

—Dale MacKay, Motor Machinist Mate

Throughout the day the ships of Force "B" waited, circling slowly, maintaining their position until the time came to close in and deliver their vehicles and men to the beach. The first news they received from Omaha Beach was not good, troops were being bottled up by stiff German resistance and finally the order was given to delay further landings until there was a breakthrough and some of the congestion on the beach could be cleared. Finally, as dusk began to settle in, Force "B" received the order to turn south and make their approach to the Omaha Beach assault area.

Our first trip across was filled with fear and apprehension. We were loaded with trucks, jeeps, big guns, ammo and all other war commodities. Our tank deck was full and topside was so crowded you could hardly move! The personnel we were carrying usually played cards, chummed with our guys and/ or slept. A lot of them worked hard to get their guns and gear in order. A fond memory I have was to look up at the sky. By that, I mean it was like a two-way highway. We saw the contrails of the fighters and bombers going to Normandy and the others coming back. What a sight!

—Harold Westerfield, Ship's Cook

That sight as we approached the Normandy beaches from far out in the Channel that first trip of the thousands of tracers arching up through the sky as shells were being fired, major explosions all along the lines of beaches creating thousands of multi-colored lights across the horizon like some giant waterfall. Anchored just off Omaha Beach that first trip we were able to witness the duel between a U.S. destroyer and a German 88 located on a concrete bunker in the hill behind the beach. The final tracer we saw was from the destroyer. Then there were the medics in the wardroom that first night after wounded had been brought aboard who were removing legs and making such repairs to mangled bodies as were possible. We were a hospital ship first and before long, we became the means of transporting German prisoners back to England.

—Ted Duning, First Lieutenant

The ships of Force "B" slowly made their way to Omaha Beach all through the night and into the morning of June 7. Off in the distance, flashes of gunfire from the beach periodically lit up the horizon. After midnight, the occasional flare dropped by enemy aircraft glowed off in the distance, but none came close enough to the convoy to be of any real concern. At 0735, the French coastline finally came into view. The LSTs in the middle column of the formation changed course and separated from the convoy's main body, and at 0943, the *LST-325* dropped anchor off the Red Sector of Omaha Beach. They opened the ship's outer doors and ramp and the first three DUKW's drove off the ship and began making their way in towards the shore. Meanwhile, deckhands cast off the rhino tug and causeway section from the stern cable lines; the tug taking the causeway in tow and guiding it towards the beachhead.

> *We stopped off Omaha Beach and released the rhino barge. Pillboxes were spraying the incoming ships attempting to beach and I recall the ships lobbing shells against the pillboxes, which were the last of the German defenses. The pillbox was under assault by gunfire point-blank from two cruisers and an assortment of Navy ships. The pillbox appeared to attract the most attention as the beach, almost secured, had pockets of resistance. We observed volleys of rockets directed to the beach that presented a carnival atmosphere.*
>
> **—Dick Scacchetti, Pharmacist Mate**

The first DUKWs had a difficult time making the trip in to the beach, so after the tug and rhino ferry were clear of the ship, the *LST-325* raised anchor and moved in closer to the beach. Even now, on the second day of the invasion, they still had to be wary of German artillery, still in action and protected by concrete bunkers. After the *LST-325* had anchored, the thirteen DUKWs remaining onboard were launched. As the last one drove off the ramp, a LCM came alongside with two wounded soldiers evacuated from the beach, soon followed by another with five more casualties onboard. After the wounded had been transferred to the ship, the two LCMs moored alongside and some of the ships crewmembers handed down food and water to their exhausted crews.

> *My battle dressing station as a Pharmacist Mate was in the hatch closest to the bow on the port side. A step outside provided a sweeping view of Omaha Beach. Landing craft of all descriptions lay offshore and took opportunities to discharge troops, vehicles and equipment. An LST made an effort to*

approach a landing. The enemy pillbox "88's" opened up by bracketing the LST. Geysers exploded on each side, and the LST realizing the next volley would be fatal, made a slow but deliberate "U-turn" and proceeded out to deeper water. Surprisingly we may never know why the third and certainly fatal shot never happened.

—Dick Scacchetti, Pharmacist Mate

That afternoon, the second platoon of the 30th Chemical Decontamination Company loaded into DUKWs, LCMs, and LCVPs and was taken ashore. Their main task was to take defensive measures against gas weapon attack, should the Germans resort to using them against the invasion forces, and setting up smoke generators to create a smoke screen in case of an aerial attack. Fortunately, the Germans did not use chemical weapons now or at any other time during the war.

Shortly after the aid station on the beach transferred a second group of wounded evacuees to the ship, one of the soldiers from the first group of casualties, Private Raymond Prince of the 116th Regiment, 29th Infantry Division, died from his wounds. Later, his body was returned to the beach for burial.

A little later, the *LCI-414* brought ninety-eight merchant sailors out to the ship. These sailors had been among the crews that sailed a number of old merchant ships from England to Omaha Beach. Once off the beach, the crews maneuvered the merchant ships into position and then deliberately sunk them, in order to create a protective breakwater for the beachhead.

At 1845, the *LCT-550* docked on the bow of the *LST-325*, and three bulldozers, a jeep and trailer, and three of the 2½-ton trucks unloaded to the craft. After unloading on the beach, the *LCT-550* returned to the ship, this time transporting two cranes, three jeeps and four 2½-ton trucks. The last vehicles to be unloaded from the *LST-325* on June 7 were the last of the three cranes on board, a bulldozer and two 2½-ton trucks, taken to the beach by the *LCT-625* just before midnight.

We were there at H-hour, but there was no way a ship as large as an LST could hit the beach until some of the obstacles and resistance was eliminated. Of course, we didn't know that, we thought we'd be going right in. We did some unloading by small boat as we lay offshore. Our planes kept the sky buzzing. Destroyers, cruisers, battleships and rocket launching craft kept pounding the gun emplacements in the hills and cliffs. I think our first cou-

ple of trips back were with wounded. Plasma bottles were hanging every-where. Some soldiers died on the way back.

—Stanley Barish, Engineering Officer

We were not real early in the movement. We were on the way in the dark, and when it was getting light, we went up to see what it looked like. It was a sight I will never forget! There were ships in every direction as far as you could see. A lot of them were ahead of us, which was not bad. The air was full of planes, looked like hundreds of them. They had all been painted with wide white stripes on the bottom of the wing. They were all headed in the same way we were, and we hoped it was going to help with the landing of the GI's. We took on some wounded as we were unloading. Some of them the same GI's that left our ship on "Ducks" earlier.

—John Roberts, Electricians Mate

There was a city burning on our port bow. We anchored out and let a "Duck" off our ramp loaded with soldiers. It hit a mine near the beach and blew up. There was a large bomber coming in that was flashing a signal from a side opening. It made a sharp turn to the left and crashed, burned all day. There were many sunken trucks and jeeps on the beachhead, we loaded ours onto LCT's to be taken in. There were soldiers bodies floating by the ship...The wounded were brought aboard and they operated on our mess tables. Many stretcher cases of soldiers were on our tank deck. The night of the invasion I was going to sleep on my gun station because of the surgery and death in the main compartment where my bunk was located. A Pharmacist Mate offered to let me sleep in his bunk in the port side passage. While I slept a shell hit right where I had intended to sleep and poured shrapnel into my equipment that I had left there. My life was definitely spared. Thank God!

—Leo Horton, Gunners Mate

Just as the last of the vehicles were being offloaded from the ship, some of the nearby ships opened fire on a small number of German fighter aircraft that had flown in over the beach. Gunners on other ships immediately followed suit and soon thousands of crisscrossing tracer rounds lit the night sky. As the gunfire started to ease up, another fourteen wounded men were transferred onboard and taken to the crew's quarters, which had been turned into a temporary medical ward and surgery.

The next morning, the unloading operation continued as soon as there was enough light in the sky for the men to see by. The barrels of fuel, oil and water designated for the beach were unloaded first onto the *LCI-86*. Then the *LCT-22* moored to the bow of the ship and five 2½-ton trucks, eight jeeps and an ambulance were loaded aboard. A rhino ferry docked to the ship's bow and the last remaining vehicles were unloaded onto it. As it was preparing to undock from the ship's bow the medical team brought down the body of another soldier to the tank deck of the ship, Corporal J. McMurray of the 37th Engineers. After being evacuated to the ship the day before, the surgical team could not save him. They put his body onboard the rhino to take back to the beach, where he could be given a proper burial.

At 1223, the engineers started the main engines as the final troops onboard, the 1006th Navy "Seabees" detachment, were loading into landing craft for the trip in to the beach. The ship then withdrew from the beach and anchored in the area designated for the convoys returning to England. While the ship waited for sailing orders, nine more wounded men were brought out to the ship, bringing the total number of evacuees onboard to thirty-eight. The doctors transferred one of the men to a Royal Navy hospital ship whose wounds required treatment beyond the facilities aboard the LST.

It was very rough. I will always think of the poor boys we had to take over and how they had a rough go. We tried to be good to all of them when we had them on our ship. Some we left off that day we hauled back in a day or two in bad shape.

—Ellsworth Easterly, Chief Motor Machinist Mate

We started taking wounded soldiers until the tank deck was full and we returned to England. We operated by surgical teams in the crew's quarters. Some died. Some we amputated limbs. I remember being somewhat sick to my stomach…I was only eighteen years old…and my condition was joined by others.

—Dick Scacchetti, Pharmacist Mate

I think we were in the third wave in; we let off three amphibious Ducks somewhere around 6:00 AM and didn't get in to unload until sometime around 5:00 PM. We had several wounded loaded for our return trip to England. We had an Army doctor aboard and extra Pharmacist Mates to take care of the wounded aboard. From the time we left Falmouth until we beached at Utah Beach I was at my 40mm GQ station. We stood watch four hours on and four hours off. The only time we left was to eat.

—Emil Kolar, Motor Machinist Mate

The Normandy Invasion was a significant experience in the lives of all of us. We were in a major, one-time, historical event the likes of which was never seen before and will never be again. What a colossal feat of planning, logistics, equipmentation, strategic misleading of the enemy and a large measure of good luck. And the unbelievable courage of the men who stormed the beaches, who dropped in by parachute and those who arrived to fight, if at all, by gliders, many of which crash landed with loss of life for troops onboard. To me those troops and the Navy seamen who took troops to the beaches will always be the No. 1 heroes of the Normandy Invasion.

—Ted Duning, First Lieutenant

The *LST-325* reached England the afternoon of June 9 and anchored overnight near Weymouth, before continuing on to the Hard in Portland the next day. During the night, another of the wounded soldiers onboard died, Private Thomas Legacy of Company G, 299th Combat Engineers Battalion. As soon as the ship docked in Portland, medical personnel immediately unloaded the casualties and rushed them to the base hospital. The ship then received medical supplies to replace that used during this first trip, along with jerry cans of gasoline, lube oil, blankets and Army rations. That afternoon vehicles and troops from the 980th Field Artillery Battalion were loaded onboard.

On the 11th, the *LST-325* began her second trip to France in Convoy EPL-410. As the convoy neared the French coast that evening it split into two groups, the *LST-325* following the group led by the *LST-262* to the Utah Beach area, the other group of LSTs continued on to Omaha Beach. As the convoy neared the Utah assault area an explosion rocked another of the ship's in the group, the *LST-499*, after they struck an underwater mine. Immediately the ship began to settle down by the stern. The escort ships moved in to rescue the stricken ships crew, while the remaining LSTs continued on and anchored near the Isle of St. Marcouf.

At 0350 in the morning of the 12th, the *LST-325* beached on the Sugar Red sector of Utah Beach and waited for the tide to go out. The crew kept a close eye on the ship as the tide went out, looking for any signs of stress to the hull. They commenced unloading trucks and artillery at 0700. When the ship was empty, sixty-eight German prisoners were marched out by an MP escort and put in a holding area on the tank deck. As the tide returned and the ship became water-borne, the crew made another inspection of the hull for signs of leaks or hull stress from beaching and drying out. The *LST-325* then retracted from the beach and anchored in the North Bound Assembly area.

As far as prisoners were concerned, the majority were glad it was over, but the SS troopers were nasty and belligerent.

—Bill Hanley, Motor Machinist Mate

Carrying prisoners could be interesting. Older ones were anxious for the war to end while the younger ones were a bit arrogant, but well informed.

—Dale MacKay, Motor Machinist Mate

I remember the prisoners down on the tank deck and they were quite docile since they realized how lucky they were to be captured. The war was over for them.

—Ted Duning, First Lieutenant

The *LST-325* got underway in a convoy the next day, as it neared Southampton the ship detached and entered the harbor, where they anchored overnight. At 0600 the next morning, the ship moored to the Hard and unloaded the prisoners. Seventy-one U.S. Army vehicles and 148 officers and men were loaded onto the ship, after which the *LST-325* anchored in the western channel off the Isle of Wight, waiting for the rest of the convoy to assemble. Lieutenant Mosier, the convoy Senior Officer, gave the order for the convoy to get underway just before midnight.

As the convoy neared France during the morning of June 15, a mine exploded next to an LST in the column of ships opposite of that which the *LST-325* was in, but the ship made no damage report. A second explosion followed from the rear of the convoy, when the *LST-133* struck a mine. At 1125 the convoy split, the *LST-325* leading the ships designated for Utah Beach while the others continued on to Omaha. After the *LST-325* had beached and dried out, they began to unload; it took until the early morning until all the vehicles were off the ship.

Several times during the night heavy anti-aircraft fire was seen coming from the vicinity of Port-en-Bessin, near the Omaha Beach sector.

After the last vehicle had unloaded, seventeen wounded American soldiers were loaded onboard. As soon as the ship had retracted, they started the trip back across the Channel to England. Also onboard the *LST-325* during this trip was CBS Radio news correspondent Paul Manning, who worked under the legendary Edward R. Murrow. After the war Manning wrote two books on the war; *Hirohito: The War Years* and *Martin Bormann: Nazi in Exile.*

The *LST-325* arrived at Portsmouth late that evening, anchoring in the eastern approach to the harbor until 0200, when the Port Director cleared them to enter the harbor and proceed to the GH Hard. After the ship had anchored a thick fog had settled in over the harbor, and as they got underway the Captain ordered the port and starboard running lights and masthead light turned on. As they inched their way through the harbor, suddenly another vessel loomed out of the misty darkness, directly on a collision course for the ship. Lt. Mosier immediately ordered both engines "back full" and the two ships desperately tried to maneuver around one another, but they collided with a sickening crunch and rending of metal. The vessel, a British-manned LCT, struck along the ship's starboard bow, cutting a fifteen-foot gash in the hull, approximately ten feet above the waterline. Even though the LCT did have its running lights lit, no one aboard the *LST-325* saw any sign of the craft until it was almost on top of them. After the two ships separated, the LCT kept going and disappeared again into the fog. After making a quick survey of the damage to the ship, the *LST-325* continued to the Hard and moored alongside the *LST-8.*

After daybreak, the *LST-325* moored to the Hard and turned over the wounded soldiers to a Royal Army Medical Corps unit. The ship then retracted and anchored in the eastern approach of the harbor to make temporary repairs to the hole in the ship's bow. That night, shortly before midnight, German bombers attacked Portsmouth and Southampton. The crews manned their guns but the planes were well out of range, all they could do was watch on as the guns on the bases opened fire on the raiders.

The ship reentered the harbor the next morning to complete repairs to the ship's bow, after which they moored to the GH Hard and began taking on the tanks and vehicles of the British Seventh Royal Tank Regiment under the command of Major M. R. Wellby. Once the last vehicle was secured, the ship again anchored in the eastern approach where two pontoon causeway sections were brought out by tug and attached to the stern towing cable with a two-line towing bridle.

The *LST-325* left Portsmouth on the morning of June 19, headed to Juno Beach where the British army had come ashore on D-Day. As the ship left the harbor and began picking up speed, one of the lines to the towing bridle parted. The Captain ordered the ship's speed reduced, but the last remaining cable soon snapped under the added strain and the two causeway sections were lost. Since leaving the protection of the convoy would be foolish, all that could be done was to log the position of the causeways and continue on.

By the time the convoy reached the French coast that afternoon, storm clouds were already beginning to gather overhead. Soon the wind was at gale force strength, driving the rain viciously before it. Over the next three days one of the worst storms to hit the Channel in the last hundred years hammered the Normandy beaches and the fleet now huddled off the coast. Winds averaging thirty knots and waves eight to ten feet high ravaged the coastline. Many smaller landing craft, and even a few of the larger ships, were sunk or severely damaged, and the artificial harbor that had been constructed in England and towed across the Channel to the American beaches was destroyed. During the first day of the storm, the *LST-325* was forced to relocate three times trying to find a secure anchorage against the onslaught of wind and waves.

Later that evening, the ship's lookouts for the first time spotted a German *vergeltungswaffe-eins*, or V-1, pilot-less rocket bomb, screaming overheads toward England. Known as "buzz bombs" because of the noise they made while passing overhead, the V-1 was Hitler's "revenge weapon", its only purpose to blindly strike at the civilians of London and other cities within its range throughout southeastern England. Armed with an 1800-pound warhead, this weapon of terror carried just enough fuel to bring it over the target area, once the fuel ran out the bomb would fall to earth and explode.

As dawn approached on the 21st, the storm finally began to diminish, and by mid-afternoon the landing craft ashore could finally get to shore and begin unloading. The *LST-325* unloaded the British tanks four miles north of Courseulles-sur-mer, then retracted and anchored offshore. That night the German bombers returned, concentrating their attack on the forces ashore and again ignoring the ships. Throughout the rest of the night the lookouts aboard the *LST-325* recorded seeing the flash of far off artillery from the landward horizon.

As the ship prepared to get underway the next morning, a cable attached to a flotation buoy, torn from its anchor during the storm, fouled the starboard propeller. Unable to clear the propeller, the ship had to beach once again on Juno and wait for the tide to go out. While the crew worked to clear the cable from the propeller, the British Medical Corps brought aboard 254 wounded, most of them stretcher cases. When the tide returned the ship retracted and anchored to await until the next convoy formed for the return trip to England.

After midnight the order to start the smoke generator came after lookouts spotted a German twin-engine bomber overhead. German bombers were using the remote-controlled glider bombs like those used against the convoy the *LST-325* had sailed with from North Africa the previous November. The Germans made several raids on the ships and the forces along the beach that night, during one of the attacks there were reports that the Germans had dropped parachute mines into the bay. When the *LST-325* and the rest of the convoy got underway the next morning they had to make a wide sweep around a group of minesweepers busily clearing out the mines. The *LST-325* reached Southampton that evening and turned the British casualties over to the Medical Corps.

> *We had a lot of stretcher cases. Some didn't make it on the way back to England. The Harbor Captain told Mosier to wait. Captain Mosier reported back, "I have 250 stretcher cases onboard and I am NOT waiting!" He came into port!*
>
> **—Don Martin, Motor Machinist Mate**

The next morning all the additional medical personnel assigned to the *LST-325* for the invasion were detached from duty and disembarked. After loading the trucks of the 441st Quartermaster Truck Company the ship was making its way to the convoy assembly area when the air raid sirens began to wail. Seconds later another V-1 rocket bomb streaked across the sky from the southeast, no more than 2000 feet up.

The *LST-325* sailed for France on June 25, anchoring near the island of St. Marcouf, off Utah Beach. They beached there the next morning and unloaded; afterwards 796 German prisoners were brought out to the ship and placed under Army Military Police guard on the tank deck.

> *We had to bring back several hundred German prisoners. I remember most vividly that they loaded up on the tank deck with large, burly Marines standing guard with machine guns! I did not want to feed them but I did so under direct orders from Captain Mosier.*
>
> **—Harold Westerfield, Ship's Cook**

> *Later we took prisoners back in the tank deck. Toilet facilities consisted of 50-gallon drums with some water in them. Once, the ranking German*

*officer wanted accommodations befitting his rank. He got the same toilet
drums as the others.*

—Stanley Barish, Engineering Officer

After retracting, the *LST-325* anchored near the *HMS Ceres* in the North
Bound Convoy area. The Convoy Control Officer aboard the *Ceres* gave the
LST-325 orders to tow the *LCT-276* back to England. The *LST-325* got underway with a convoy for Southampton that afternoon. The ships anchored in the
eastern approach to the harbor overnight, continuing on the next morning. The
LST-325 paused in the Calshot Collecting Area long enough to leave the LCT
moored alongside the *LST-49*, then continued to the S1 Hard to unload the German prisoners.

The *LST-325* left Southampton after midnight on June 29 with vehicles and
men of the Royal Army Medical Corps. The convoy reached Sword Beach
around noon, anchored offshore, and waited for the order to beach. The British
Beachmaster gave the *LST-325* orders to beach well after the tide was beginning
to ebb, and the ship ground ashore too far from the beach. Even at low tide, the
water around the ship was too deep to drive a vehicle through without drowning
it. To further complicate matters there was a five-foot deep depression in the
beach right under the bow ramp. Unable to unload, they had no choice but to sit
and wait for the tide to return.

When the tide returned the next morning, the *LST-325* was able to move in
another hundred feet closer to the shoreline. This time when the tide went out
they were able to unload the ambulances and trucks off the ship. After the last of
the vehicles were gone, a squad of British soldiers brought twelve German prisoners out to the ship. Just before the incoming tide returned a Royal Navy bomb
disposal unit brought a crate onboard that contained two German underwater
mines. Their instructions were to return these mines to England and turn them
over to the custody of the British Admiralty Department in London for further
study.

When the *LST-325* prepared to get underway during the morning of July 1,
they received orders to take the *LST-493* in tow. While attempting to beach, the
LST-493 had settled down on top of their own anchor, punching a hole through
the bottom of their hull and flooding the engine room. The *LST-325* shackled
their stern anchor line to a towing line from the bow of the damaged LST and
got underway for the port of London.

As the convoy approached the English coast, they sailed into a heavy fog bank.
Visibility was so poor at times that the Convoy Commander ordered all ships to

drop anchor until the conditions improved and they could again proceed safely. By noon on July 2 the fog had cleared and the ships could continue to London without further delay. That evening, after the *LST-325* anchored near the Tilbury docks in London, a tugboat came alongside, bringing a British naval officer to inspect the two German mines stored onboard. The German prisoners and their British guards then disembarked to the tug. The *LST-325* continued on to the West India piers where the *LST-493* was unshackled from the towline and two tugboats maneuvered her into dry-dock. As midnight approached, the ship passed through the Thames tidal locks and moored at the Hard. Just as the last line was secured, an air raid siren went off just seconds before several V-1 rockets slammed in and around the area of the docks.

> *We went up the Thames to London for one trip. We were delivering a German mine for study. While there a buzz bomb fell close enough to shake the ship.*
>
> **—Bill Bliss, Quartermaster**

> *There was our sail up the Thames River, which was an interesting one, particularly as we neared the city of London and watched buzz bombs coming in overhead and then seeing their flame-out, signaling their fall toward what would become their target in the city.*
>
> **—Ted Duning, First Lieutenant**

As the ship was being loaded with Royal Army Signal Corps vehicles the following morning, personnel from the Admiralty Office unloaded the German mines. Afterward the ship anchored in the Thames River estuary, sailing that evening with a convoy for the Gold Beach assault area near the French town of Arromanches.

The convoy reached the French coastline shortly before midnight on July 4 and anchored with orders to beach at noon the following day. There were a number of air raid alerts during the night and at times heavy anti-aircraft fire was seen coming from the guns on shore, providing the only fireworks the ship would see this Independence Day. The *LST-325* beached as ordered the next day and unloaded, returning to Southampton the next morning as part of Convoy FTM-29.

In Southampton, the *LST-325* loaded with U.S. Army vehicles and soldiers, delivering them to Omaha Beach on July 8. As a routine inspection of the ship was being made drying out, they discovered a foot-long section was missing from one of the propeller blade tips. Shortly after beginning the return trip to England the next morning, one of the escort ships began dropping depth charges directly ahead of the convoy, at the same time signaling the ships to make an emergency 45° turn to port. The enemy submarine was forced to break off their attack and the convoy continued on to Portland without further incident.

During the last two weeks of July the *LST-325* made six more trips between England and France. After returning to Portland on the 28th, the crew had a few days to rest and to catch up on some of some long overdue maintenance. Since June 6 the *LST-325* had made thirteen round-trips across the English Channel and had been continuously active bringing supplies and reinforcements to the armies now fighting west to the port of Cherbourg and eastward towards Paris.

July 30 was LtJG. Stan Barish's last day as part of the *LST-325* crew. He had served as the Engineering Officer since the ship had been commissioned, and he was highly respected by the men who served under him.

> *After 18 months on the 325 I was, sadly, transferred to the LST-369. Skipper didn't know why. I went to group headquarters and asked. They said the 369's engineer wasn't getting along with his Skipper and they thought Mosier could handle him. I understand that Mosier got rid of him in a couple months. On the 369 I was given a choice of Engineer or Gunnery jobs. I opted for Gunnery so I could experience deck duty, conning the ship, etc. I'm glad I did.*
>
> **—Stanley Barish, Engineering Officer**

The next day technicians from the repair ship *USS Melville* began installing the ship's new navigation radar, and finishing the temporary repairs the crew had made to the damage caused in collision with the British LCT the month before. That night a movie projector was set up on the tank deck of the ship and the officers of the *LST-325* invited the crews of the *Melville* and the LSTs anchored nearby to join them for a small slice of home and a brief escape from the realities of war.

> *After Normandy D-Day we made several trips to the French coast. Finally, we were all getting stomach nerve pains because of the stress. John Roberts and I went to Cardiff, Wales on leave. We stayed at a Red Cross canteen. We had beans on toast every morning. Laid on the lawn in the sun until the*

bars opened up. Quietly got a little drunk, slept it off and did the same the next day. We got back to the ship and felt fine.

—Don Martin, Motor Machinist Mate

8

Victory

On the morning of 6 August 1944, the *LST-325* moved from alongside the repair ship *Melville* to a mooring buoy out in Portland Harbor. After morning muster, a quarter of the ship's company disembarked on a five-day leave. Later that day, the ship moored to the R2 Hard and loaded aboard vehicles and troops of the 773rd Tank Destroyer Battalion. The *LST-325* left Portland on August 8, returning the following day after unloading the 773rd on Utah Beach.

On the 10th, the *LST-325* moored at the R2 Hard and loaded lube oil drums, medical supplies, blankets and supplies for the crew. Early the next morning the vehicles of the 945th Field Artillery Battalion were loaded onboard. That afternoon an officer from the *USS Melville* reported aboard to assist the ship's radar technicians with operating the ship's new radar equipment. And, on August 11 the Captain's promotion to the rank of Lieutenant Commander became official.

The *LST-325* left Portland on August 12, with Lt. Cdr. Mosier the convoy's Senior Officer. The ships beached that evening five miles west of Grandcamp. It was after midnight when the last vehicle was offloaded, after which U.S. Army Military Police brought 471 German prisoners out to the ship. The convoy began the return trip to Portland after daybreak, arriving late that afternoon.

We made a lot of visits to Portland. Weymouth nearby was a tourist town and catered to servicemen. Movies, teashops and dancing. One of my local friends invited me to a lobster feast. The best lobster I ever had. Better than Maine's. Excellent hiking all over this area.

—Bill Bliss, Quartermaster

On August 16, the *LST-325* sailed from Portland in Convoy FBC-55 for Swansea, Wales, arriving there the following day. During the morning of the 18th, sixteen tanks and their crews under the command of Captain Walter Wade were loaded onto the ship. The ship remained in Swansea until August 20, sailing as part of a convoy of nineteen LSTs and five merchant ships. The next afternoon, the convoy sailed into a severe storm as they made their way south along the English coastline. After struggling against wind and wave throughout the night, the ships sought shelter in the entrance to Portland Harbor on the morning of the 22nd.

By daybreak on the 23rd the storm had passed and the convoy left Portland, reaching Utah Beach that afternoon. The *LST-325* remained anchored offshore until 0300 the next morning. After the last tank was driven off the ship, the motor was engaged to begin raising the ramp. Suddenly both hoist chains snapped and the ramp thudded back down on the beach. The ramp then had to be raised by using the gear-drive backup system. Once the ship returned to Portland the ramp chains were replaced.

The *LST-325* made two more trips to France before the end of August. Before the ship retracted on the second trip, the army began loading the ship with crates of artillery shells. The *LST-325* would deliver this ammunition to St. Michel-en-Greve on the western side of the Cotentin peninsula, in support of the troops driving west to the port city of Brest.

It wasn't until the afternoon of September 2 before the last crates were aboard. Altogether, more than 400 tons of ammunition was loaded onto the tank deck. That evening the ship retracted and got underway, and after a difficult passage through heavy seas, they reached St. Michel before dawn on September 5. After daybreak, the ship beached and they began unloading the ammunition onto army trucks until the incoming tide forced them to suspend operations.

Do others remember the stormy passage near the Guernsey and Jersey Islands to a beach south of Normandy; our tank deck loaded with ammunition the Army needed for the siege of Brest? Once unloaded of that cargo quite a few of us were granted liberty and John Sarbaugh and I plus a couple of others hitched a ride in one of the Army's 4X4's taking the ammunition inland. We were dropped off first at the cottage of a French couple who insisted we come in to help them celebrate their liberation with a bottle of wine. From there, we went on to a small village where the local hotel had a bar serving calvados. After a couple more stops we returned to the beach, where we heard there was another bar just down the way. As John and I headed toward this new attraction two MP's took us by the arms, one on each side, turned us towards the waters edge and escorted us to the liberty boat waiting there. It seems we were being involved in a roundup of 325 crewmembers who some-

one felt would be better off aboard their ship than to remain on the beach. I still remember that the bow doors were opened and the ramp lowered for the most practical way to get the participants in the afternoon's liberty excursion aboard. Few would have made it up a ladder over the side.

—Ted Duning, First Lieutenant

The ammunition was unloaded by September 6, and the ship began the return trip to Portland, sailing with the *LST-393*, *LST-72* and three merchant ships. The *LST-325* remained in Portland until the 11th, giving the crew a few days of rest and to restock the ship's stores. On the 10th, they began loading the trucks and guns of the 358th Field Artillery. As the ship was being loaded, the ship's port side boat davit was damaged after being struck by the bow of another LST trying to moor alongside the *LST-325*.

On September 15, the *LST-325* started out on her twentieth trip to France since D-Day, carrying vehicles and men of the Channel Base Section Communication Zone, under the command of Colonel Squire. After beaching near the town of Port-en-Bessin that evening, 500 tons of ammo for delivery to St. Michel was loaded onboard. The *LST-325* sailed for Cherbourg with the *LST-521* the morning of the 17th. There they were joined by four LSTs and two merchantmen and then continued on to St. Michel, where they beached the afternoon of September 18. It took four days to unload all the ammunition. The convoy then returned to Cherbourg and on the 23rd, the *LST-325* set off for Portland.

After anchoring in Portland the night of the 23rd, the harbor was hit with gale force winds and driving rain. About an hour after the storm began, the *LST-325*, buffeted about by the high winds, began to drag its anchor. The engineers quickly brought the main engines on-line and the ship moved to a more protected anchorage. Twice more the ship had to relocate until a secure anchorage was found. Shortly afterward, a British LCT spun past the *LST-325's* bow, adrift and out of control. Some quick-acting deck hands managed to pass a line to crewmembers of the LCT and then tie it off to the stern, but before more lines could be passed to secure the LCT, the first line parted. The Captain immediately had an emergency message radioed to Base Operations, and a tug was sent to rescue the drifting craft.

After making one more trip to Utah Beach the *LST-325* returned to Portland for a few days of R&R. On September 30 Commander Pattie, the commanding officer of LST Group 34, held an inspection of the ship and crew. He was accompanied by Lt. Quareau and LtJG. Gibson from the *LST-317*. When the personnel inspection was over, the crew demonstrated a series of collision, fire, abandon ship and general quarters drills. After the inspection party had left the ship, Lt. Cdr. Mosier had the crew mustered again on the main deck of the ship. He then presented the Purple Heart to Motor Machinist Mate 2/c Lloyd Mosby, awarded for the wounds he suffered during the air raid in Bizerte in September 1943.

On October 1, seventy members of the British Home Guard came aboard for a tour of the ship. The Home Guard was a group of civilian volunteers, many veterans of W.W.I, who performed certain tasks for the military in order to free up servicemen for the business of fighting the war. As the Guardsmen were being shown around, the 527th Engineers began loading their vehicles aboard. The *LST-325* got underway the next morning, returning to Portland on October 3.

The *LST-325* left Portland on October 6 with a full load of trucks on the main deck and tanks below. As the convoy approached the French coast, they were hit with winds in excess of forty miles an hour. The *LST-325* was tossed about so severely that some of the securing chains snapped and a couple of the tanks below began to slide into each other and into the bulkheads of the tank deck. The Captain ordered the *LST-315* to take over as lead ship and then put the ship on a course that would reduce the pitching and rolling and relieve some of the strain on the chains. After getting close enough to shore to receive some protection from the pounding waves, the Captain had the ship anchor. They stayed here for two more days before the storm passed and they could continue on and unload near Grandcamp.

After returning to Portland, the *LST-325* then sailed to Southampton. From October 14–22 the *LST-325* made two trips between Southampton and Utah Beach. On the return trip to Portland on the 22nd they brought back three officers and eighty-one sailors from the crew of the *LST-512*. While attempting to retract from the beach, the *LST-512* had broached and broken her back. Her crew stayed in France until temporary repairs were made to their ship; she was then taken back to England before being towed to the United States with only a skeleton crew. The remainder of the crew, the men the *LST-325* brought back on this trip, was reassigned to other ships in the fleet.

The *LST-325* left on October 26 for Falmouth, where they would remain until November 12. During this time the main engines were overhauled along with the generators and the fire and bilge pumps and additional first aid boxes and supply racks were also installed. On the 12th, the *LST-325* went into dry-dock to have the hull cleaned and repainted and to replace the ship's propellers. On November 1, LtJG. Art English was transferred to the *LST-357*, his duties as the ship's First Lieutenant were taken over by Ensign Ted Duning. On November 13, Lt. Gordon Keene, the *LST-325's* Executive Officer, was transferred to the *LST-373* to take over as that ship's Captain. Lt. Robert Smith replaced him as the ship's Exec. By the 15th all shipyard work was completed, and after a final inspection by Ensign Duning, the ship was towed out into the harbor.

My first act as First Lieutenant was to meet with Chief Hughes ("Boats") of the Deck Division to say I recognized that he had a lot more knowledge of what the Division required and how to work with the men there than I. He was to "carry on" and advise me from time to time the best ways to keep the Division up to standards that would suit the Skipper. I respected "Boats" and we got along quite well. Our GQ station was on the port side of the fore-castle one deck down, which if I remember correctly, was the control room of the bow doors and ramp. Chief Hughes and four or five others were assigned to this station with me.

— ***Ted Duning, First Lieutenant***

Every liberty was a story of its own. Lots of wine, women and song. One that stays with me is when one of our medics onboard went on liberty stone drunk. We lowered him into the small boat, which was our transportation to shore. When we hit shore he couldn't make it out of the boat. We covered him up with life vests and they took him back to the ship. Next day we asked him about the blonde he was with on liberty. He said he didn't know, but he sure had one helluva time! He didn't realize he didn't even leave the ship.

— ***Chet Conway, Motor Machinist Mate***

I used to attend the Plymouth Brethren Church although I was Baptist. It was the only fundamental group I could find. Different ones would invite the men in uniform to their homes for Sunday dinner. One family gave me the key to their house and told me to make it my home anytime we were in port. I went there to study on my high school course by correspondence. I ate there and was included in their evening family devotion time.

— ***Leo Horton, Gunners Mate***

The *LST-325* left Plymouth in the afternoon of November 22 for Portland. After docking at the Hard in Portland early the next morning, vehicles from the 44th Mechanized Cavalry were loaded onboard. On the 24th, the *LST-325* sailed from Portland as part of Convoy PVL-14. That afternoon two of the escort ships made sonar contact with a submarine and began dropping depth charges. As they pressed their attack, the convoy continued on, anchoring in the harbor at Le Havre near the mouth of the River Seine. The following day a river pilot came aboard to guide the ship up the lower half of the Seine. At village of Villequier they exchanged pilots, the upper river pilot guided them the rest of the way to the city of Rouen, roughly 120 miles from the mouth of the river. Rouen, an ancient city whose origins dated back before the time of the Romans, was where Joan of Arc was burned at the stake in 1431. The *LST-325* anchored in the river overnight before mooring to the Hard after daybreak. After unloading, the ship retracted and then returned downriver, reaching Le Havre late that afternoon.

> *We went up the Seine River to Rouen, France. I saw one of the biggest Catholic cathedrals in France. I stood Shore Patrol duty with a .45 automatic on my hip. Talked with a French girl with a phrase from the "Stars & Stripes", "Vous etes belle, Cherie", which meant, "You are so beautiful, darling." She laughed and went on.*
>
> **—Leo Horton, Gunners Mate**

> *I liked the trip up the Seine to Rouen. There was wrecked and destroyed enemy equipment strewn along the banks. There were interesting manor houses, some of which appeared to be centuries old. One was reputed to be a residence of William of Normandy at one time. Then too, there were the ships sunk by the Germans in the river channel around which we had to do some fancy maneuvering since there was a pretty good current running. I remember the French pilot requested coffee from time to time in which to pour his calvados.*
>
> **—Ted Duning, First Lieutenant**

Shortly after returning to Le Havre, the *LST-325* set off alone back across the English Channel. About halfway across the Channel they sailed into a storm that grew steadily worse as the night went on. By dawn gale-force winds and driving rains were hammering the ship mercilessly. After finally reaching the English coast, the ship sought shelter near Lymimgton. They anchored there until the storm passed on the 29th and the *LST-325* could continue to Portland. The next day a working party from the Navy base in Exeter installed new navigational radar equipment on the ship.

I don't recall where it happened, the Channel more than likely, but while we were underway about midnight we were riding in some big swells. Next thing the stern of the ship kept rising to an extreme degree, then the ship practically fell into the next hollow. We hit bottom with such force that the bunk chains gave way and sleeping sailors were piled up wondering what had happened. I was coming off watch, which was a big advantage. Just a shake-up, no one was hurt, but one could expect anything with such a drop.

—Dale MacKay, Motor Machinist Mate

During the early part of December, the *LST-325* made three more crossings between Portland and Rouen, the first two through miserably cold and wet weather. When the ship docked in Portland on December 18, they received orders from the base commanding officer to be on the alert for enemy activity during the night. The German's had begun a last-ditch offensive just two days before in the area of the Ardennes in Belgium, in what would soon be known as the Battle of the Bulge. The American divisions in the region of the Ardennes were caught completely by surprise, and there were reports that German saboteurs had been captured behind the lines in American uniforms. The Allies were taking no chances and security was tightened all along the lines of supply. During the next few nights, the Captain had a security watch armed with machine guns posted on the forecastle and the fantail of the ship.

I remember in December 1944, when the final German onslaught was underway, we were warned to keep special watch around the perimeter of the ship in port or any suspicious activity and be ready to shoot to kill should proper identification not be forthcoming. One of the reasons I joined the Navy was that it was unlikely I would ever be in face-to-face personal combat with the enemy. The question on my mind as I walked the perimeter of the ship at that time was could I really shoot to kill?

—Ted Duning, First Lieutenant

We made many trips to and from Normandy but the worst one I remember was we were supposed to have liberty for about one week. But we hadn't got used to it because the Battle of the Bulge broke out. We were ordered to load

up, real fast, and we hit the Channel again. We made three or four trips,
hurriedly I must say before we had any time to relax.

—Harold Westerfield, Ship's Cook

On December 20 the ship, carrying twenty-seven tanks and their crews, left
for Cherbourg in Convoy PEL-2, their thirtieth trip to France in the six months
since D-Day. When they arrived back in Portland Lt. Robert Smith received
orders transferring him to the base in Vicarage to await transfer back to the
United States. LtJG. Bill Bodiford then assumed the duties of Executive Officer,
and LtJG. Sarbaugh took over as the Navigation Officer.

On Christmas Day, the ship got underway from Portland, again sailing to the
Seine River and unloading at Rouen the next afternoon. Fog and drizzling rain
slowed their trip back downriver and they had to anchor overnight before reaching Le Havre the next day. After leaving Le Havre during the early morning of
December 28, the ship received a message from a passing transport ship that a
troopship ahead of them had been torpedoed. Lt. Cdr. Mosier ordered full speed
ahead, and along with the *LST-532* and the French corvette *K-572* they raced to
assist the crippled ship. Soon they picked up the ship on radar, directly ahead and
nine miles away. At 1645, they made visual contact with the ship, now sitting
quite low in the water and settling down by the stern.

The stricken ship was the *HMS Empire Javelin*, an English LSI (Landing Ship
Infantry) and she had been carrying a full compliment of troops when torpedoed.
As the *LST-325* approached the scene, The Captain passed the word to all hands
to prepare to take on survivors. They hove to near the site of the sinking ship and
the French corvette *K-267* came alongside, the decks of the small warship nearly
overflowing with survivors they had rescued from the water. The crew draped
cargo nets over the side of the LST to the deck of the smaller destroyer, and the
exhausted survivors climbed aboard. Moments later the muffled rumble of explosions could be heard coming from deep within the *Empire Javelin*, and in seconds
the ship, her bow now vertical, slipped beneath the waters of the English Channel. The decks of the *LST-325* were overflowing with 645 shivering soldiers of
the 15th Army Headquarters and 34 members of the *Empire Javelin's* crew.
While the ship's crew brought the survivors hot coffee, blankets and whatever else
they could offer to make the weary men comfortable, the *LST-325* and the ships
with the other survivors onboard made full speed for Le Havre.

One of the outstanding events in my memory was the SOS call received
while crossing the Channel from France and joining another LST with full

speed ahead to the site of the torpedoed troop ship, already down by the stern off of which 1400 troops had been taken aboard a French destroyer. The LST's, each in turn, pulled alongside the destroyer to take off 700 troops each at some risk to these men since a rather heavy sea was running and they had to climb rope ladders from the destroyer deck up to the much higher decks of our ships. Once these were aboard we looked over to where the doomed ship was now three-quarters under water with the bow straight up and we watched as she slowly slipped down, out of sight. The sight of a ship going down like this is not one likely to be forgotten.

—Ted Duning, First Lieutenant

After returning the *Empire Javelin* survivors to Le Havre, the *LST-325* resumed the return trip to Portland. On the 30th, a machinist from the base came aboard to inspect the portside propeller. At some point while in the Seine River, the ship had struck a submerged log and bent two of the propeller blades.

The *LST-325* began her first cross-channel trip of 1945 on January 3, with a load of tanks and support vehicles. It had been a stormy and windy morning and after the ship left the protection of the harbor and faced the full brunt of the storm, she began to pitch and roll wildly. The chains securing the tanks to the deck of the tank deck were under tremendous strain as the weight of the tanks were continually shifting from side to side. Soon a few of the chains began to snap. When the word came up to the bridge about what was going on below the Captain immediately signaled to the rest of the convoy that the *LST-325* would be falling out of formation and returning to the harbor. At first his superior officers were upset that he had brought the ship back to port, but when the Captain heatedly invited them to come aboard and see the damage the tanks had caused to the ship they quieted down. With the tanks again secured the *LST-325* got underway the following morning.

The *LST-325's* next trip across the Channel was on January 7 carrying thirty-eight American tanks. For most of the trip, the convoy sailed through blinding snowstorms that turned to rain and hail as they approached Le Havre on the 8th. After the *LST-325* unloaded the tanks on the Hard in Le Havre, they retracted and attempted to swing the ship into the teeth the wind. A French tug, seeing that the ship was having a bit of a struggle completing the turn, decided to come to their assistance but failed to radio their intentions to the ship. Before anyone aboard the *LST-325* knew what it was doing the tug came alongside, but it had misjudged the ships rate of turn and slammed into the portside bow. Fortunately, the only damage suffered by the LST was a dented hull plate.

After unloading their next cargo of tanks and artillery in Le Havre on January 12, the *LST-325* set off for the return to England in a convoy of LSTs. Just after dark one of the escort ships radioed they had spotted a torpedo wake on an intercepting course with the convoy. General Quarters was immediately sounded and the men who had battle station's topside anxiously watched for any sign of the incoming torpedo. Finally, as the seconds ticked by it became apparent that the torpedo had missed and the crew breathed a collective sigh of relief. The escorts had already picked up the contact and started dropping depth charges, but the submarine managed to elude them.

The ship remained in Portland for a few days after returning from Le Havre, using the time to complete some overdue maintenance to the main engines and restocking the ship's stores and provisions. During this time, most of the crew received five-day liberties.

On January 18, the *LST-325* docked on the Hard to begin taking on the next load of vehicles and troops. It was a windy and rainy morning, and by the time the ship had left the Hard and anchored, the harbor was being pounded with driving rain and sleet, severe lightening and winds in excess of 40 miles an hour. The storm continued throughout the night, but began to diminish as dawn approached. By the afternoon normal harbor traffic resumed and the ships of Convoy PVL-57 sailed for Rouen.

The *LST-325* made three trips between Portland and Le Havre during the end of January and the first part of February. During the return trip the night of February 14, with twenty-eight Navy Construction Battalion men onboard, the convoy the *LST-325* was sailing with encountered dense fog. Shortly before midnight, lookouts spotted another convoy of ships dead ahead and bearing down on them. Lt. Cdr. Mosier, the convoy's Senior Officer, ordered an emergency 45° turn to the port to avoid the oncoming ships. The two convoys passed without incident, but as soon as they were clear and had resumed their base course, the Captain ordered the ships to begin sounding fog warnings on their ship's whistles. Even after taking this precaution, an hour later the *LST-30* collided with an English LCT passing in the opposite direction and had a foot wide hole punched in her side. The fog only grew thicker as the night went on and the Captain ordered the convoy's speed reduced. Another collision was narrowly avoided at 0830 the next morning when a LCT appeared out of the fog directly in front of the *LST-325* and continued all the way through the convoy between the two columns of LSTs. The convoy managed to reach Portland a few hours later without further incident.

> *One trip to France I had my pockets full of the Gospel of John written in French. That trip we went to Le Havre, a seaport instead of the beach as usual. We diverted to Le Havre where we had liberty. There was a storefront where I stood, with a group of young ladies sewing cloth. At first they were afraid of me, but then opened the door on a chain holder. I slipped the Gospels to them and there was just the right number for the number of women. Each one got one and started reading them right away. That was a real blessing to me.*

> **—Leo Horton, Gunners Mate**

From February 16–24, the *LST-325* made two more trips from Portland to Le Havre. On the 24th, the *LST-325* and *LST-279* left Portland for Falmouth, where the two LSTs were scheduled for a routine overhaul of their main engines. The *LST-325* returned to Plymouth on the 28th to go into dry-dock.

On March 2 a tug maneuvered the *LST-325* into the dock, then the *LST-506* was moved into position directly astern of them. Once the dock was emptied and the two ships securely resting on keel blocks, the ship's crew began the arduous task of chipping and scraping the bottom of the hull. The work on the ship continued until the 8th. While the crew had chipped, scraped, wire brushed and then repainted the hull bottom, the base maintenance people had adjusted the bearings on both propeller shafts to bring them into alignment and the port propeller with the two bent blades was replaced. Both rudders were also chipped and repainted with anti-fouling paint. In addition, the welders from the base installed strengthening brackets to the four inside corners of the elevator and cargo hatches. LtJG Duning and Ensign Batsel, the Engineering Officer, made a thorough inspection of all the finished work and after everything met with their approval the docks were flooded and the ship moored to the Turnchapel Hard.

The *LST-325* remained at the Turnchapel Hard until March 18 while the crew finished repainting the topside and finished a number of small mechanical repairs and adjustments to some of the ship's equipment. On the 18th the ship got underway to conduct tests on the newly overhauled main engines. Onboard the ship to observe the tests was a Navy officer and a Chief Motor Machinist Mate from the base maintenance shop. Returning to Plymouth after the completion of the test run, two Royal Navy officers came aboard and calibrated the ships degaussing system. Meanwhile an American naval officer and his assistant reported aboard to calibrate the ship's magnetic compass.

The next day the *LST-325* returned to the Turnchapel Hard. That afternoon the British army began a training exercise loading vehicles onto the LST. The ship remained here on the Hard, assisting the British army with their training and completing routine ship maintenance until the exercises were finished on the 29th.

The *LST-325* sailed out of Portland on Tuesday, April 3, carrying forty-five British Army vehicles and eighty-nine U.S. Navy and Coast Guard sailors to Cherbourg. After unloading at the Hard in Cherbourg and anchoring offshore, sixty-three French Marines were ferried out to the ship and embarked for passage back to England, along with two British civilians that had boarded the ship while on the Hard. The *LST-325* returned to Portland that night with Convoy EWL-99, reaching Portland and mooring alongside the *LST-393* at daybreak on the 5th.

The *LST-325* remained in Portland until April 10. Welders from the *USS Melville* came aboard on the 9th to add additional bracing under the main deck. On the 10th, the ship moored to the Hard and began loading aboard the vehicles for this, the ship's forty-fourth and *final* trip to France. After unloading in Le Havre the next afternoon, *LST-325* hoisted anchor at 2100 and for the final time, left the French coastline behind them. That night the convoy's escorts were kept busy, as they made contact with Germans submarines on two separate occasions, both managing to get away without having an opportunity to fire their torpedoes. Just before noon, the *LST-325* entered Portland harbor, mooring alongside the *LST-335*.

On April 12, the crew of the *LST-325* was shocked, as were Americans everywhere, to learn that President Franklin Roosevelt had died that day from a massive cerebral hemorrhage. It was difficult to accept the fact that the man that had led the nation's recovery from the Great Depression and guided them through four terrible years of war was now gone, especially with victory so near at hand. On the 14th the crew mustered on the main deck in full dress uniform to observe five minutes of silence in respect for the late President.

On the 17th, the *LST-325* left Portland for the final time. They entered Plymouth Harbor the following day, staying here for the rest of the month while they got ready for the trip home. Workers removed the ship's navigational radar and installed LCT loading skids on the main deck, and the main engines were re-inspected once again.

The *LST-325* entered the #5 Basin in Devonport on April 26, where the *LCT-954* was hoisted onto the ship's main deck. Once the LCT was securely fastened to the deck, an LCM was then loaded into the LCT while two fork trucks, a fire pump, crates of spare LCM parts and fifty bottles of hydrogen were loaded onto the tank deck. After the ship returned to its mooring off Yonderberry Point, welders from the repair ship *USS Adonis* came aboard and welded additional pad-eyes and supports for the LCT and LCM onto the main deck. On the 28th, the *LST-325* docked on the Turnchapel Hard and a crane was loaded into the tank deck.

The Commanding Officer of LST Amphibious Craft 12th Fleet came aboard on Monday, April 30, to conduct a material inspection of the *LST-325*. After he completed his inspection the crew loaded aboard a few last minute supplies, then the ship retracted from the Hard and anchored alongside many other LSTs gathering in the harbor, all waiting to begin the journey home.

At 1215 on May 5, the Captain ordered the main engines started and the crew prepared for getting underway. At 1350, the *LST-325* passed through the Plymouth Harbor boom gates; the final time the ship would sail from an English port. Emotions were mixed among the crew, the excitement of returning to the United States tempered by that fact that some were leaving very dear friends behind.

> *I had been transferred off in Plymouth and saw the* **LST-325** *leave and tears came to my eyes. I had gone through a lot with some great guys. They performed their jobs so I'm alive, and I performed my duty so they were alive.*
>
> **—Don Martin, Motor Machinist Mate**

> *I had a lump in my throat as the British Isles faded off in the distance, knowing I was leaving some dear Christian friends behind which I would never see again in this life.*
>
> **—Leo Horton, Gunners Mate**

> *I was a little sad to leave the ETO due to leaving my wife and child, but I knew that we were going home and that she was coming along with a troop transport with our flotilla. But, it was not meant to be. She came to the United States later on.*
>
> **—Harold Westerfield, Ship's Cook**

The convoy made their final stop before heading across the Atlantic, entering the harbor at Belfast, Ireland on May 7. The next day they received the official announcement that all German forces in Europe had surrendered to the Allies. At last, the long war in Europe was officially over. That evening the fortunate members of the ships company that had liberty joyously joined in the wild victory celebrations in Belfast.

We were in the Irish capital at the time of VE Day and we fell in with a conga line around the capital building. We were on our way to the States now.

—Dale MacKay, Motor Machinist Mate

I had the good fortune of getting liberty when we put into Belfast, Ireland on VE Day. The partying started in a large downtown hotel ballroom where men and women of all ranks and in every branch of the services, foreign and domestic, were singing, dancing and enjoying a bit of libation. Churchill came in over a loudspeaker with his commentary on the ending of the war in Europe. I remember John Sarbaugh was in our group and at the invitation of a couple local lasses we wound up with around ten people in an all night party in a house out in the suburbs. This was the only party I ever attended where there was a break every hour or so for tea and cakes. Lest you wonder, wild as it sounds, every aspect of the partying was based on fun and good fellowship only.

—Ted Duning, First Lieutenant

Actually, it was hard to believe that the European conflict had ended as quickly as it did. We did bring supplies to Rouen about the time of the Battle of the Bulge. After that, the Germans were in retreat and in a matter of months the war was over.

—Dale MacKay, Motor Machinist Mate

During the evening of May 11, the crew of the *LST-325* began made preparations for getting underway and secured the ship for sea. They hoisted anchor at midnight and finally, after more than two years of service in Europe and the Mediterranean and having taken part in three major invasions, they were on their way home. They were sailing as part of Convoy ONS-50, with the Captain of the

SS *Empire Cabot* the Convoy Commodore. At 0400, the ships turned to a heading of north-northwest to begin the long journey across the North Atlantic.

> *The joy of returning home was enormous. We realized that we would head towards the Pacific after our return. After celebrating V-E Day in Belfast, Ireland, we would face the Japanese after we returned. Fortunately that never occurred, as we celebrated V-J Day in New Orleans.*
>
> **—Dick Scacchetti, Pharmacist Mate**

Two days from Belfast, the convoy sailed into the fiercest storm the crew of the *LST-325* had yet encountered. Monstrous waves, thirty to forty feet in height, pounded the convoy. Winds of near hurricane strength whipped the rain and blinding spray from the bow into driving needles that stung the skin. There was no chance of maintaining the convoy's formation and soon the ships were scattered in the merciless storm. Time and again, the creaking and groaning ship would crest one monstrous wave only to slam head on into the next. Each time the ship went over a wave the screws would come up out of the water and the engines would wildly race, and without constant vigilance on the throttles the engines would have shutdown because of the automatic over-speed cutoff.

Shortly after midnight, the ship crested one more enormous wave and as her flat bottom slammed down into the wave's trough a horrible shudder vibrated through the hull. Immediately the call came to the bridge from the auxiliary engine room that water was now pouring into the bilges through cracks in the forward bulkhead. LtJG Duning was the officer on the conn at the time, but the Captain was on the bridge immediately and ordered an assessment made of the damage. A few minutes passed before the damage reports started to come back. The worst of it was that there was a four-inch crack in the main deck plates, extending outward from the forward starboard corner of the cargo hatch. There were more cracks where welded seams between deck plates on the portside had separated and ruptured plates further forward where longitudinal support brackets to the cargo hatch had pushed through the deck. Several support brackets in the tank deck had separated from the deck plates, and numerous cracks appeared in the bulkheads from the tank deck all the way to the tanks and voids on the fourth deck forward of the auxiliary engine room. The ship was literally beginning to crack in two.

> *I had the conn on the dog watch in the midst of that storm in the North Sea when we were being battered by very heavy swells running before the high*

winds. Suddenly, as if hit by a giant battering ram on the bow, the ship shuddered, arched with the flat bottom slamming down into the trough of the seaway and the mast shook as though it would come down on the conn. The Skipper was on hand immediately and a report came to the conn from the engine room through the voice tube that eighteen cracks had appeared along the bottom of the hull at the main frame and were taking on water. We are indebted to the Skipper and the Lorenz twins for the damage control solution of welding water pipes taken from the troops quarters across each of the cracks in the hull. When we got to the dock in Norfolk an inspection was made of the hull and I heard a Lieutenant from the shipyard say we should never have made it across. But we weren't the only ones in trouble in the storm that night. I can still see those breakdown lights on the masts of one or two ships nearby and no ship seemed able to stay on station in the convoy as we prayed for that storm to end.

—Ted Duning, First Lieutenant

We were in the North Sea in very rough weather when our ship started to crack in the area in front of the superstructure. The Captain was signaled that he could go back if he wanted to, but he said no. We laid in the swells sideways as our talented shipmates welded big patches over the cracking areas. We got further behind the convoy.

—John Roberts, Electricians Mate

At 0800, the shipfitters began welding brackets to the bulkheads in the auxiliary engine room and across the ruptured main deck plates as the crew worked to save their crippled ship. The Captain knew that if he kept the ship heading directly into the hammering waves that she could split in two, so he risked having her capsize by angling the ship sideways to the waves. The shipfitters continued welding additional plating over the cracks in the bulkheads and on the main deck, even resorting to taking the tubing off the bulkheads in the troop quarters to use as brackets across the crack. Finally, the storm diminished during the evening of May 15, and the convoy that had been scattered by the fury of the storm could begin to regroup.

We left Belfast on May 8, 1945 and the first five days were very rough seas. The bottom of the ship in the auxiliary room was cracked and every time we hit a big wave water would squirt into the bilge. We ha to pump the bilges about every three hours. Then we hit smooth seas all the way back to Norfolk.

—**Emil Kolar, Motor Machinist Mate**

The absolute most frightening experience was when we left England to come home. We hadn't been out to sea very long and we encountered the most horrific Atlantic storm. Our helmsman had to keep the "old ladies" bow into the waves, which I recollect were twenty-five to thirty-five feet high and we knew that if we went broadside we would have capsized! Thank God for our engine crew keeping the screws turning. It was terrible to see the bow hit those waves and the stern coming out of the water, making the whole ship shudder! Terrible. Also thank God for the Lorenz twins for getting those plates welded onto the deck in front of the deckhouse. If not for them I would no doubt not be telling you this story.

—**Harold Westerfield, Ship's Cook**

Our ship cracked across the main deck when we started for the States. The Captain signaled a British vessel, "I got her over here and I intend to get her back." We went on by ourselves and finally made it to the States in one piece. The North Atlantic stayed unusually calm for our trip back. Again Praise the Lord! A good storm might have finished us.

—**Leo Horton, Gunners Mate**

Fortunately for the crew of the *LST-325* and their hastily repaired ship, the seas were as calm as a millpond during the next few days. At 0845 on May 27, the convoy received a radio message instructing the LSTs to proceed to Norfolk while the rest of the convoy continued on to New York.

On May 31, as the Virginia coast was sighted off the starboard bow, Captain Mosier ordered the "homeward bound" pennant hoisted on the main mast. The long narrow pennant, with its narrow blue field and long red and white stripes, is traditionally flown on the day that a U.S. Navy ship arrives back in an American port after a deployment overseas. At sunset on the day of arrival, it is lowered and then cut into small sections and divided among the crew. Just before 0700, the convoy of LSTs passed the Cape Henry Lighthouse, and an hour later they began working their way up the James River towards Norfolk. As the ships entered

Hampton Roads near the Norfolk Navy Base, the order came, "to all ships, act independently and seek anchorage." At precisely 0919 the anchor was released, the chain rumbling through the hawse pipe behind it.

The *LST-325* was home.

9

Home

Shortly after the convoy of LSTs arrived in Norfolk, a Navy doctor and medical team came aboard the *LST-325* to give the crew a medical screening, required by all servicemen returning home from overseas. Afterward, the *LST-325* temporarily moored alongside Pier #4, where a crane lifted the LCM off the LCT on the ship's main deck, after which the ship returned to its assigned anchorage offshore.

> *We went into Norfolk and thinking how great it would be to go ashore on arrival but we were not allowed to leave. We were told all we could do was send telegrams. From a list of messages many of them came out wrong. Then we went for six more days to New Orleans.*
>
> **—John Roberts, Electricians Mate**

The next morning, June 1, the *LST-325* got underway from Norfolk, along with the *LST-338, LST-304, LST-388* and *LST-393*. Their orders were to proceed to New Orleans for refitting and preparing the ship to go to the Pacific. As the ships rounded Cape Hatteras the following morning, they encountered more stormy weather and rough seas and again the LSTs took a severe pounding. Soon leaks were springing up around some of the repairs the ship's welders had patched together in the North Atlantic, but they held and the ships pressed onward.

Before dawn on June 9 the LSTs passed through the South Pass entrance and into the mouth of the Mississippi River. Before reaching New Orleans, the *LST-325* moored to the ammunition dock at Little Rock, Louisiana and began unloading all of the ammunition remaining onboard. Then they passed under the drawbridge into the New Orleans Inner Harbor. The *LST-325* moored to the Florida Avenue Wharf at the Pendleton Shipyard, where the LCT was lifted off the deck of the ship by the immense tandem derrick on the wharf. From there, the ship went to the Naval Base at Algiers, where a Navy ordnance party came onboard and began the task of removing the guns from the ship.

Summer in New Orleans is hot. I recall perspiration dripping into my dinner tray from my brow and feeling roasted just walking to Canal Street. The riverboat steam-wheeler "President" was a popular liberty spot with the cruise dance. Quite a few 325'ers could be found there.

—Dale MacKay, Motor Machinist Mate

When we arrived in New Orleans, being the ship's mail carrier, a buddy shipmate and I were sent ashore to pick up some ships mail. We got the mail OK, but decided to have a few at the bar. Well, we woke up about 6:00 a.m. The mail was still OK. We got back to the ship and was questioned by the Captain. We told him we had gotten lost.

—Harold "Icky" Allgaier, Radioman

I was in the skeleton crew kept aboard the 325 for a portion of the refit period in New Orleans. Life aboard was a bit rough during the refit activity but during liberty there was the chance to meet new friends down at the USO and to enjoy some of the great food and hospitality that we found in that city during the war.

—Ted Duning, First Lieutenant

I had a Christian friend aboard ship overseas who worked in the galley, a black man by the name of Calvin Brock. But when we got to New Orleans we decided not to go on liberty together there because of the danger from racists.

—Leo Horton, Gunners Mate

All the guns were removed by the next morning and the fuel remaining onboard was pumped off the ship to a fuel barge. The ship was then towed to the Todd-Johnson dry-dock facilities. After the water had been pumped from the dock the outer hull was given a complete inspection, then the dock was refilled and the ship returned to Pendleton Shipyard. The ship remained in the shipyard until June 22, undergoing repairs to the damage suffered while crossing the Atlantic. The ship was then towed back to the Todd-Johnson dry-dock, where the bottom of the ship was sandblasted and repairs continued to the damaged hull and framework. On June 28, the dock was flooded and the ship moved back to the Pendleton shipyard. Workmen then began making extensive alterations to the ship, including the addition of what was known as the "Brodie Device" for launching and retrieving small liaison aircraft from the deck of an LST.

Named for its inventor, Lt. James Brodie, U.S. Army, the Brodie Device was basically a cable stretched between two tall masts, mounted along the port side of the ship. Attached to the cable was a specially designed sling, which would catch a hook mounted to the top of an L-4 aircraft, the military version of the Piper Cub. A special brake system would bring the aircraft to a stop within the distance of the two masts. Then the L-4 could be launched from the cable, or lowered down to the deck of the ship for refueling or other purposes. One of these rigs was installed aboard the *LST-776* and had been successfully used during the invasions of Saipan and Okinawa. Despite its circus type flair the Brodie Device proved to be a successful way to launch and retrieve observation aircraft from an area that would otherwise be too small for an airplane. Originally, twenty-five LSTs were contracted for the Brodie Device, but only eight, including the *LST-325*, were complete by the time the war ended. The advent of helicopters would eventually make the Brodie Device obsolete.

On July 7, while the while work was still underway on the ship, Lieutenant Robert Chitrin replaced Lieutenant Commander Clifford E. Mosier as the Captain of the *LST-325*. As he explained in a letter he wrote to the crew many years later:

> *"I have often regretted my failure in not obtaining all your names and addresses but my departure from the ship in New Orleans happened very fast. About the second day after arrival there, My Exec informed me that an officer from the base was waiting to see me. The moment I saw him, I knew he was a psychiatrist. They always have a sneaky look. He asked me just one question, "Do you sleep well at night?" My answer, mixed with a few choice cuss words, convinced him otherwise. I think he may have also interviewed some members of the crew and some one told him, "The old man is driving us crazy." Anyway, I shortly got orders which, clearly stated "IN THE PUBLIC INTEREST," transferring me to a new and larger LST being out-fitted in Baltimore. Md."*

For most of the ship's company this would be the last time they would see Clifford Mosier, but none of the men who served under him during those two and a half years would ever forget him. He had been a pillar of strength and a source of courage that the officers and crew could depend on during the darkest times of fear and uncertainty. The crew of *LST-325* loved and respected Clifford Mosier and the ship would never be the same with him gone. Mosier reciprocated those feelings. At the conclusion of his letter to the crew he said, *"I have often said, and I will repeat it here. I know I had the best crew and the cleanest ship of any LST in the Navy, I was proud of you then, and I still am."*

> *He was a real leader, a man who was respected. He was a gentleman, and a brave risk-taker. We called on him in California after the war. He looked great, but his wife had Alzheimer's. However, she was delightful and happy.*
>
> **—Don Roy, Signalman**

> *All you had to do was be square with him and he'd be square with you. He wasn't afraid to get his hands greasy. He saved our butts on the way to Oran when the clutch went out on one of the main engines. He used to be an engineer in the Navy before Officer Candidate School. He was a real good ship's pilot too. He could get that damn tub in and out of places no one else could. We once towed a damaged LST from Normandy to the West Indies Dock in London. He put that cripple in her berth and didn't use a tugboat. In Bizerte the Germans had sunk ships in the Channel and he got in the harbor without the pilot.*
>
> **—Don Martin, Motor Machinist Mate**

> *I reported to the Main, and I do mean the "Main Man" and Captain Mosier. None finer in the U.S. Navy. There aren't enough words in the English dictionary to describe this man. One helluva officer, honest, loyal and smart. If it wasn't for Captain Mosier I don't think the boys on the LST-325 would be around today, at least most of them.*
>
> **—Chet Conway, Motor Machinist Mate**

On July 15 the *LST-1050* came alongside the *LST-325* and pumped aboard 8500 gallons of fuel oil into her tanks. The main engines were started, the harbor pilot came aboard and the ship got underway on her own power for the first time in more than a month. The ship moored to the Florida Avenue wharf, where the crew began loading the ship's equipment back onto the tank deck. Afterwards, the ship returned to the Pendleton Shipyard, remaining there until the 17th when they passed through the locks and into the Mississippi River. The ship then moored to the Harmony Street Wharf.

On the 18th the bulk of the crew reported back onboard from the Navy Receiving Station on the base at Algiers. Some of them were part of the original crew reporting back from thirty-day leaves, or replacements for those that had been transferred elsewhere. After running some last tests on the engines and the new Mk.14 gun sights and gun fire control systems, the ship was moved to the Navy Supply Dock on July 23. The next two days were busy with restocking the ship with provisions and water and topping off the fuel tanks. The ship moved to a quarantine anchorage area below New Orleans, and on the 26th the ship moored to the Navy Ammunition Docks to take aboard a supply of ammunition.

Finally, on August 2 the ship left New Orleans for Galveston, Texas, where they would take part in flight tests with the new Brodie Device. The ship arrived at Galveston late Friday afternoon and prepared for the tests scheduled to begin on the 8th. But before the ship even reached Galveston the world's first atomic bomb was detonated above Hiroshima, followed by a second over Nagasaki, and suddenly the end was within sight.

The *LST-325* stood by and observed flight operations aboard the *LST-388* on August 8, before conducting operations with their own Brodie gear the next day. However, instead of mentally preparing themselves to go to the Pacific for the invasion of the Japanese homeland, the crew's thoughts were on returning to New Orleans and going home. The ship left Galveston on August 9 for New Orleans, where on the 13th the ship unloaded all the ammunition onboard at the ammunition docks in Little Rock, Louisiana. On 15 August 1945, the Japanese signed the formal surrender documents aboard the *USS Missouri* and the war was over.

> *I went with a bunch of shipmates on the night the war was over. We all went to the boat called "The President" and I ended up on the shore in my shorts. Some way I was rolled but good, and they took $200 I had saved up to go home on leave. My shipmates and I never knew who did it, but always figured it was some of the President's crew.*
>
> **—C. J. Mitchell, *Chief Motor Machinist Mate***

On August 25 the first group of ship's company to be transferred off the ship was sent to the Receiving Station at the Navy Repair Base in Algiers, their first step towards going home. In the days and weeks ahead, there would be a steady trickle of men away from the *LST-325*, some transferring to other duties in the fleet, some to separation centers around the country to be discharged.

On August 29, Lt. William Hoppe relieved Lt. Cdr. Robert Chitrin as the Commanding Officer of the *LST-325*. Lt. Hoppe would stay in command of the *LST-325* for the next eight months, until being relieved by Lt. Siedenburg on 29 April 1946.

The *LST-325* made a short trip to Burnwood, Louisiana, bringing furniture, supplies, and twenty-two sailors of the Burnwood Naval Frontier Base back to Algiers. They then prepared to leave New Orleans on September 13 for the Panama Canal Zone to pick up sailors from the Navy base at Coco Solo. They reached Coco Solo on September 24 and the next morning 106 Navy and Coast Guard sailors, along with their gear, embarked for the voyage home.

The *LST-325* arrived back in New Orleans on October 1. On the 5th the *LST-325* left New Orleans with orders to proceed to the St. Johns River Reserve Fleet anchorage off Green Cove Springs, Florida. The ship made its way up the St. Johns River on October 9, anchoring alongside several other LSTs and destroyer escorts. This would be the final time that the *LST-325* got underway under her own power, except for one small move on December 6 to relocate to another nest of LSTs.

Now began the waiting game. For the crewmembers that were part of the Naval Reserve, the wait was to accumulate enough points for discharge. For the men in the regular Navy it was waiting until their four-year enlistment was up. The numbers of men onboard trickled down during the final months of 1945 and into 1946, most sent home for discharge, some transferred to other parts of the fleet. Finally on 2 July 1946, the skeleton crew remaining onboard mustered on the main deck of the ship, where at precisely 1025 Captain C. E. Parsons, Commander Sub Group 5, decommissioned the ship. Among the eleven enlisted men remaining onboard was MoMM 1/c Emil Kolar, the only sailor to serve aboard the *LST-325* from the time she was commissioned until now. After the simple ceremony was over the last few men were transferred to another LST nested alongside the ship, and the long proud history of the *LST-325* was complete.

Of the men who served on her though, the memories of the events, the places the war took them, the things they experienced, and most importantly, the friendships they formed while aboard the *USS LST-325* would never be forgotten. After leaving the ship and the service, each man went his separate way and began life as a civilian again. Most of them returned to the hometown they had left when they had enlisted, a lot of them to the same jobs they had left behind.

Some of them married their sweethearts who had been waiting for them all this time. Some took advantage of the GI Bill and went to school. But wherever they went, and whatever they eventually did, each man took with them the memory of those years aboard that proud, ungainly lady, and of the men, the "band of brothers," with whom they served.

Dick Scacchetti, Pharmacist Mate

(Served aboard LST-325 from 12 May 1944 to 4 January 1946)

When LST-325 was in Florida I was transferred and served aboard LST-527. I was the Medical Rep on several LSTs tied together in Green Cove Springs. I just waited patiently to return to civilian life. I returned to New York University and later took a Masters at Stevens Institute. I became a Business Manager in New York and Washington, D.C. I worked for General Foods, Touche Ross and fifteen years as a General Manager of the American Hotel and Motel Association. I resided in New Jersey, Washington, D.C. and now in Sarasota, Florida.

I was proud to be part of a ship's company on a ship in the United States Navy. I volunteered to serve in the Navy. I volunteered to go overseas and I volunteered to serve in the Medical Corps. I was proud to serve with my shipmates and Captain Mosier. I organized the first reunion in New Jersey as I had numerous hotel and motel contacts, then I organized the reunions in New Orleans and Laredo, Texas. Others have taken over the reunions to the present day.

My service days forced me to grow up and be responsible for my actions, to conform to neatness and to become somewhat independent. I made up my mind to finish college...my short year of accelerated courses was almost failing...and to make something of my life. I worked hard to do so after I returned to civilian life, but it took my marriage to my wonderful wife, Gay, to make my life more complete. Navy life gave me pride and made me a more positive person and to attempt to achieve positive goals in my life.

Don Roy, Signalman

(Served aboard LST-325 from 23 February 1943 to 7 December 1945)

I was discharged on 13 December 1945. I went to work at Honeywell. Married Betty Lou Smith on 29 December 1945. We are the proud parents of five children born to us and one child we adopted. We have twin grandchildren.

Everyone on the ship got along pretty good. Lt. Sarbaugh was the best officer beside our Captain who was the best!

Richard "Rem" Martin, Motor Machinist Mate

(Served aboard LST-325 from 5 March 1943 to 20 December 1945)

I was an architect. I have a daughter who is a rehabilitation counselor for the Pennsylvania State Office of Vocational rehabilitation. She has two children. I have a son who is a District Justice and he has two children. One is a son at the University of Tennessee studying architecture. His daughter is at Hofstra University studying English.

All the crewmembers, especially the engineers, were my friends. Dale MacKay was an usher at Jackie and my wedding. I was best man for Dale in his wedding to Betty. Being in the service was good for me. I got to see other countries with a great bunch of shipmates. I think you learn to look at things differently and appreciate your home, family and country even more.

Gerry Murphy, Motor Machinist Mate

(Served aboard LST-325 from 12 May 1944–19 July 1945)

I left the ship in dry-dock in New Orleans. I went home for a thirty-day leave. I was discharged on 6 May 1946 in New York. I went to school to be a plumber and steam fitter.

I guess being in the service did change me. I got used to taking orders and doing a job the best I could. I believe I grew up fast. It was a big change in life for me.

Dale MacKay, Motor Machinist Mate

(Served aboard LST-325 from 5 March 1943 to 5 December 1945)

I left the 325 in December 1945 in Green Cove Springs. I was discharged in Boston in mid-December. I went to college, starting in 1946. I have an AB from Clark University in Worcester 1949, and a Masters in Education from Boston University in 1954. I started teaching in the fall of '49 in Rutland, Massachusetts, I was married in the spring of '51 and we raised three daughters.

It is not easy to spot changes in yourself and I can only say that possibly being in the service made a change in my sleeping habits. That being a change from a sound sleeper to a light sleeper. Perhaps standing night watches and experiencing General Quarters alarms could be responsible.

Rem Martin, Don Martin and Tommy Combs were good friends. The friends you had onboard depended a lot on which liberty section you found yourself in. Most of our crew was made up of eighteen to twenty-two year olds, adjustable good-natured young men. Our crew was well organized, capable and had respect for one another. The Captain set a good tone for the crew. Our Chief Petty Officers probably did more to unify the crew than anyone. We had our share of colorful characters to round out the crew. Bruno and Bill Donovan to mention a couple, kept us from being too serious.

James "C. J." Mitchell, Chief Motor Machinist Mate

(Served aboard LST-325 from 1 February 1943 to 1 November 1945)

After the war, I went to work in the oil fields. Centralia had an oil boom starting in 1939 and it was still booming. I wanted to get a little cash ahead. I then got a job at Tri-State Sales and Service. I then went to work as a Chevrolet salesman and then became a Chevrolet dealer. During that time, I met my wife, Joyce Pfeffer, and we were married in 1948. We have three children—Susan, Carol and David—who are all married and we have six grandchildren.

They were a great group of shipmates, the kind you never forget.

Emil Kolar, Motor Machinist Mate

(Served aboard LST-325 from 1 February 1943 to 2 July 1946)

I was on the half of the crew that was to stay on the 325, so I was first with a thirty-day leave. Most of the refit was done when I got back from leave. I was the only original crewmember when the ship was decommissioned on 2 July 1946. I was discharged on 31 May 1947 at Jacksonville Air Base, Florida. I worked for the White Haines Optical Company until November 1977, and with the Walman Optical Company until retirement in February 1988. I got married in September 1947 and have one son and two daughters, I was divorced in March 1981.

My best friends aboard ship, Jim Bronson was a great person. Donald Martin, Richard Martin and Dale MacKay also were great friends. They were people you could depend upon. Today I feel I was very lucky to have served with the men I did. Back then it might have been a different feeling, but hindsight makes it much better.

Bill Bliss, Quartermaster

(Served aboard LST-325 from 1 February 1943 to 25 August 1945)

My best friends were Paul Meehan, Ed Karlinski and Moe Malen. I keep in touch with Paul, he's pretty feeble now. Paul was well liked by all the crew and had a good sense of the ridiculous. Ed Karlinski is now gone. He was very quiet, very competent. I *used to write his letters to his wife for him. Moe was a professional seaman, very competent. I never had any social contact with him during the war, but after the war my wife and I visited him and his wife in Coral Gables where they lived. Probably the most popular man on the ship was Ellsworth Easterly, Chief Motor Machinist Mate. I had no contact with him during the war, but afterwards in 1978 or 1976 my wife and I visited him and his wife at their home in Litchfield, Illinois. They were very nice people. I hear each year from Ernie Ninness, a nice man.*

After the war I moved to Colorado. My first job was as a Circulation Manager for a newspaper. Then I worked as a prison guard in Englewood. I tried door-to-door sales. Then I moved to New York City where I worked for my father. Then I moved to Ft. Lauderdale where I started my own business. I married Virginia Clark on 7 October 1939. We had no children. Virginia died on 15 August 1995.

John Roberts, Electricians Mate

(Served aboard LST-325 from 1 February 1943 to 12 September 1945)

I was in the first half to get leave in New Orleans. I went home on thirty days leave and got married. I brought the wife down and stayed until it was over, August 1945. I was discharged in New Orleans in September. I went back to work at the same electrical shop I had been with before. Spent over thirty years there as part owner for part of that time. My wife and I had four children, one boy and three girls. Nine grandchildren and two great-grandchildren.

How can I name any of them best friends, there were all of us! We all thought the world of each other, regardless of any personalities that could have come into play. We were shipmates! Getting back to best friends, I will start with the best...Jim Bronson, Jack Greenly, Bill Hanley, Mosby, Conway, Ninness, Meehan, Tierney, Brown, Dessinger, Kolar...the whole crew, I can't list them all! If I were to choose a place, or a group of guys to go anywhere with I could never have chosen better. I'm so glad for the experience and I feel sure all of my buddies are too. I guess being in the service did change us. I can't describe how. In many ways I guess. We were not the same guys that left, I'm sure. How could we be after two or more years on that great ship. I hope it's brought back for all to see. It's the best ship! LST-325!

Harold "Icky" Allgaier, Radioman

(Served aboard LST-325 from 1 February 1943 to 19 July 1945)

I worked in a large department store in Lincoln, Nebraska. I married in 1947 and had one son. We were later divorced. I remarried and moved to Casper, Wyoming in

'56. I have a total of six children, five boys and one girl, two grandsons, two grand-daughters. My wife Norma passed away in October 1997.

We were such a close-knit group. We actually lived closer than brothers at home do. I would tell any young man today that if they were thinking of joining the military to join the Navy. As I mentioned the excitement, it was quite dull when I was discharged and came home. It took me awhile to adjust. I always and still do crave excitement.

Leo Horton, Gunners Mate

(Served aboard LST-325 from 13 May 1944 to 19 July 1945)

I left the ship in New Orleans and went to Michigan on a thirty-day leave. Japan surrendered while I was home. My orders were changed and I was ordered to go to the Amphib Base just out of Norfolk, Virginia. There I was given my preliminary discharge papers and sent back to Great Lakes. I was discharged at Great Lakes on 18 October 1945.

I went back to finish high school on the GI Bill, a special setup for returning veterans. We took all the regular courses, but studied at our own speed. I finished the eleventh and twelfth grades in twelve months of steady studying. When I graduated in 1947, I went to college also on the GI Bill. I went to Northwestern College in Minneapolis in 1951, BA in History and Bible. Morris Harvey College, Charleston, West Virginia, 1961, BS Education. Marshall University, Huntington, West Virginia, 1968, MA Education and Administration.

William Hanley, Motor Machinist Mate

(Served aboard LST-325 from 1 February 1943 to 19 July 1945)

I left the 325 in New Orleans when the ship returned from the ETO. I was discharged one and a half years later. Points didn't matter I was regular Navy. The remaining time was spent in receiving stations and finally onboard ATF-159, the USS Piute, a sea-going tug stationed in Bermuda. After the service I wound up back at my old job mold making (toolmaker). I went through some more schooling and threw over the anchor and took up matrimony. We have four children and two grandchildren.

I stuck close to the engineering group, as far as friends were concerned. John Roberts, Frank Jaworski, Don Martin, Chester Conway, Paul Meehan…they were all good buddies. One striking fact stands out, you could leave your wallet and money on your bunk, come back two or three hours later and it'd still be there.

In the service, I learned the social abilities to live with others, to cooperate with others, learning to perform duties you normally would bypass. There is a Navy saying, "the best ship in the navy is the one your leaving and the one you are going to." That is not true by me, I would go out of my way to see the crew of the 325. Let my record speak for itself, I have yet to miss a reunion. My wife Betty is a great influence there. When you consider that all of us were not of any experience on the seas, outside of the Captain and Chief Boatswain Hughes, that we learned and performed our duties to a high degree. It was a credit to the cross section of the USA. When there was a job to do, there was always somebody that got the job done. The war and the Navy took five years of my time. When I look back it was a privilege to be part of the crew of LST-325.

Ellsworth Easterly, Chief Motor Machinist Mate

(Served aboard LST-325 from 1 February 1943 to 25 August 1945)

I returned to the Brown Shoe Company in Litchfield, Illinois, for several years in the cutting department where I had been before the war. Then I went to work for the International Paper Company for twenty years. I retired in 1979. I got married in 1945, have one son, James Easterly. Named after my real good Navy friend, Jim Bronson.

I liked all my shipmates. Always had more likes for my engineers, they were a real good bunch of guys. You could always depend on them if you needed help. Always think of when I got married in '45, Jim Bronson and four other mates came to my wedding. I had to run them home; they had a good time with the girls in Litchfield! Jim Bronson and my sister stood up with me at my wedding. He had a green Olds and they had it all decorated up. I would not want to go through any time like we had to again, but if I had to I would want the same crew we had at that time. I was a very lucky guy to have the good fortune to have a good and honest bunch of shipmates that would do and help out on anything that needed to be done. Being in the service made me think how lucky we are to live in a free country and can come and go as we please, after seeing how some of those poor people live in the other parts of the world. We are very fortunate.

Donald Martin, Motor Machinist Mate

(Served aboard LST-325 from 5 March 1943 to 3 May 1945)

I was discharged on 26 December 1945. Our family was complete again as my brother was in the Navy Construction Battalions and had also been discharged. He had been overseas for 27 months in the Pacific and had gotten home twenty-one days before I did. My mother went into the hospital on January 2 and never got back home. She died knowing her two sons were safe at home. I got married in 1950, I have one daughter who taught in Australia and still lives there and our son Rem is a family physician here in Fargo, North Dakota. My wife died of breast cancer in 1980. I remarried in 1983. All is well that ends well! I farmed all my life. I retired in 1984, six miles from where I was born.

My friends aboard ship were Bill Hanley, he was my co-worker in the auxiliary room. Dale MacKay slept under me. He had a chuckle that was good to hear. Richard E. Martin, "Rem," one of my buddies and I even named my son Richard E. Martin and we had everyone in Westhope know him as "Rem." Then there was "Bummie," Lander Bumgarner. He was a good solid man. Emil Kolar, we went on liberty in Plymouth all the time. My Rem's middle name is Emil. So you see what I mean. Everyone was great or you stayed away from him. Thus, there was no fighting on the ship.

I was born on a farm in northern North Dakota and attended a rural consolidated high school from which I graduated at sixteen years of age. When I enrolled at North Dakota State University I soon learned the most not from books, but by living and being in an institution of higher learning. I guess I learned the most in being tolerant to other's ideas, religion, mood and feelings. Being a farm raised son with my own ideas the ol' Boatswains Chief Hughes would say, "Martin, you're going to get into trouble, you're thinking again!" The "Navy Way" was not the only way, or the best!

Chet Conway, Motor Machinist Mate

(Served aboard LST-325 from 1 February 1943 to 7 December 1945)

After the war I stayed at home with my dad, he had cancer. After he died I got a job at the Amoco oil refinery. I lost that job due to a scale down, and I ended up in the steel mills. End result of my marriage, three girls, a blonde, brunette and redhead. They are great kids.

I love 'em and the Good Lord bless 'em all. I had many good memories. All the guys were my best friends. All brothers, all honest, all knew their jobs aboard ship, and above all, all "goofs" with a great sense of humor. I learned to grow up and above all the friendship I received from good people. The service changed me in many ways, hopefully for the better. One thinks he knows it all at a young age. Serve a few years aboard ship and live with people from all walks of life and see how little you know about life and all life's experiences.

Ted Duning, First Lieutenant

(Served aboard LST-325 from 3 December 1943 to 24 July 1945)

I was detached from the 325 in New Orleans around the end of July 1945. It was my first leave time at home in over eighteen months and while there the atomic bombs were dropped on Japan. My new duty station was Norfolk, Virginia. As a single person with less active duty time than many it didn't take me long to figure out I wouldn't be discharged soon and could be sent out to the Pacific as a replacement for someone with far more discharge points than I. So, I quickly applied for and obtained orders to report to Great Lakes for demobilization instruction. Following two weeks of training there I was sent back to Norfolk. But I wanted to be back in New Orleans, not Norfolk of all places, and sure enough, orders came through to report to New Orleans on 1 January 1946. I began dating a local girl who, along with four friends, rented a flatbed trailer to decorate and put in the famous Mardi Gras parade. An invitation was sent to a girl I had gone with back in high school and college days to come with her husband and join us on the float. The Mardi Gras celebration was almost as much fun as VE-Day in Belfast, but not quite. The major thing that happened, an event that was to change the rest of my life, my guest's arranging a blind date with a college acquaintance, Waverly, whom she chanced to meet on a New Orleans street. We met March 6 on that blind date, we got engaged on March 18 and married in Waverly's hometown, where we live today on 1 June 1946. In June 2001 we will celebrate our 55th anniversary. Right choice.

Civilian life started the day I married, the last day of my terminal leave. I saved some money by not having to buy a new suit for the wedding. The uniform was fine. The bachelor quarters I had reserved at the University of Michigan Law School had to be switched to married quarters that were obtained in the rental houses at Ypsilanti, Michigan, built for the workers at the Willow Run bomber plant. Upon graduation in January 1949 a friend from law school and I set up practice in Richmond, Indiana. Not really satisfied in law practice I organized a federal savings and loan association in Waverly's hometown, Lewisburg, Tennessee, which opened for business 1 July 1955 and which I continued until merging the association with a larger one in 1984. I had practiced some law while running the savings and loan and I continued by practicing in the office of a local lawyer until 1988. We've been fortunate to be able to engage in travel, foreign and domestic, and to keep busy with involvement in many community affairs during these retirement years. We have two daughters and two sons, all of whom are college graduates and have established their own homes. They are the parents of our seven grandchildren who can sometimes be a worry, but who are mainly a great delight for us.

Lloyd Kurz and I were Ensigns right out of Midshipman School when we reported aboard the 325 in November 1943 and we've kept in contact down through the years. John Sarbaugh was probably my closest friend. He gave me the idea of attending law school upon getting out of the service. In private life we were in John's home near Chicago two or three times prior to his death. Since then we've been in touch with his widow, M.E. and his son Thomas. Arthur English was another good friend onboard, but I lost contact with him after he left the ship. We stopped for lunch with Bill and Bebe Bodiford in Tallahassee, Florida, several years ago and exchanged Christmas letters until Bill's recent death. I had a good telephone chat with Stan Barish a couple years ago too. In recent years Richard E. Martin and I have been corresponding at Christmas time. Incidentally, here's a coincidence we've shared with Lloyd and Phoebe Kurz. They have a daughter-in-law who we learned a few years ago has a desk practically adjoining our daughter-in-law's desk at the Gannett office of USA Today Weekend in Arlington, Virginia where both of them are associate editors.

My final thoughts on the men and officers with whom I served is to affirm that thinking of them and the time we spent together on the 325 brings back memories that I truly relish. We had quite a cross-section of personnel onboard, both in the geographical diversity of hometowns and the diversity of cultures in which we grew up. The experience with them was a part of my growing up and learning more about and gaining respect for others. I only got to one of the 325 reunions, but I thoroughly enjoyed being back with this group with whom I had shared part of my life. I remember thinking at the reunion, "Gosh, these guys sure have changed a lot," and then I took a look in the mirror back at the hotel room showing how much I had aged. I take a great deal of pride in my country and I'm also proud of the group of men with whom I was fortunate enough to serve with on the LST-325 during the time of war.

Did the service change me? A particular change that comes to mind is my learning to accept risks and hazards that arise for everyone throughout life with a degree of equanimity. This change began when my transportation from New York City to England was aboard a large tanker filled with aviation gasoline. For worry about what would happen to me if a torpedo hit us on the way I got no sleep that first night out. Then I realized that if a torpedo did hit us all of us aboard would probably be wiped out instantly. Throughout the rest of the times I was at sea I accepted the fact that all of us were continually at risk out there and that was the life you lived in a war situation. The war experiences are long past, but that outlook has continued for me down to the present...accepting whatever is to be, both from a pragmatic standpoint and from religious convictions. I sincerely believe that this makes the journey through life, whatever time it will last, easier to handle. For none of us is ever in total control of what life brings. So, we need to direct and manage what we can and accept the rest with equanimity.

Stanley Barish, Engineering Officer

(Served aboard LST-325 from 1 February 1943 to 30 July 1944)

We (the crew of LST-369 to which I had been transferred in July 1944) left Rose-neath, Scotland on the old Ile de France. After a stormy seven-day passage across the North Atlantic, we arrived in Boston on 21 December 1944. By this time the Navy was well organized. Like a smooth running machine they got everyone their leave papers and on their way home by 23 December. I had Shirley and our parents meet me in New York and we were married by a Navy chaplain for the second time for the benefit of our parents. We never told them about our first marriage until five years later. I had a thirty-day leave, another thirty days at the Philadelphia Navy Yard in Damage Control and Fire Fighting School and then…what luck…assigned to teach Ordnance at USNR Midshipman School at Columbia University…the same place I had gotten my training. While I was there the war in Europe and Japan ended. I also got my second full stripe, Lieutenant instead of Lieutenant junior grade. I was "detached" from duty on 19 April 1946 at Third Naval District, New York. After two months and twelve days on leave…which I had accumulated but not used…I was released from active duty on 2 July 1946, exactly four years after I reported for training at Midshipman School.

During the two month and twelve day leave period I just relaxed and had a good time with family and friends. I took up golf. Then six months taking baby pictures, six months in a wall washing business, then bought a very, very small local camera store. After four years I moved the store to the prime location in this area, not downtown. Business grew steadily, if not spectacularly. I have two sons, a daughter, and the same wife. I took up sailing at age fifty and am still doing it on Lake Erie.

My shipboard friendships were different that those experienced as a youth and young adult, playing in the streets, going through years of school together, double dating, etc. On the ship we had serious responsibilities. When not busy with them there was sleep to be had. And we didn't get to shore that much. But what we were going through together, what we were doing, created a very strong emotional bond with the other officers, the men in my Engineering divisions, and to a lesser degree with everyone on the ship, and to the ship itself. My final thoughts are 99.5% good. They were a wonderful bunch of men, really just boys doing a man's job. I was only 23 myself. We moved aboard ship after just a couple months to learn the way of the Navy and war.

We learned together and without realizing it became an efficient unit, depending on each other and on the ship. It was a strong bond, a bond that exists today. I'll never forget the 325 and its men.

Harold Westerfield, Ship's Cook

(Served aboard LST-325 from 1 February 1943 to 19 July 1945)

We docked in New Orleans in June. I had enough points to be discharged but Captain Mosier wanted me to stay on and make me a Chief Commissary Officer. I elected to go home. I was discharged in New Orleans and went home to Canton, Illinois, to see all my brothers and sisters, uncles and aunts, Mom and Dad. After a thirty-day leave I went back to work at Caterpillar Tractor Company. It was not easy to get back to civilian life again but it got easier with time. After a short while my English wife and son arrived in New York, where I met them. We returned to Peoria and set up house keeping in a trailer. I later bought a house and we live there while I worked at "Cat." In 1956, I was transferred to Caterpillar in Decatur, Illinois, as a Quality Control Supervisor. My wife and I and my son lived there until 1961 when we were divorced. In 1963, on a blind date, I met my lovely and wonderful wife, Jo Ann. We were married and have been happy for 37 years. I have two stepsons, Van and Kevin, whom I think of as my sons. We have a wonderful life here in Sun City and are happy.

Most of the crew aboard ship were my friends. Yet, they called me "The Belly Robber." Some of my good friends were Gordon Bjargo from Austin, Minnesota and Lemieux from Massachusetts. The Pharmacist "Doc" Hutchens was also a good fellow.

Service changed me in few ways. But I was reminded that all of us guys worked together and got a job done. No, I didn't think about us making history, but I guess we were! My thoughts of the men and officers I served with cannot be written! They were so wonderful to be with and we worked together as a team. I cannot say enough about them. Thank God, they were my friends and fellow shipmates! The one thing that my experiences from the war taught me was to be more tolerant of all people and notions. To phrase a comment, "war is hell" is so right. All my memories bring back the hardships that the people in England went through, the German people endured, and our own personal sacrifices we made serving our country. But I would do it again in a heartbeat! Serving my country was the greatest honor I have ever known.

Afterword

The *LST-325's* story did not end after being decommissioned in July 1946. On 12 June 1951, she was one of five LSTs transferred to the Military Sea Transport Service, or MSTS. The transfer of two of the five ships was quickly cancelled and the other three, *LST-1072*, *LST-287* and *LST-325* all became part of the MSTS fleet used to support operations in the Arctic. After being transferred the ship was re-designated as the *T-LST-325* and given a civilian crew of merchant marine sailors, along with a very small contingent of Navy crewmembers. Typically they would be loaded with material and beached. Then they would shuttle out to larger ships, dock alongside and load up and then run again into the beach.

In late 1951, she returned from service in the Arctic after suffering heavy damage in an ice flow. She lost one of her engines and had to limp back to New York on the one remaining engine. In 1954, she was outfitted with two ten-ton booms to facilitate cargo offloading without the need to beach the ship. They had found that the Arctic region was very rocky and dangerous to these craft, and instead favored transferring cargo ashore in smaller landing craft. In 1955 and 1957, the *T-LST-325* was also used in larger operations in the Arctic in support of the DEW Line Programs, the early warning radar installations above the Arctic Circle whose purpose was to detect any potential Soviet nuclear missiles coming towards the United States over the North Pole. According to the MSTS records, the *T-LST-325* remained part of their fleet until 30 January 1961 when she was stricken from the Naval Vessel Register and turned over to the Maritime Administration for inclusion in the National Defense Reserve Fleet.

The record of the ship's MSTS service is quite sketchy and will need to be researched further in the future.

The *LST-325* was returned to the Navy in 1963 and was modernized for further use under the Military Assistance Program. In 1964 she was transferred as grant aid to Greece, where she was re-designated again as the L-144 *Syros*. The Greeks give their LST's the names of islands and *Syros* was named after an island in the Cyclades, a complex of islands in the central Aegean. She remained in the service of the Hellenic Navy for the next thirty-five years until decommissioned again in December 1999.

This would have been the end of the *LST-325*, except for the efforts of the United States LST Association and a few incredible volunteers. It is beyond the scope of this book to tell the story, but suffice it to say that in late 2000 and early 2001, and with great fan-fare and considerable attention from the national media, the *LST-325* returned to the United States with a crew of aging veterans who rescued the ship with the intent of making her into a memorial ship for our country's LST sailors. I will leave that story for another author to tell.

USS LST-325 Mission Summary for Invasion of Sicily (Operation HUSKY)

8 July 43—Task Group 86.1218 from La Goulette, Tunisia to Gela, Sicily. 73 vehicles, 31 officers, 242 enlisted men, 1st Armored Signal Battalion, 1st Armored Corp Reinforcements. Lt. Col. W.B. Latta commanding. Returned on 12 July 43. No cargo.

15 July 43—From La Goulette, Tunisia to Gela, Sicily. Unspecified number of vehicles, 19 officers, 247 enlisted personnel, U.S. Army. Returned 18 July 43 via Scoglitti carrying 310 Italian POW's.

21 July 43—From La Goulette, Tunisia to Gela, Sicily. Unspecified number of vehicles, 4 officers, 165 enlisted men, 814th Engineers, 1059th Signal Battalion, 1941st Quartermaster Company, Major A.J. Scholt commanding. Returned 24 July 43. No cargo.

26 July 43—From La Goulette, Tunisia to Licata, Sicily. 62 vehicles, 9 officers, 211 enlisted men. A Company 205th Quartermaster Battalion, F Company 19th Engineers, 1st & 2nd Platoon 3407th Ordnance Company. Major P.E. Arneson, 45th Division, Senior Officer. Returned 29 July 43 carrying 730 Italian POW's.

1 Aug 43—From La Goulette, Tunisia to Syracuse, Sicily. 86 vehicles, 41 officers, 241 enlisted men, British 15th Army Group. Lt. Col. Hodson commanding. Returned 3 Aug 43. No cargo.

6 Aug 43—From La Goulette, Tunisia to Licata, Sicily. Unspecified number of vehicles, 202 men, 55th Squadron, Royal Air Force. 4 officers, 241st Squadron U.S. Air Corps. Returned 8 Aug 43 carrying 3 officers, 188 enlisted men, 71st and 72nd Signal Companies, U.S. Army.

14 Aug 43—From La Goulette, Tunisia to Palermo, Sicily. 65 vehicles, 1 officer, 28 enlisted, 437th Signal Construction Battalion (Aviation), 2 officers, 158 enlisted, 255th Squadron, Royal Air Force, 2 officers 256th AMES, 103 enlisted 1st Air From. Sig. Returned 16 Aug 43 to Bizerte, Tunisia.

USS LST-325 Mission Summary for Invasion of Italy (Salerno) (Operation AVALANCHE)

13 Sept 43—From Bizerte, Tunisia to Salerno, Italy. 63 vehicles, 16 officers, 369 enlisted, 40th Battalion Royal Tank Regiment. Captain E.J.P. Roberts commanding. Returned 15 September to Palermo, Sicily. No cargo.

17 Sept 43—Convoy PSS9 from Palermo, Sicily to Paestum, Italy. 136 vehicles, 41 officers, 662 enlisted men, 3rd Division, U.S. Army. Lt. Col. F.W. Sladin commanding. Returned 18 Sept 43 in Convoy SPS10 to Termini Imerese, Sicily.

20 Sept 43—From Termini Imerese, Sicily to Paestum, Italy. 62 vehicles, 27 officers, 265 enlisted men, 400th CA Battalion (AA). Lt. Col. E.B. Hempstead commanding. Returned 23 Sept 43 to Triploi, Libya.

27 Sept 43—From Tripoli, Libya to Salerno, Italy. 55 trucks, 4 British officers, 125 enlisted men, 657th GT, Royal Army Service Corps, Ceylonese Detachment. Capt. W.E.R. Trelor commanding. Returned 1 Oct 43 to Bizerte, Tunisia.

USS LST-325 Mission Summary for Invasion of Europe (Operation OVERLORD)

5 June 44—Task Group 126.4 from Falmouth, England to Omaha Beach (Fox Red). 59 vehicles, 31 officers, 408 enlisted. 30th Chemical Decontamination Company, 5th Engineer Special Brigade. Captain Moore commanding. 19 men, 1006th US Navy Construction Battalion, W/O A.K. Butterfield commanding. Returned on 8 June 44 carrying 38 casualties. 98 merchant sailors from ships scuttled for breakwater.

11 June 44—Convoy EPL4-10 from Portland-Weymouth, England to Utah Beach (Sugar Red). Vehicles and personnel of 980th Field Artillery. Captain A.J. Reid commanding. Returned on 13 June 44 carrying 68 German POW's, 4 U.S. Army MP escorts.

13 June 44—Convoy EPL-8W from Southampton, England to Utah Beach (Sugar Red). 71 vehicles, 148 officers and men, U.S. Army. Returned 16 June 44 carrying 17 casualties, and Paul Manning, war correspondent.

19 June 44—Convoy EWL-13 (Mosier SOPA) from Portsmouth, England to Juno Beach. Vehicles and personnel of 7th Royal Tank Regiment. Major M.R.

Wellby commanding. Returned on 23 June 44 in Convoy FTM-16 carrying 254 English casualties.

25 June 44—From Southampton, England to Utah Beach. Vehicles and personnel, 441st Quartermaster Truck Company Captain A.A. Slickers commanding. Returned 27 June 44 carrying 796 German POW's, 9 U.S. Army MP escorts. Towed LCT(5)-276.

29 June 44—Convoy EWL-21 from Southampton, England to Juno Bach (Mike Green). 48 vehicles, 217 officers and men, Royal Army Medical Corps. Lt. Col. Jones commanding. Returned 1 July 44 carrying 12 German POW's, 12 British guards. Royal Navy Bomb Disposal Unit with 2 German underwater mines. Towed LST-493.

3 July 44—From London, England to Gold Beach (Jig). 59 vehicles, 8 officers, 163 enlisted men, Royal Army Signal Corps. Captain Graham commanding. Returned 6 July 44 in Convoy FTM-29. No cargo.

8 July 44—Convoy EPL-30W from Southampton, England to Omaha Beach (Fox White). 66 vehicles, 7 officers, 107 enlisted men, U.S. Army. Returned 9 July 44. No cargo.

11 July 44—Convoy EPM-3 from Portland-Weymouth, England to Omaha Beach (Fox Green). 76 vehicles, 2 officers, 117 enlisted men, U.S. Army. Captain Haut commanding. Returned 12 July 44. Professor Dudley M. Newitt, FRS, aboard for transportation.

14 July 44—From Portland-Weymouth, England to Utah Beach. 67 vehicles, 13 officers, 420 enlisted men, U.S. Army. Captain K.E. Schmidt commanding. Returned 15 July 44 in Convoy FPM-6. No cargo.

17 July 44—Convoy EPM-7 from Portland-Weymouth, England to Utah Beach. 75 vehicles, 21 officers, 293 enlisted men, Headquarters Company, 687th Field Artillery Battalion. Major M.E. Billingsley commanding. 53 bags U.S. Mail. Returned 19 July 44. No cargo.

21 July 44—Convoy EPM-11 from Portland-Weymouth, England to Omaha Beach 64 vehicles, 11 officers, 243 enlisted men, 229th Field Artillery Battalion, Captain Clark commanding. Returned 23 July 44 in Convoy FOM-16 carrying U.S. Navy officers, 9 enlisted men. Lt.(jg) R.G. Gustafson commanding.

26 July 44—Convoy EPM-16 from Portland-Weymouth, England to Utah Beach. 65 vehicles, 16 officers, 303 enlisted men, 390th AAA, AW Battalion, (SP). Captain J.L. Porter commanding. Returned 28 July 44. No cargo.

7 Aug 44—Convoy EPM-28 (Mosier SOPA) from Portland-Weymouth, England to Utah Beach (Tare Green). 59 vehicles, 10 officers, 235 enlisted men, Recon Company, 773rd Tank Destroyer Battalion, Captain H.R. Emhardt commanding. Returned 8 Aug 44 in Convoy FPL-12 (Mosier SOPA). No cargo.

12 Aug 44—Convoy EPM-33 (Mosier SOPA) from Portland-Weymouth, England to Utah Beach. 69 vehicles, 14 officers, 287 enlisted men, 945th Field Artillery Battalion, Lt. Col. W.V. DeLoach commanding. Returned 13 Aug 44 in Convoy FPM-35. 471 German POW's, 7 U.S. Army MP escorts.

20 Aug 44—Special Convoy from Swansea, Wales to Utah Beach (Tare Green). 16 tanks, 4 officers, 104 enlisted men, U.S. Army. Captain Walter O. Wade commanding. Returned 24 Aug 44 in Convoy FPL-16. No cargo.

27 Aug 44—Convoy EPM-46 from Portland-Weymouth, England to Utah Beach. Vehicles, 2 officers, 77 enlisted men, 147th Ordnance MVA Company, Lt. A.G. Dobrick commanding. Returned 29 Aug 44 in Convoy FPM-45. No cargo.

31 Aug 44—Convoy EPM-50 (Mosier SOPA) from Portland-Weymouth, England to Omaha Beach. 61 vehicles, 9 officers, 164 enlisted men, U.S. Army. Captain B.M. Nostrup commanding. Returned 3 Sept 44 in Convoy NAB-7 (Mosier SOPA) to St. Michel-en-Greve with 410 tons mixed ammunition.

11 Sept 44—Convoy EPM-60 (Mosier SOPA) from Portland-Weymouth, England to Omaha Beach. 63 vehicles, 14 officers, 183 enlisted men, 358th Field Artillery Battalion, Captain Ray Floyd commanding. Returned 12 Sept 44. No cargo.

15 Sept 44—Convoy EPM-64 (Mosier SOPA) from Portland-Weymouth, England to Omaha Beach. 50 vehicles, 32 officers, 70 enlisted men, Channel Base Section (Comm Zone) ETO. Colonel D. Squire commanding. Returned 17 Sept 44. To St. Michel-en-Greve with 500 tons mixed ammunition.

26 Sept 44—Convoy EPL-37 from Portland-Weymouth to Utah Beach. 71 vehicles, 12 officers, 173 enlisted men, U.S. Army. Lt. Col. C.F. Fiore commanding. Returned 28 Sept 44. No cargo.

2 Oct 44—Convoy EPL-43 from Portland-Weymouth, England to Utah Beach. 60 vehicles, 1 officer, 89 enlisted men, 527th Engineers, 2nd Division. Captain R.C. Anderson commanding. Returned independently on 3 Oct 44. No cargo.

6 Oct 44—Convoy EPL-47 (Mosier SOPA) from Portland-Weymouth, England to Utah Beach. 61 vehicles, 17 officers, 229 enlisted men, U.S. Army. Lt. Col. Childness commanding. Returned independently on 10 Oct 44. No cargo.

14 Oct 44—Convoy WFM-5 (Mosier SOPA) from Southampton, England to Utah Beach. 41 vehicles, 25 enlisted men, U.S. Army. Returned 16 Oct 44 carrying 4 officers, 192 enlisted men, U.S. Navy Construction Battalion, Lt. S.W. Beed commanding.

19 Oct 44—Convoy WFM-9 (Mosier SOPA) from Southampton, England to Utah Beach. 42 vehicles, 5 officers, 204 enlisted men, 547th Port Company. Captain V.T. Foster commanding. 10 officers French Army, Captain Robert Martin commanding. Returned independently 21 Oct 44 carrying 3 officers, 81 enlisted men (crew of LST-512). Lt.(jg) J.H. Doherty commanding.

24 Nov 44—Convoy PVL-14 from Portland-Weymouth, England to Rouen, France. 63 vehicles, 8 officers, 195 enlisted men, 44th Mechanized Cavalry.1st Lt. C.F. Huff commanding. Returned independently on 27 Nov 44. No cargo.

1 Dec 44—Convoy PVL-20 (Mosier SOPA) from Portland-Weymouth, England to Rouen, France. 51 vehicles, 16 0fficers, 274 enlisted men, U.S. Army. Lt. Col. T.W. Riggs commanding. Returned 4 Dec 44. No cargo.

9 Dec 44—Portland-Weymouth to Rouen, France. 59 vehicles, 14 officers, 241 enlisted men, U.S. Army. Col. R.M. Broberg commanding. Returned 11 Dec 44 carrying 43 vehicles and 37 enlisted men. Captain E.W. Hothorn commanding.

14 Dec 44—Convoy PVL-29 (Mosier SOPA) from Portland-Weymouth, England to Rouen, France. 76 vehicles, 1 officer, 56 enlisted men, 758th Field Artillery Battalion, Captain J.S. Mayne commanding. Returned 17 Dec 44. Col. James E. Slack, Chief of Staff, NYPE, onboard for transportation.

20 Dec 44—Convoy PEL-2 (Mosier SOPA) from Portland-Weymouth, England to Cherbourg, France. 27 vehicles, 5 officers, 108 enlisted men, U.S. Army. Captain R.L. Ameno commanding. Returned 21 Dec 44. No cargo.

25 Dec 44—Convoy PVL-36 (Mosier SOPA) from Portland-Weymouth, England to Rouen, France. 52 vehicles, 9 officers, 183 enlisted men, U.S. Army. Captain E.C. Klein commanding. Returned 27 Dec 44. Took aboard 645 soldiers from 15th Army Headquarters, 34 English merchant men from HMS Empire Javelin, torpedoed in English Channel. Took survivors to Le Havre, France.

3 Jan 45—Convoy PVL-45 from Portland-Weymouth, England. 56 vehicles, no personnel. Returned to Portland-Weymouth after two tanks broke loose from securing on tank deck.

4 Jan 45—Convoy PVL-46 (Mosier SOPA) from Portland-Weymouth, England to Le Havre, France. 56 vehicles, no personnel. Returned 5 Jan 45 in Convoy VWL-44 (Mosier SOPA) 1 U.S. Navy passenger.

7 Jan 45—Convoy PVL-49 (Mosier SOPA) from Portland-Weymouth, England to La Havre, France. 38 vehicles, 1 officer, 86 enlisted men, U.S. Army. 1st Lt. A. Stansby commanding. Returned 8 Jan 45 in Convoy VWL-47 (Mosier SOPA) No cargo.

11 Jan 45—Convoy PVL-53 (Mosier SOPA) from Portland-Weymouth, England to Le Havre, France. 8 vehicles, 8 gun trailers, 20 tanks. No personnel. Returned 12 Jan 45 in Convoy VWL-57 (Mosier SOPA). No cargo.

19 Jan 45—Convoy PVL-57 (Mosier SOPA) from Portland-Weymouth, England to Rouen, France. 99 vehicles, 24 officers, 53 enlisted men, U.S. Army. Captain M.F. Schlather commanding. Returned 21 Jan 45 in Convoy VWL-58. No cargo.

25 Jan 45—Convoy PVL-63 from Portland-Weymouth, England to Le Havre, France. 49 vehicles, 4 officers, 147 enlisted men, U.S. Army. Captain J.T. Elliot commanding. Returned 26 Jan 45 in Convoy VWL-63. No cargo.

4 Feb 45—Convoy PVL-69 (Mosier SOPA) from Portland-Weymouth, England to Le Havre, France. 56 vehicles, 4 officers, 139 enlisted men, U.S.

Army. Captain C. Manning commanding. Returned 5 Feb 45 in Convoy VWL-73 (Mosier SOPA). No cargo.

7 Feb 45—Convoy PVL-72 (Mosier SOPA) from Portland-Weymouth, England to Le Havre, France. 41 vehicles, 150 personnel, U.S. Army. Lt. Col. Adams commanding. Returned 8 Feb 45 in Convoy VWL-76 (Mosier SOPA). No cargo.

13 Feb 45—Convoy PVL-75 (Mosier SOPA) from Portland-Weymouth, England to Le Havre, France. 56 vehicles, 6 officers, 144 enlisted men, U.S. Army. Captain L.J. Suadja commanding. Returned 14 Feb 45 in Convoy VWL-82 (Mosier SOPA) carrying 28 U.S. Navy Construction Battalion personnel. CCM R.S. Hollingsworth commanding.

16 Feb 45—Convoy PVL-77 (Mosier SOPA) from Portland-Weymouth, England to Le Havre, France. 60 vehicles, 3 officers, 153 enlisted men, U.S. Army. Captain R.C. Archenbold commanding. Returned 17 Feb 45 in Convoy VWL-85. No cargo.

21 Feb 45—Convoy PVL-79 (Mosier SOPA) from Portland-Weymouth, England to Le Havre, France. 48 vehicles, 4 officers, 136 enlisted men, U.S. Army. Captain O.W. Holtz commanding. Returned 23 Feb 45. Convoy VWL-90 (Mosier SOPA). No cargo.

3 Apr 45—Convoy PEL-32 from Portland-Weymouth, England to Cherbourg, France. 45 Royal Army vehicles. 3 U.S. Navy officers. 89 U.S. Navy and Coast Guard enlisted men. Returned 4 Apr 45 in Convoy EWL-99 carrying 1 U.S. Navy, 1 U.S. Army, 2 British civilian and 63 French Navy personnel for transportation.

10 Apr 45—Convoy PVL-113 from Portland-Weymouth, England to Le Havre, France. 51 vehicles, 7 officers, 173 enlisted men, 1288th Engineer Construction Battalion. Captain J.W. Cosky commanding. Returned 11 Apr 45 in Convoy VWL-38. No cargo.

Bibliography

Books:

Ageton, Arthur A.: *The Naval Officer's Guide*. New York: McGraw-Hill, 1944.

Barger, Melvin D.: *Large Slow Target: A History of the LST*. Toledo, Ohio: United States LST Association, 1986.

Blumenson, Martin: *Sicily: Whose Victory*. New York: Ballantine Books, Inc., 1968.

Duning, Theodore P.: *Remembering the 325: Recollections of the Life and Times Aboard the U.S. LST 325 from November 1943 to July 1945*. Self-published.

Gavin, James M.: *On To Berlin*. New York: Viking Press, 1978.

Gawne, Jonathan: *Spearheading D-Day: American Special Units In Normandy*. Paris, France: Histoire & Collections, 1998.

Hoyt, Edwin P.: *The Invasion Before Normandy: The Secret Battle of Slapton Sands*. Lanham, Maryland: Scarborough House, 1999.

Lewis, Nigel: *Exercise Tiger: The Dramatic True Story of a Hidden Tragedy of World War II*. New York: Prentice Hall Press, 1990.

Lorelli, John A.: *To Foreign Shores: U.S. Amphibious Operations in World War II*. Annapolis: Naval Institute Press, 1995.

Morison, Samuel Eliot: *History of United States Naval Operations in World War II Volume IX: Sicily-Salerno-Anzio*. New York: Little, Brown and Company, 1954.

Morris, Eric: *Salerno: A Military Fiasco*. New York, Stein and Day, 1983.

Stratton, Bill: *Box Seat Over Hell: Volume II*. International Liaison Pilots and Aircraft Association.

United States Naval Institute: *The Bluejacket's Manual*. Annapolis: United States Naval Institute, 1943.

United States Navy Department: *General Training Course for Non-Rated Men*. Washington, D.C.: United States Government Printing Office, 1943.

Witter, Robert E.: *Small Boats and Large Slow Targets: Oral Histories of the United States' Amphibious Forces Personnel in WWII*. Missoula, Montana: Pictorial Histories Publishing Co., Inc., 1998.

Official Documents:

Deck Log, *USS LST-325*, 1 Feb 1943 to 2 July 1946.

Commanding Officer, *USS LST-325*, Action Report, Bay of Tunis to Landing off Gela, Sicily, July 8–12, 1943. 1 August 1943.

Commanding Officer, *USS LST-325*, Action Report, Bay of Bizerte to Landing at Salerno, Italy, September 13–15, 1943. 15 September 1943.

Internet Sources:

Haze Gray and Underway: www.hazegray.org
Naval Historical Center: www.history.navy.mil/index.html
Nav Source Naval History: www.naval-history.net
Navy History.Com: www.navyhistory.com
U.S. Navy in World War II: www.ibiblio/hyperwar/USN/index.html
U-boat.Net: The U-boat War 1939–1945: http://uboat.net
The Luftwaffe 1933–1945: http://www.ww2.dk

Articles:

The Stars and Stripes at Sea: Vol. 1 No. 1, 26 June 1943
The Stars and Stripes at Sea: Vol. 1 No. 2, 27 June 1943
The Stars and Stripes at Sea: Vol. 1 No. 3, 28 June 1943
The Stars and Stripes at Sea: Vol. 1 No. 4, 29 June 1943
The Stars and Stripes at Sea, Vol. 1 No. 5, 30 June 1943
The Stars and Stripes at Sea, Vol. 1 No. 6, 1 July 1943
The Stars and Stripes at Sea, Vol. 1 No. 7, 2 July 1943
The Stars and Stripes at Sea, Vol. 2 No. 1, 3 July 1943
The Stars and Stripes at Sea, Vol. 2 No. 2, 4 July 1943

The Stars and Stripes at Sea, Vol. 2 No. 3, 5 July 1943
The Stars and Stripes at Sea, Vol. 2 No. 4, 6 July 1943
The Stars and Stripes at Sea, Vol. 2 No. 5, 7 July 1943

Dougherty, John H.: *The USS LST-481*. 1995.

Written Interviews with LST-325 Crewmembers:

Allgaier, Harold	17 November 1999
Barish, Stanley S.	3 December 2000
Bliss, William	31 December 1999
Conway, Chester W.	13 December 1999
Duning, Theodore P.	24 May 2000
Easterly, Ellsworth L.	2 December 1999
Hanley, William J.	26 January 2000
Horton, Leo L.	13 December 1999
Kolar, Emil	4 February 2000
Kramer, Howard F.	7 April 2000
MacKay, Dale	13 December 1999
Martin, Donald L.	12 December 1999
Martin, Richard E.	9 December 1999
Murphy, Gerry F.	17 January 2000
Roberts, John G.	1 December 1999
Roy, Donald O.	4 June 2000
Mitchell, Charles J.	10 January 2000
Scacchetti, Richard V.	1 July 2000
Westerfield, Harold	25 May 2001

Other:

Bodiford, William: Personal Diary, 3 Oct 1942–25 Dec 1943

0-595-31399-X

Printed in the United States
88093LV00002B/391-465/A

9 780595 313990